Sheen

Carol MacLean lives in the Glasgow area. She began by writing pocket novels, having 18 published before deciding to write historical saga.

When she's not writing, Carol can be found visiting museums or walking around the city looking for traces of old Glasgow to inspire her next novel.

Also by Carol MacLean

The Kiltie Street Girls

Jeannie's War
Elsie's Wartime Wish
Kathy's Courage
Sheena's Promise

Sheena's Promise
CAROL MacLEAN

hera

First published in the United Kingdom in 2025 by

Hera Books, an imprint of
Canelo Digital Publishing Limited,
20 Vauxhall Bridge Road,
London SW1V 2SA
United Kingdom

A Penguin Random House Company

The authorised representative in the EEA is Dorling Kindersley Verlag GmbH. Arnulfstr. 124, 80636 Munich, Germany

Copyright © Carol MacLean 2025

The moral right of Carol MacLean to be identified as the creator of this work has been asserted in accordance with the Copyright, Designs and Patents Act, 1988.

All rights reserved. No part of this publication may be reproduced or transmitted in any form or by any means, electronic or mechanical, including photocopy, recording, or any information storage and retrieval system, without permission in writing from the publisher.

No part of this book may be used or reproduced in any manner for the purpose of training artificial intelligence technologies or systems. In accordance with Article 4(3) of the DSM Directive 2019/790, Canelo expressly reserves this work from the text and data mining exception.

A CIP catalogue record for this book is available from the British Library.

Print ISBN 978 1 80436 487 1
Ebook ISBN 978 1 80436 486 4

This book is a work of fiction. Names, characters, businesses, organizations, places and events are either the product of the author's imagination or are used fictitiously. Any resemblance to actual persons, living or dead, events or locales is entirely coincidental.

Printed and bound in Great Britain by Clays Ltd, Elcograf S.p.A.

Look for more great books at
www.herabooks.com
www.dk.com

For Rosie, Dinah and Charlie

Chapter One

September 1944

'I'm very sorry, dear. I wouldn't ask if it was anyone other than my sister.' The landlady looked distressed as she stood in the neat dining room with its crystal bowl of wax fruit and lovely sea view framed by thick pre-war brushed silk curtains. 'You see, she and my nephews and nieces have been living with our cousin since Coventry was blitzed but now my cousin isn't well and can't cope with five lively children, so I felt it only right and proper to ask them to come and live with me,' she explained.

'I quite understand, Mrs Porter. Please don't worry about it. I'm sure I'll find another place.' Eileen Sheena Boyle smiled reassuringly.

Only, inside, she didn't feel at all confident of that. The tiny village of Budleigh Salterton on the Devon coast was full of evacuees, service personnel and women like her who wanted to live close to their husbands or boyfriends who were serving in the forces.

'Only… they're coming in the next fortnight,' Mrs Porter said. 'It's rather short notice, I know, but I'll need your room back by then.'

'A fortnight. Goodness…' Eileen said faintly.

'You speak so fondly of your parents. Surely they would have space for you?'

Going home to Glasgow. She hadn't thought of it. Eileen hadn't been back to Glasgow in over a year. She had moved down to Devon in the hope that her fiancé, Jimmy, might get leave and he'd certainly find it easier to visit her in the south of England, or so she thought, rather than the west of Scotland. As it turned out, Jimmy hadn't made it back to Britain at all. She had last seen him in June 1940, and it felt like a very long time indeed.

'I'll write and ask. You needn't worry, Mrs Porter. I'll be out of here in the next couple of weeks one way or another.'

With a firm nod, Eileen went up to her rented room and sank down onto the bed, her mind frozen with panic and indecision. Jumping up again, she paced the small space and then looked out the window. It was the gorgeous view of the sea and the beach that had made her fall in love with these lodgings. Not even the barbed wire and barricades across the beach could mar its beauty. Mrs Porter was a kindly soul who had mothered her since she arrived. Being in the countryside, the food was more plentiful than in Glasgow and all in all, Eileen felt like she'd landed on her feet. She'd been homesick, yes, but soon got over it and kept busy by joining the Women's Institute and making jams and pies and helping as a teacher's assistant with the evacuees who had swelled the numbers of children in the local school.

This sense of despair wouldn't do. She was prone to moments of loneliness and often had to shake herself free of it. Now was one of those very moments. Eileen sat at the tiny desk under the windowsill and took a sheet of precious writing paper. She folded it once and made a sharp crease with her fingernail before tearing it carefully. She had two letters to write. One to her mother to say she'd be moving back home and one to Jimmy, care of the army postal service, to let him know. She wrote to him every week. Jimmy's letters came back sporadically and lately none at all. She kept his letters in her suitcase. Many of his earlier ones were stained with sweat and sand from the African desert and creased where he had kept them in his pocket in between finishing them. The stains added their own stories and filled in the gaps where Jimmy's descriptions and the censor failed to tell her what he was doing, although she had worked out he was now fighting in Europe. She loved that the letters had lain so close to his heart and held them to her cheek as if she could feel his touch on her.

She put down the fresh piece of paper and took the bundle of Jimmy's letters out of her suitcase as she had done so many times before. She unfolded the most recent, which had arrived a month ago, and smiled fondly as she read it.

My darling Sheena, Jimmy had written in his poor handwriting. *It's evening and the lads and myself have a wee moment to smoke or polish our buttons or write to our girlfriends and wives. So forgive the smear of ash on this here scrap of paper. I love you and while I don't feel like telling you what's going on here too much I can't wait to hear your stories about teaching the weans and what kind of jam you've boiled up. When we're married, I'd like you to make me jars of strawberry jam, it's my favourite. Will you do that, Sheena dear? All my love, your Jimmy.*

Jimmy was the only person to call her Sheena. It was Eileen's middle name and Jimmy had claimed it when he found out. 'I like the name Eileen well enough,' he'd told her honestly, 'but I like Sheena better and I want you all to myself, so you'll be my wee Sheena from now on if you don't mind.'

Eileen didn't mind one bit. It made her feel special and loved when Jimmy called her that.

She kissed his letter and carefully tucked it in with the others and replaced them in the suitcase before she picked up her pen and began to write her own letters.

–

Her mother's reply came back a week later.

> *Dear Eileen*
>
> *You must not think of coming back here. Your father is still recovering from his latest heart attack. He needs the utmost peace and quiet. I cannot have more people in the house.*
>
> *You should stay in Devon. I am sure there are other guest houses in the area.*
>
> *Do you need money? I will send a postal order.*
> *From your mother,*
> *Agnes*

A few years ago, before the Clydebank blitz, Eileen would have felt hurt by such an abrupt response. However, after she and her mother survived a bomb blast together, she had finally understood why Agnes found it difficult to show her emotions. It turned out that Agnes had lost her first child, Ronnie, before Eileen was born and couldn't bring herself to love Eileen as she should, as it would be too painful if she lost her too.

Eileen now knew her mother loved her even if she didn't always demonstrate it. Offering to send money was her way of saying she loved and cared for her daughter.

Eileen's father, Robert, had a heart attack before the war, and Agnes fretted over his health. A second attack this spring had terrified them all. But he was quietly getting better.

She bit her lip in thought. Picking up her pen, she wrote another letter. She walked to the pillar box in the hot summer sunshine, greeting people she knew. She crossed her fingers as the letter slid away. She only had another week left before she had to move out. She knew Mrs Porter was nervous that she was still there. She walked round the village again, looking for vacancies, but there were none advertised. Besides, she had made up her mind to go home. Maybe not to her parents' but to Glasgow… somewhere. She had given Devon her best shot, but Jimmy hadn't had leave in all that while. She'd miss the children in the school, and she had made some friends among the teachers and other assistants but no one special.

She was making a half-hearted start on packing up her meagre belongings days later when the neighbour's little boy ran up and knocked on her open door.

'There's a telephone call for you, miss. At the corner shop.'

'Thank you, Ben. I've been expecting it. Here's a penny for you.'

Ben beamed as he clamped his dirty hand over the penny and scampered off down the stairs. With a lighter heart, Eileen followed him down more slowly and set off to the village shop, which wasn't far away.

'Hello, Jeannie?' she said into the telephone mouthpiece. 'Is that you?'

'Aye, it's me. I got your letter. Maybe it's selfish but I'm that excited you're coming home.'

Eileen smiled and her heart warmed to hear her best friend's voice. 'How's Flora? Are you all keeping well?'

'I can't believe you haven't met her yet. She's almost four months old and hard work but I love being a mammy. When are you travelling up?'

'I've to be out of my lodgings by the end of the week.' Eileen spoke into the mouthpiece and tried to ignore the customers in the tiny shop whose ears were pricking up. News in the village spread fast. She could be sure the school would know before she told them she was leaving. She hadn't said yet because she wasn't certain. Oh well. The cat was truly out of the bag now.

'And you're sure your mother won't let you stay with them?'

'Och, you know my mum. She worries about my father. I can't go home, Jeannie.'

'I was just checking. Anyway, you're in luck. There's a room and kitchen empty at number eight in Kiltie Street. The woman who lived there did a moonlight flit. It's furnished and got the stuff she left behind or so I'm told by that Frankie Bett. He's the landlord.'

'You're a good pal,' Eileen said, feeling relief flood her body. She wasn't going to be homeless. 'Do you know of anywhere taking folk on? I need a job too.'

'There's Fearnmore.' Jeannie named the munitions factory where she and Eileen had first met back at the start of the war and became good friends. 'I could ask Miss McGrory for you.'

Eileen shuddered. She had never got along with the supervisor, who had been sharp and unpleasant to the girls and particularly disliked Eileen. 'I hoped she might have moved on to another job.'

'No such luck. She's no' that bad these days. If you don't fancy Fearnmore then I heard someone say they're hiring at Greenbank.'

'The carpet factory at Glasgow Green?'

'That's the one. Only it's no' carpets these days they're making. It's army blankets. Do you still like your sewing?'

'Aye, I do. Greenbank might suit me very well. Thanks, Jeannie. I don't know what I'd do without you.'

'Me neither,' came the cheeky reply, making Eileen grin and long suddenly to be back in Glasgow where she'd be sure of a warm welcome from Jeannie and her family in Kiltie Street, if not at the Boyles' house.

—

Mrs Porter gave Eileen a warm hug when she left and Ben's father, the local milkman, gave her a lift on his cart to the train station and helped her with her luggage, putting her cases on the rack above her seat in the train carriage with a ready smile.

'Thank you. I hope I haven't made your milk deliveries late,' Eileen said.

'Not at all. It's all I can do to say thank you for looking after Ben at school. You improved his spelling no end, Miss Boyle.' He tipped his cap to her, and she watched him through the steam on the platform until his back disappeared behind a group of soldiers boarding the next carriage.

A chapter in her life was ending, she mused as the train's whistle blasted and the engine chugged into action. The countryside, so green and gentle, passed by as she tried to adjust to leaving Devon and anticipated heading north into cooler weather and towards Glasgow's familiar grimy, soot-covered tenements and busy city streets. She felt older than her twenty-three years. So much had happened since war broke out. She had left her job as a maid in a big house, worked in a munitions factory, met her lovely friends and fallen in love with Jimmy, and ended up in the English countryside. So although a period of her life was ending, she was also at the start of something new again. Eileen smiled and settled in to read her book as the train moved steadily north.

—

'It's a month's rent upfront,' Frankie Bett informed her.

She was hard put not to stare at his Adam's apple bobbing up and down in his scrawny neck like a ball in a stocking. His hand had lingered on hers too long when she shook it. She'd had a strong desire to wipe her hand on her skirt afterwards.

'Yes, I can pay that,' Eileen said, glancing about at the drab room that doubled as a bedroom and living area.

There was an iron-framed double bed with a stained mattress and two lumpy pillows. A rickety table and chair stood under the window and a dark wood wardrobe graced the far wall. There was a bed recess with cupboard doors across it. The curtains at the flat window had seen better days and Eileen was sure the holes in the fabric were due to moths. So much for the blackout; any lamp would show through those. Already her thoughts were turning to her beloved sewing machine. She could fix those curtains easily.

Frankie kicked a suitcase out from under the bed, making her start.

'The previous tenant left this. You can make use of the contents, but I'll take the case.'

She watched him dump a pile of women's clothes onto the mattress. It was obvious he already knew what was in the suitcase. His ferrety eyes flicked from her to the clothing as if he was doing her a huge favour. Eileen didn't say anything. She knew she could use the material or maybe adapt the clothes for herself. She didn't want Frankie Bett to know that. If he thought the clothes had value, she was fairly sure he'd take them along with the suitcase.

The sound of a motor car drew her to the window. She looked out to see the vehicle drive past to the end of Kiltie Street and park at the pavement. As she watched, a middle-aged man got out. Despite the warm day, he was wearing a long leather coat with an astrakhan collar. She couldn't see his face, shaded as it was by a black homburg hat.

Frankie came and stood beside her, far too closely. She smelled his body odour.

'Ah, that's Mr Mearns from number one. He inherited the property from his mother, who passed away last month. A man of means, so he is.' Frankie's chest swelled proudly as if he was personally responsible for the man's good fortune.

'Let me pay the rent, Mr Bett. I've kept you too long. You must be a busy man.' Eileen gave him her prettiest smile and tried to hold her breath against the stink of unwashed armpits.

'I am that.' Frankie swaggered. 'But I'll be back next month for your rent so make sure it's on time.'

Eileen knew from Jeannie that it was Frankie's father who was the landlord. Frankie was only permitted to gather the rents under his father's beady eye. His fingers touched hers deliberately as she passed back the signed rent book. She wasn't worried. She had met enough Frankie Betts over the last few years to know how to handle him. Eileen knew she was attractive, but she wasn't vain. She didn't want men's attention. The only man she wanted was Jimmy Dougal.

She managed to escort him out the door, all while he was still prattling on about the flat and how lucky she was to get it. With a long expulsion of air, she leaned against the closed door and stared at her new home. From the tiny hallway she could see into both the kitchen and the room.

'And where will I take my guests?' she asked herself. 'If I have any, that is.'

There it was again. That sharp, little pang of loneliness. She missed Jimmy and she didn't have any friends apart from Jeannie. What was wrong with her? She hadn't tried too hard to make friends in Devon because she knew she'd leave eventually. The problem was that men liked her too much and women disliked her for the same reason. Her looks. She made other young women feel jealous or insecure and they didn't like her around their boyfriends or husbands.

'I'll have to entertain in here.' Eileen continued to chat to herself as there was no one else.

She walked into the kitchen. It was a dark, grimy area and the previous occupant clearly hadn't enjoyed housework. The range was smeared with grease and the linoleum floor was sticky under her shoes. She picked up a heavy griddle pan that lay on top of the range and grimaced when encrusted soot and old food came off on her fingers. She wasn't a good cook but she had to eat and that meant she'd have to scrub everything before she could begin. At least she knew now how to fill her day.

She was familiar with the layout of the kitchen as it was the same as the rest of Kiltie Street. Eileen had lived for a while with Jeannie's family in number four, after the Boyles' home was destroyed in the blitz. There was a fireplace, a coal bunker, a press and an overhead pulley for hanging damp clothes. There was also another bed recess covered with faded red curtains. When she peeked inside, she saw the bed was made up but didn't look as if it had been used recently. Well, she wouldn't need that either. There was only her after all.

Eileen managed to get the range lit to boil water. She decided to have a cup of tea before using the rest of the heated water to scrub the range and all the kitchen equipment and the horrible floor. She thought of Jeannie and how much she was looking forward to seeing her the next day.

She and Jeannie had met in Fearnmore munitions factory soon after the war began. They started on the factory floor on the very same day along with other girls, including Annie and Janet. The four had become fast friends but she was particularly close to Jeannie. Jimmy was Jeannie's older brother,, and she had fallen in love with him at first sight when he came home to recuperate from his wounds after the retreat from Dunkirk. She was thrilled to think that one day she'd be her friend's sister-in-law and knew Jeannie felt the same. They were already as close as sisters.

Jeannie had fallen in love with a Canadian soldier, Bill, and now they were married and had a baby daughter, Flora. Eileen couldn't wait to meet her. One day soon, Flora would officially be her niece, Eileen thought happily as she went through to the bedroom and rummaged in her suitcase for her tea ration and teapot.

She sat back on her heels suddenly, the teapot still in her hand. She was nervous of what awaited the next day. She needed a job, but would she pass the interview at Greenbank? And what if Jeannie was wrong and there were no jobs going? It was all so unknown. She sat in her new kitchen with a cup of tea, surrounded by its shabbiness and the smell of stale food, and wondered if she had made the right decision coming back to Glasgow.

Chapter Two

The next day, Eileen walked over to number four Kiltie Street to collect Jeannie. She had forgotten how neighbourly the small row of tenements was. There were only eight in the row, which came to a dead end with the back of another tenement building. Kiltie Street itself turned onto the main road with a handy bus stop and plenty of shops. Near the end of the street there was a bench and a square of grass where the local children played when they weren't rolling marbles along the pavement or playing hopscotch with chalks. Today, the women were hanging out of windows to shout across and gossip to each other. They waved to Eileen as she passed under their homes to knock at the Dougals' door.

Jeannie gave a shriek of delight and hugged her when the door opened, and over her friend's shoulder, Eileen saw Jeannie's mother, Mary, and her husband, Harry, smiling and coming towards them. It felt like coming home, she thought. The Dougals' home was always full of love and warmth.

After saying hello to them all and Jeannie telling Mary they couldn't stay because Eileen was hoping for a job interview, the two young women managed to get themselves organised to head down to the city centre. They got off the bus and walked down High Street to Glasgow Green with Jeannie pushing Flora in her pram.

'Mammy was that pleased to see you. I thought I heard your ribs crack when she hugged you.' Jeannie laughed.

'I was pleased to see her too. She's been like a second mother to me. In fact, she shows me more affection than mine ever has,' Eileen replied with a wry grin.

'At least you know why your mum has her limitations. Poor Agnes. I don't know how I'd bear it if I lost my wean.' Jeannie gave a shudder and leaned down to tuck Flora's light blanket over the baby's kicking feet.

'I understand Mum better since she told me about Ronnie, but I wish I had a mother like yours who dishes out the hugs and kisses without a moment's thought.'

'I'm envious of the peace and quiet at yours, though,' Jeannie said. 'Evie and Dennis are very noisy, and Flora has a good set of lungs too.'

Eileen thought how lovely it would be to have family living with her. She'd love to have noise and bustle to complain about. As an only child, she had often asked God to give her a sister or a brother, but it had never happened. After Ronnie, Agnes had not wanted another child – and Eileen's arrival had been a surprise.

'I wish—' she began, but Jeannie cut across her with an exclamation.

'Och, I'd forgotten what a grand building Templeton's Carpet Factory is. Like something out of a storybook, so it is.'

Eileen followed her friend's stare. She was right. Eileen hadn't been down towards Glasgow Green for years and she'd forgotten how big the park was and how fine a setting it made for the main carpet factory. Templeton's was designed by the famous architect William Leiper, and it was said he had modelled the building on the Doge's Palace in Venice. Eileen had never seen pictures of the

Italian palace, but she gazed in wonder at the amazing yellow and green zigzag-patterned tiling and the many windows, some circular and others curved at the top. Jeannie was right. It belonged in the *Arabian Nights* or similar. The building had had its share of tragedies. During building works, the façade collapsed, killing twenty-nine women working in the weaving sheds. Later, in 1900, a fire had killed more workers, all women. She hoped that Hitler's bombs wouldn't add more casualties, especially if she was going to be working nearby. The Greenbank building sat adjacent to the larger factory, looking like a drab poorer relative.

'Me and Flora will wait outside for you and take a wee turn round the park,' Jeannie said. 'Good luck. I hope they *are* hiring.'

So did Eileen. She needed work. Jimmy sent some of his pay home to her, but it wasn't a lot, not when he also sent money to his mother, as was only right and proper. She needed an income and quickly to pay her rent and buy enough food.

A half-hour later, Eileen practically skipped out of the carpet factory. Not only had they taken her on right away once they found out she could sew, but the floor supervisor was a jolly older woman who seemed kind and friendly. Eileen looked forward to starting there tomorrow. She was so preoccupied looking for Jeannie and Flora that she almost collided with another young woman.

'Oh, I'm so sorry. I wasn't looking where I was going,' Eileen said, flustered.

'You were fair storming through.' The other girl laughed, her dark eyes creased in amusement. 'I'm Morag, by the way. Are you working here too?'

'I'm Eileen. Yes, I think so.'

'You think so? Are you not sure?' Morag grinned.

'I've just been taken on. I'm starting tomorrow. I'm so relieved to have a job; I moved up to Glasgow yesterday and I was worrying about how to manage.'

'It's a good place to work and our supervisor is nice. So, I'll see you tomorrow then?' Morag said. 'No need to run, though,' she teased.

Eileen laughed. She waved goodbye to Morag and thought that maybe she'd made a friend already at the factory, which would make the next day easier to face.

—

'Is it army blankets, then?' Jeannie asked as they wheeled Flora past the wide River Clyde, which flowed along the western edge of the Green.

'Aye, it is. You should see it inside. The factory floor's massive and you can see nothing but rows and rows of sewing machines with women's heads bent over them. It smells of wool and thread and it's more than a mite dusty. I was coughing when I came out. But I think I'll like it.'

'That's good you're sorted. Shall we head back home? This young lady's getting restless and needs a nappy change.'

Eileen picked up a newspaper on the corner where a boy in a cloth cap and ragged trousers was shouting out the headlines and selling them. When they were on the bus, with Flora on Jeannie's knee and the pram stowed at the side, she looked at it. The front page had a big, bold title. *Siegfried Battle Zero Hour is Drawing Near*, it proclaimed, and in smaller font, *Allied Forces Sweep Over Moselle*. That had to be good news, didn't it, even if she had no idea where the Siegfried Line was nor what or where the Moselle was. *The moment when the Allied armies will hurl themselves against the Siegfried Line seems approaching fast. Allied formations are sweeping over the Moselle and Meuse at an ever-increasing number of places*, she read. She felt a surge of hope that perhaps the war was nearly over. After all, they had liberated Paris only a fortnight ago. When she turned to page two, there was an article about the home front, which promised *relaxation of the blackout, of fire-watching and Home Guard duties as from the middle of September...* There was a very real sense that the war was almost won, reading that. She wondered where Jimmy was and if he too was sweeping over the Moselle and Meuse. Her stomach lurched. *Please stay safe*; she sent a silent prayer into the air.

'What's wrinkling your nose?' Jeannie said, kissing Flora and glancing at her friend.

'I was praying for Jimmy. That he'll be all right. It's reading all this... seems like our lot are doing well, taking back Europe and all that, but soldiers will be dying in the battle. Jerry isn't going to just lie down and take it, is he?'

Jeannie frowned. 'Best not to imagine it. My brother's called Lucky Jim by his friends. If anyone makes it home, it'll be him.'

Eileen sighed. 'You're right, but it's hard not to wonder where he is and what he's doing.'

'Go on, cheer us up by telling us what's on at the cinema.'

Eileen sighed again as she flicked to the entertainment pages.

'Remember when we used to go to the dancing?' she said to Jeannie wistfully.

Eileen loved to dance. As a parlour maid in a big house in Cambuslang, before the war, she used to spend her half day off dancing at Green's Playhouse. She had gone back there with Jeannie and their other friends from the factory and to Locarno's too. There were adverts for both in the paper. *Green's Playhouse Ballroom Last Week of Oscar Rabin and his band with Harry Davis. Victor Silvester and his ballroom orchestra, 'the band that's grand to dance to'*, and then in big, bold letters: *Locarno*.

Jeannie nodded. 'Those were the days. Fat chance I'd have now with this wee one. You could go, though?'

Aye, but who with? Eileen thought. She didn't fancy it by herself.

'Have you heard from that brother of mine?' Jeannie asked, cuddling Flora, who gurned quietly.

'I haven't had a letter in the past few weeks but it's sometimes like that. Then they'll all come at once in a bundle tied with string.'

They got off the bus and walked down from the main road into Kiltie Street. Eileen's room and kitchen was in number eight, which was the first tenement off the split in the road, but she walked along to number four to keep Jeannie company. She helped lift the pram up the stone steps and into the close where it was stored. Jeannie took Flora into the flat and Eileen waved as they promised to meet up soon. She felt a bit deflated as she stepped back down onto the pavement. She was on her own again, going back to an empty flat.

'Oh, I do beg your pardon.' A man's voice broke into her thoughts, and she looked up to see a bulky figure in front of her, touching the brim of his hat respectfully.

He looked vaguely familiar as she took in the homburg, the thick, black moustache and pouchy cheeks and a rounded stomach under the leather coat. Then she remembered the motor car from yesterday.

'Leo Mearns at your service, madam.'

He gave a small bow, which made Eileen want to giggle, but something in his face made her stop. He took himself seriously, she thought. He was waiting and she realised he wanted to know who she was too.

'Eileen Boyle. I've just moved into number eight, a flat at the top,' she said, and instantly wished she hadn't.

He had cold, dark eyes and his smile was reptilian. She disliked him immediately. He glanced at her left hand and raised his hat.

'Miss Boyle. Delighted to make your acquaintance. Welcome to Kiltie Street.'

She could have told him she knew the street well and had indeed lived here before but instead she gave a polite nod and turned away towards her flat. Her skin prickled unpleasantly, and she knew he was watching her go. She ran up the steps and into her flat, slamming the door and locking it. He was just another daft man taken with blonde curls and green eyes. But she couldn't help moving over to the window and carefully looking out, trying not to be seen as she did so. Leo Mearns was staring back and Eileen gasped and darted out of sight. When she looked again, he had gone.

The room darkened, and she realised it had started raining. She went into the kitchen to prepare her dinner. Not being a great cook, it was only bread and jam and a small piece of cheese from her weekly ration. She ate it sitting on her bed, watching the raindrops drizzle down the window pane.

She ought to be celebrating. She had a place to live, near to her best friend, and a new job beginning the next day. Instead, she felt unsettled and wary. As if something bad was coming.

Chapter Three

'They've taken on some new workers. A really nice bunch of girls. I think I'll make some new friends. I had a chat at tea break with a girl called Eileen; she's moved here from down south. She reminds me of Lana Turner, such lovely blonde curls and big eyes. She's got a fiancé fighting in Europe and you can tell she's deeply in love with him.' Morag Kincaid took a moment to pause in between her chatter, bending down to shove a shepherd's pie into the oven.

She glanced over at her husband, George, who was hidden behind the newspapers. Pipe smoke wafted up. He grunted to show he had heard. Morag rolled her eyes, knowing full well he hadn't paid any attention.

'And we also saw Herr Hitler himself. He came to see how we were getting on sewing army blankets.'

George grunted again but the papers didn't move. Morag felt a wave of tiredness wash over her. Every day she worked a full shift at Greenbank, her head bent over her sewing machine, and by the evening, her neck and shoulders ached. She was only twenty-two but sometimes she felt like seventy. After her shift she always hurried home to cook the evening meal for herself, George and their two long-term lodgers. She rinsed the dirt off the carrots, home-grown from their tiny garden, and stuck them in a pot of water to boil. The tatties were simmering away nicely. She loved the smell of them. It reminded her of her childhood home, growing up in Bridgeton in a wee house not far from where they lived now.

Mr McLeod put his head round the door, withered neck stretched out, reminding Morag of an elderly tortoise.

'Will it be long till tea, Mrs Kincaid?'

'Not too long, Mr McLeod. I'll call you once it's on the table.'

Morag smiled at her lodger as he shuffled back out. They had the same conversation every evening. Mr McLeod liked everything just so. He had his routines and became quite agitated if they were disrupted. When the air raids and bombings were at their worst, three years ago, it had been very difficult for him and for those who lived in the same house, trying to reassure him amid the uncertainty and fear that they all felt.

Morag's other lodger, Miss Linton, was quite the opposite. She was a dainty but frail old lady with a penchant for mint humbugs who quite happily accepted whatever was going on and never complained if meals were late or ingredients missing due to rationing or scarcity. Food was hard to come by in the city and rations had to stretch further these days than ever before. Miss Linton also reminded Morag of an aged Lana Turner with her soft, fluffy, faded blonde hair and her good bone structure.

Morag chuckled to herself at the absurdity of that. Two Lana Turner lookalikes in her life. She wanted to share the joke with George and opened her mouth to do so but closed it again. George wasn't one for whimsy. He didn't really understand her sense of humour. Never mind. She loved him anyway. They had been married almost four years but sometimes it felt brand new to her.

She looked around her kitchen with pride. They actually owned this house, thanks to George inheriting it from his parents. Not many folk could say the same. Most people rented flats in the red sandstone tenements nearby. Bridgeton lay east of Glasgow Green. It was a working-class area full of engineering firms and factories, a busy and interesting place to live. Morag loved the grand Olympia Cinema, which was a five-minute walk away and boasted over fifteen hundred seats. Luckily, George loved seeing films too, and they often went on a Saturday evening. If they didn't fancy what was on at the Olympia, then the King's Cinema in James Street, a wee bit closer to the Green, was their other option. There were cheap wooden seats at the front where they often sat as they were 'saving their pennies', as George put it.

When the meal was ready, Morag set it out on the dining room table using the matching crockery that had belonged to George's mother and took pleasure in how the cutlery glinted since she had polished it with a tea towel. Mr McLeod took his seat quickly. For an old man he could be sprightly when there was a meal on offer. Miss Linton walked more slowly, and Morag frowned. Her lady lodger looked pale.

'Are you quite all right, Miss Linton?' she asked with concern.

'Yes, dear, thank you for asking. I have a little dyspepsia, that's all. I'm afraid I won't be able to eat all my dinner. Could I ask you to put half aside for tomorrow? I don't want to waste any.'

'Of course. That's no problem. George, will you pull Miss Linton's chair out for her, please, while I cover up half the portion.'

George courteously pulled out the chair and ushered Miss Linton into it in a gentlemanly manner. He winked at Morag, who hid a smile as she took half the old lady's meal back into the kitchen in the pie dish and covered it with a cloth. He had very nice manners, her husband, she thought. Could charm the birds from the trees, as her mother would say. She felt a flush of pleasure that he'd chosen her to court and marry. Friends often said what a good match they were, with George's wavy fair hair and her own dark, thick brown locks. They were both good-looking, young and ambitious to do well for themselves. George was a clerk in the shipyards at Govan and hoped for promotion.

'They like the right sort of chap,' he had told Morag. 'That's why I've got to dress well and polish my shoes and get the right accent. Then I'll go far. I'm certain of it.'

Mr McLeod gave a small cough. This generally indicated an announcement and today was no different.

'They're lifting the blackout, I see. Calling it the dim-out. Good thing too now that Jerry is on the run. Won't be long now until the war is won, mark my words.'

'Oh, that is good news,' Miss Linton cried. 'Won't it be lovely to see the city lights once again.'

'Steady on. You won't see the lights, I'm afraid. No, indeed. They simply mean that you can ditch the blackout curtains and use normal curtains. Direct lights are still forbidden and if the sirens go it's back to full blackout.'

'It's still a very good sign,' Morag said warmly, seeing Miss Linton's disappointment. 'Maybe it really will all be over by this Christmas.'

'Well, as they've said that every other Christmas, I doubt this one will be any different.' George laughed.

Mr McLeod shook his head and went back to concentrating on the shepherd's pie, demolishing it steadily with his knife and fork.

After the evening meal, the lodgers usually sat in the parlour and listened to the wireless or played cards while Morag brought them a pot of tea and a small selection of biscuits. Once she had done that, she went back into the kitchen to wash up the dishes. George came in and sat at the table. In the early days of their marriage, she had suggested he dry the dishes while she washed but he had gently pointed out that it was women's work. He more than did his part by working in the shipyard offices and doing any heavy work around the house, fixing anything that was broken and so on. Morag had wanted to remind him that she worked her shifts, queued for food, made the meals and looked after their lodgers along with all the housework but she knew that George's parents had had a very conventional marriage and that he wanted the same. Besides, she was very much in love with him, and they were newly married, so it didn't seem right to argue.

Sometimes, like tonight, when her muscles ached, she wished she had made a stand right at the beginning. It was too late now to complain. When the pots and dishes were washed, dried and put away, she sat at the table too. Honestly, she could put her head down on the polished wooden surface and sleep. She yawned.

'Darling, are you sleepy?' George said lightly. 'Come here and I shall kiss you awake.'

Morag smiled. She slipped from her chair and sat on George's lap, her arm around his neck. His kiss was warm and comforting.

'Mrs Kincaid, you are a tonic, so you are,' George said with a sigh. 'Do you know, Morag darling, I think about you when I'm at work striving to do my best so that the managers will notice me. You make me want to be a better man and make money so that we will be more comfortably off.'

'We are comfortable, George. That's why you suggested we take in our lodgers. And you were right. This house is too big for just the two of us and their rent brings in the cash.'

'I know, but I also want that job… Did I tell you that Rob Gunn was made up to supervisor over me? What has he got that I don't? I've been in there longer than him by six months.'

'His uncle is one of the managers. That's how,' Morag said.

She kissed him on the mouth, trying to distract him. She was a little bit sick of hearing about Rob Gunn and his promotion. George couldn't understand why he hadn't been picked and kept going on about it. Nothing Morag said could soothe him.

'You should see if there's any promotion prospects at the carpet factory,' George said suddenly. 'If they've taken more women on, they must need more supervisors.'

So he had noticed what she said earlier.

'There's been no mention of that,' she said. 'I don't think there will be more supervisor posts.'

George's shoulders slumped. 'We have to plan for our future, darling. The war won't last forever, and we have to be ready to make the most of what comes after. That means better jobs for both of us. The sooner we can get those, the better. We're lucky we own this house outright and that Mum and Dad left us all the furniture too, but I want us to have savings for more than a rainy day.'

'If we have children, I won't be able to work so I'm not sure I should be looking for advancement,' Morag said tentatively.

'Darling, we agreed we won't try for children. Not now. Didn't we?' George squeezed her hand.

You agreed. I didn't, Morag thought but managed a weak smile. He was very careful when it came to their lovemaking, so there was no chance of her conceiving.

'I'd... I'd love to have our own wee baby,' she said softly. 'Imagine it, George. A wee boy who looks like you with gorgeous fair curls and brown eyes. Wouldn't it be marvellous to have someone to call you Daddy? Someone we would love so very much. Wouldn't that make life worthwhile?'

'One day we will. But not now, we both know this isn't the right time. Babies are expensive items. Besides, we've only been married a few years. I want you all to myself, Mrs Kincaid.' George stood up, taking Morag with him, and swung her in a waltz across the kitchen floor before kissing her. 'Now, I think I'll join Mr McLeod to hear the BBC news. Will you join me?'

Morag shook her head. 'I have to blacklead the range. I'll be through in a while. You go on.'

She didn't reach for the tin of black lead when he had gone. She leaned against the range, feeling the hard metal dig into her back. She counted her blessings. She was in love with George and that was the main thing. They had a lovely house. The lodgers were good people who paid their rent on time. Her parents lived not far away. She had made some new friends at her work. All these were good things. So why did it feel as if there was a terrible hole in her life that could only be filled by a baby?

—

Eileen wore her favourite blue dress to visit her parents. She had made it herself from a roll of cheap printed cotton she'd found in a market in Glasgow a few years ago, a real bargain. Once it was made up into the dress pattern, she thought it looked quite smart and cheerful, especially as she had embroidered the pockets and sewn on pretty buttons. Blue suited her blonde curls. She applied her crimson lipstick and brushed her hair until it shone. Her utility shoes with wooden heels were at least hard-wearing if not fashionable, and they would have to do.

The bus left her off at the western end of the city, where Agnes and Robert Boyle rented a small house in a street not far from where their own had been destroyed by the bombing. Eileen walked past the crumbled remains of their old home and shuddered. They had been lucky to survive in their Anderson shelter that night. She had taken a bump to the head and didn't remember all of that terrible event, having woken to find herself in hospital. It was a sad sight; most of the row of houses was still a pile of rubble. The house at the end stood, but the wall was missing, so the rooms were visible like a doll's house opened up. There was a piano in an upstairs room and curtains flicking indolently this way and that in the summer breeze on a window frame with no glass except for jagged shards. At the ground floor, thieves had been at work and stripped the contents out so that only the fireplace and floorboards remained. Eileen noticed that even some of those had been prised up and removed.

A few streets away, she rang the doorbell and waited for her mother to let her in. Agnes kept the door locked and Eileen didn't have a key. She'd returned it when she moved to England. The front garden was tiny and neat with gravel and a shrub border. There was a pot with lettuce leaves and another with beans in flower, their orange-red petals a startling flash of colour against the drab pebbledash of the house.

'There you are. Was your bus late? I expected you sooner.'

Agnes popped a dry kiss on Eileen's cheek and gave her a brief hug. Eileen wanted to prolong the hug but knew her mother wasn't comfortable with displays of emotion. Especially when the neighbours might see.

'How are you, Mum? I don't think I am late. I was working a short shift this morning and got the afternoon off. They want me in full shifts next week, though, which is good.'

Agnes sniffed as if to say she didn't approve of half days but didn't comment. Instead, she stopped in the hallway. 'Don't agitate your father at all. He has to be kept quiet.'

'Is he improving? I do hope he is all right.'

'He is getting better, but I'm scared in case he has another attack and it's fatal.' Agnes folded her arms against her chest with a tight expression on her thin face.

'Oh, Mum. I'm sure that won't happen,' Eileen said, giving her mother that hug now, impulsively.

Her mum felt all sharp bones beneath Eileen's arms and made no effort to return the embrace. With an inward sigh, Eileen reminded herself yet again that Agnes was doing her best, that she loved her but simply couldn't show it well.

'Are you looking after yourself? You've lost weight,' she said.

'It's all the worry. I just don't feel hungry,' Agnes replied. 'Go and see your father now. I'll boil the kettle and we'll have some tea and scones.'

The front room was neat and tidy, just as Eileen remembered, but she saw that Agnes had made it more homely in the months she had been away. There were now three ceramic flying ducks on the wallpapered chimney breast, and a new vase with wax roses sat on the sideboard. They had lost most of their belongings in the blitz, so Agnes had gradually bought, borrowed, and somehow replaced things as and when she could.

Her father was sitting in an overstuffed armchair, his head resting on a lace antimacassar. His trusty pipe, emitting small curls of smoke, was propped on the table beside him along with a tin of Sobranie, his favourite tobacco. As a child, Eileen had loved the smell of the Sobranie as her father's long fingers wadded it into the pipe bowl.

'Hello, Dad. How are you?'

Robert nodded. 'There is very little wrong with me. Your mother fusses unnecessarily.'

Eileen shared a look with her father. They didn't often mention emotions or feelings, but she knew they were both thinking about Ronnie and all that Agnes had lost. She was scared of losing her husband too.

Agnes came in with a tea tray and Eileen took it from her and laid it on a low table in front of the fireplace. She poured the thin liquid into the cups, placed them on the matching saucers and gave them to her parents. The scones had a scrape of margarine and jam. They each took one on a plate. There was a silence while these were eaten, and a sip of tea taken to wash them down. It was an unwritten rule that they never spoke during mealtimes. Eileen had never understood why. Growing up, she had ached to share her day and hear their stories too. And between meals, there was never enough time to do so as they were all busy. She had to remind herself now that she was in their house and had to abide by their rules, but honestly, she felt quite impatient with it, having been out into the big wide world, seeing and experiencing different ways of life.

Finally, Agnes gave a small cough and spoke. 'How is that young man of yours?'

'My fiancé, you mean.'

Agnes's gaze flickered meaningfully to Eileen's fingers, bare of decoration.

'He hasn't been here to give me a ring, Mum. He wrote that we'll go and choose it together when he comes home.'

'And when will that be, do you know?'

Eileen sighed and put her cup down. 'He has no idea. How can he have when they're in the thick of the fighting?'

'Dad was reading about them being in Paris. Perhaps he's there. What was it they were saying, Robert? Not that you should be reading about all the terrible news; it isn't good for your heart.'

'I could tell you, dear, but you don't need to hear about it. Nor do you, Eileen. Women shouldn't worry their heads about all this. That's for fathers and husbands to do.'

Although women were also fighting this awful war, Eileen thought grimly. And dying in it too. Her friend Janet had been killed in the Clydebank blitz. The women making army blankets, day after day, were playing their part, as were those in the munitions factory where Jeannie worked. Jeannie's wee sister, Kathy, was a gunner girl, a dangerous occupation. There was no one who had been left untouched by the war. If it wasn't that her father was recovering from a heart attack, she'd have argued with him. Women couldn't afford ignorance of what was going on.

'Does he write often?' Agnes asked.

'When he can. The letters come patchily. I haven't had any for a week or two, but then I know one day soon, I'll get a bundle all together. The army post has its vagaries.'

'And what will you do if he doesn't come home at all?'

There was a tremor in her mother's voice, and Eileen knew she wasn't asking out of meanness or making Eileen afraid. It was Agnes's own fears rising to the top. She didn't want her daughter to experience the pain of loss as she had herself.

—

The visit hadn't been a great success, Eileen thought afterwards as she made her weary way back along Kiltie Street. She loved them both; of course she did. They were her parents, after all. But she couldn't feel close to them somehow, even though she wanted to.

She turned into tenement number eight and up the stairs to the top and decided to cheer herself up by sewing. She had mended the holes in the curtains shortly after moving in and rehung them and now she was making herself a new nightdress out of butter muslin, which she had been able to buy as it wasn't rationed. Her foot went up and down, up and down treading the sewing machine as her fingers made sure the needle pressed the thread through in the right places. It was a pattern she had used before so she was confident she could produce a reasonable nightdress. If only Jimmy could see her wearing it. After they were married, of course, Eileen chastened herself with a giggle.

The wireless blasted out cheerful songs as she sewed. She sang along to the popular number 'I Had the Craziest Dream' and laughed out loud as she enjoyed the music. She had been in the flat a week. The bed mattress was now covered in clean sheets and a blanket that she had brought with her from Devon. The pillowcases, also from Devon, were a buttercup yellow, which brightened the room. She had draped a small blue tablecloth over the rickety table to hide the cup marks where the previous tenant had carelessly set down a hot mug. There was no way of disguising the sombre colour of the wardrobe, but she had hung some of her colourful scarves from the wardrobe doors and thought they looked nice.

The flat had smelled of damp and mould, so she had squirted a little of her precious White Lilac perfume into the air and onto her scarves, where it lingered. Finally, she had set up her sewing machine in the small remaining space between the bed, wardrobe and door. She itched to adjust the clothes that Frankie Bett had so carelessly dumped on the floor when he took the suitcase. But going to work had put paid to any thoughts of sewing for the first few days, apart from mending the curtains, which was a necessity if she didn't want the ARP man to come calling and give her a telling-off and a hefty fine.

She was finishing the hem when there was a knock at the door. Thinking it might be Jeannie, she flung it open with a smile that vanished when she saw a man holding a bunch of flowers.

'Mr Mearns. Can I help you?' Her thoughts were scattered. What was he doing on her doorstep?

'Miss Boyle.' The hand that wasn't holding the flowers lifted his hat politely.

Before she knew it, they were both inside the tiny flat, and he thrust the flowers at her.

'A house-warming gift.'

She took them reluctantly, wondering how to make him leave. The flowers had a sickly sweet scent that permeated the air in the flat. She should've opened a window earlier and let the breeze in.

'They need water. Let me.'

He was in her kitchen, reaching for a jug. Her only jug as it happened. One she'd need later to pour her custard. Sudden irritation made her senses sharp. She had dealt with plenty of other men. Leo Mearns was no different. She didn't care what he wanted or why he was there. He had to go.

'How is your wife, Mr Mearns?' she asked sweetly.

The shock that passed briefly over his fleshy features was a sign that her arrow had hit the target. She had made a guess that he would be married. His face drooped as if sad.

'Ahh, the Kiltie Street gossip mill has been in motion, I see,' he said. 'I'm afraid Mrs Mearns hasn't kept good health since our second child was born. We live quite separate lives. She keeps our house in Dennistoun, and I prefer to live in Kiltie Street since I inherited it recently. You must come and visit. It is beautifully furnished thanks to my mother's good taste.'

'My fiancé wouldn't like me to visit a man living on his own,' Eileen told him.

'Congratulations to the lucky fellow. When is the happy day?' Leo Mearns said.

Was she imagining the slightly mocking tone? Oh, if only Jimmy had been able to give her a ring to show the world that they were promised to each other. She didn't care if it was expensive or not. She only cared that everyone knew she had found her perfect other half. This horrible suave man in front of her, he wouldn't dare to swan into her home in this way if she was married. She was sure of it.

'Thank you for the flowers. I'm sorry but I'm very busy so I'll have to ask you to leave,' Eileen said firmly.

She held the front door open so he couldn't mistake her message. With a small bow, he walked out. He paused then.

'We'll meet again, as the song goes. Good afternoon, Miss Boyle.'

Not if I have anything to do with it. Eileen slammed the door shut. Her heart was thudding. She didn't go to the window in case he was staring up at her. *Oh, Jimmy, where are you, my love? I love you so much. I need you*, she thought to herself. In a flash of fear, Agnes's words came back to her.

'*And what will you do if he doesn't come home at all?*'

Chapter Four

It was a dreich October day with a light but persistent rain that soaked the streets and anyone foolish enough to linger outside. A young woman, carrying a cardboard suitcase, walked along the main street in Maryhill. Her clothes were shabby and her leather boots scuffed and worn down at the heels. She had a piece of paper clutched in her hand and she stopped people to ask directions. There weren't many folk on the street. She pulled her faded blue cloche hat as far over her ears as possible. Its linen flower drooped.

'Excuse me.' She stood in front of an elderly woman dragging a reluctant terrier along on a length of rope.

'What is it, hen?' the woman said, not unkindly. The terrier yelped and sat on its hindquarters as raindrops dribbled down its fur.

'I'm looking for Kiltie Street. I know it's around here somewhere, but I can't see the turn-off.'

'Kiltie Street, is it?' The woman looked at her curiously.

'That's what I said.' Her tone changed to become softly pleasant. 'I'd be very glad of your help if you can tell me.'

'Och, I can tell you all right. You're no' far frae it the now. See down there, past the shops, turn right and there you are. It's only a short street, mind, and a dead end. You're no' local wi' that accent, are you, hen?'

But the girl only nodded her thanks, picked up her damp suitcase again and walked quickly away. The older woman made a face at her receding back. A wee chat wouldn't have hurt her now, would it. It wasn't as if they often got tourists coming to Kiltie Street and the local area. She jerked the rope, making the terrier whine.

'Whit happened tae yer face?' she shouted after the retreating figure.

—

Eileen had a day off from the factory. She had been delighted to get a letter from Jimmy in the morning post. It was over a month old, but she realised how tense she'd been, waiting to hear from him. It was proof that, at least four weeks ago, he was alive. She'd made an event out of it, waiting to read it until she'd made a pot of tea and a piece of toast with a thin smear of margarine for her breakfast. Then she settled into her chair and opened the envelope carefully.

My dearest Sheena, Jimmy wrote. The letter was dated 3 September.

> *Well, dear, today marks the start of the sixth Year of War and that must make us all feel weary. What cheers me up is remembering a certain dance hall in Maryhill and a young lady I accompanied to the dancing in June 1940. I recall she wore a red dress and had lipstick to match. Very nice she looked too, with her blonde curls. I had sore feet, mind, after being rescued from the beach at Dunkirk, but they didn't stop me doing a slow shuffle on the dance floor. You know, Sheena, I had already decided*

> *you'd one day be Mrs Dougal. Did you have the same idea? I hope so, my darling girl. Ma wee doll.*
>
> *I can't settle to write a long letter when there's so much uncertainty. Aye, we're moving forward, kicking Jerry where it hurts, but sometimes we're moving sideways or backwards too. I don't have much confidence in our commanders, but there we are. What can I do? I'm only a private who has to follow orders. I won't say more, dear. I won't describe the sights I've seen. I only want to imagine your pretty face so I can see it when I sleep.*
>
> *HOLLAND*
> *Your Jimmy*

Eileen kissed the letter, wishing it was Jimmy's mouth. His hands had touched this paper, and it was a link with him somehow. HOLLAND was the soldiers' shorthand for Hope Our Love Lasts And Never Dies. She hoped the same and knew, for her, it would always be true.

Later that morning, humming 'Little Brown Jug' to herself, she got ready to go out. She'd get her rations first from the shops and then she was meeting Jeannie up at the park for a walk and some fresh air, as Jeannie had a half-day shift. It would do them both good. It was drizzling a light misty rain as she reached Maryhill Park. Like other parks in the city, the flowerbeds and lawns had been dug up to make allotments. There was a land girl hoeing weeds in between the growing onions, beetroot and cabbages, her back bent to her task. She must have been disappointed being sent to an industrial city instead of the wholesome countryside when she joined the Women's Land Army, Eileen thought wryly. But the girl smiled and waved as Eileen went by, so she seemed happy enough.

And there was Jeannie ahead, also waving at her. She was pushing the big pram, her nephew Dennis toddling gamely alongside, and Evie, who was almost six, skipping ahead. 'Och, it's good to get a wee breather, so it is, even if it's raining,' Jeannie said as the two friends met. 'I forget there's such a thing as daylight when I'm working in Fearnmore. The windows are that high up they may as well not have any.'

'I know what you mean. Greenbank is fine for windows, but we've all got our heads bent over the sewing machines. We daren't make wobbly seams in the blankets so we can't look up and appreciate the light coming in.'

'You'll not recognise our Dennis, he's grown so much,' Jeannie said, nodding towards her nephew.

'He was only a wee baby when I last saw him,' Eileen agreed. 'You're a big boy now, aren't you?' She hunkered down to Dennis's height to greet him.

'And this here's Evie.' Jeannie smiled at the little girl holding hands with Dennis. 'I wrote to you about Kathy and her friend Violet who are gunner girls with the ATS. Evie is Violet's niece and needed a home while her auntie is fighting the war. Mammy took her in, and we are all pleased about that, aren't we, Dennis?'

'Who are you?' Evie asked, taking her hand and hopping up and down.

'I'm Jeannie's friend,' Eileen said.

Evie nodded. 'Is Auntie Violet coming home soon?'

Eileen knew from Jeannie that Evie's mother had died of tuberculosis. Her heart went out to the small girl who had lost her mother so early in life.

'I don't know, sweetheart. Jeannie's mum will tell you when she hears. I expect she'll get letters from your Auntie Violet.'

'Auntie Violet may not be getting leave just now but we won't be here anyway for a few days,' Jeannie said. 'So perhaps it's just as well.'

'Where are you going?' Eileen asked as they all walked along the wide park path.

Flora was asleep in her comfortable pram, her wee body moving under the thin blanket as the pram bumped over tree roots and cracks in the tarmac. There was no money for park improvements, just as there was no money for anything other than the war machine over the last five years.

'We're going to visit Isa and Bob on the farm. You know how they're staying with my Uncle Angus and Aunt Martha for the duration. We're invited for a few days. I can't wait, never mind the weans. It's out in the countryside and Martha's a grand cook. I'm always starving, and Evie and Dennis are like wee gannets, so they are, when Mammy puts the food down in front of them. Mammy reckons we'll be round as balls when we come back.'

Isa and Bob were Jeannie's younger sister and brother and part of the large, loving Dougal family. There it was. Eileen couldn't help it. A sharp jab of envy in her ribs, like a proper pain. Oh, but she'd love to have a favourite aunt and uncle who invited her to stay. Not on her own. No. In her imagination, it would be just like Jeannie's situation, where there were several lively children and other relatives—a whole noisy, happy household. She only had an aunt in Glasgow whom Agnes and Robert rarely saw and a cousin who was working in London for the war effort, and she'd only met her a handful of times.

'You could come, if you like,' Jeannie said, understanding her friend only too well.

'Och, no. I don't want to intrude.'

Eileen half hoped Jeannie would argue and persuade her otherwise, but her friend nodded and then dived in to split up an argument between Evie and Dennis, who were tussling over a flower plucked from the muddy grass.

'Wee devils,' Jeannie muttered once the two youngsters had scampered off screaming happily, the flower forgotten.

'When are you going?'

'Tomorrow. I've got leave to take, and it'll do the wee ones good. Gives Mammy a break too.'

Eileen nodded. She'd miss her friend, but it was only for a few days.

'How are you settling in at Greenbank, then?' Jeannie asked.

'It's fine. I like the sewing, and the other girls are friendly. There's one, Morag, who I chat to over tea most days.'

'That's good you've got a pal already.'

Morag was friendly, but Eileen didn't know if they were friends exactly. It wasn't as if Morag had suggested meeting up outside of working hours. They walked on past the tennis courts and then back along the lime tree avenue. The trees cast shadows on the path as a cautious sun came out from behind the clouds and she realised it was late afternoon.

'Aye, we'd best get back too,' Jeannie said, when Eileen remarked on it. 'Let's gather those two running wild and get on home.'

—

When they turned into their street, Dennis was tired and whining and Evie was dragging her feet. They both had mud-streaked faces and damp boots.

'I'd best get this lot inside for a wash and some grub.' Jeannie grinned at Eileen. She paused. 'Who's that on your doorstep?'

Eileen looked over to see a slim girl sitting on the top step, her arms wrapped around her bent knees and a blue hat covering her face. Beside her on the step was a suitcase. Her coat showed signs of the recent rain, wrinkled as if it had dried badly. As Jeannie went on with her brood, Eileen went slowly up the stone steps.

'Excuse me, I need to get past,' she said.

The girl raised her head, and Eileen felt a strange sense of familiarity.

'Do I know you?' she asked.

'Are you Eileen Sheena Boyle? Then I know you. I'm your cousin, Amy Boyle. I got soaked through waiting on you. Where have you been?'

'My... cousin?' Eileen was shocked and bemused.

'Can we go in and talk? I'm cold from sitting on this step.' She stood up and dragged the suitcase with her, looking impatiently at Eileen.

Eileen found herself hurrying up to the top floor to unlock her flat with Amy right behind her. She stopped once the door was open as Amy bumped into her.

'I've only got one cousin, Linda, and she's in London,' Eileen said suspiciously.

Amy gave an audible sigh. She dug about in a scuffed navy blue handbag and pushed a photograph into Eileen's hand.

'There, see. That's my dad and yours. Your dad is Robert Boyle and mine is Norman; he is Robert's younger brother.'

The photograph was not one Eileen had ever seen but there was no doubt that her dad was the tall young man on the left and little doubt that the other man was his brother. They looked identical. They were standing in a field with a broad oak tree behind them. While she stared, wide-eyed, trying to make sense of all this, Amy brushed past her into the flat and dropped her suitcase in the hall.

'Is that what you're planning for your tea?' she shouted back over her shoulder.

Eileen had set out half a loaf, a small dish of margarine and a pot of jam.

'Aye, it is. You can share it with me, if you like.' It wouldn't do any harm to let this new cousin stay for a meal so she could find out more about her and what she wanted. She felt completely bewildered.

'I can do better than that.' Amy darted back out of Eileen's kitchen. She had her sleeves rolled up to her elbows and Eileen's apron on. 'I'll make you a proper tea. You've got a little bit of cold fish here and an egg. I'll do us devilled fish and a Brown Betty for afters.'

Eileen's tummy rumbled. 'Don't go to any bother on my behalf.'

'Oh, it's no bother at all,' Amy called, and Eileen heard the clank of pots and the rattle of spoons.

She frowned at the photograph, still clasped in her hand, and went to look in the kitchen. Even without the proof of the two brothers, it was obvious now that she and Amy were related. Amy looked very like her; they could be sisters, even. No wonder she looked familiar. Her skin was pale with an unhealthy greyish tone apart, from a livid purplish bruise on her left cheek. Her hair was more mousey-brown than blonde, but their bone structure and eye colour were identical. They were even the same height and build.

She was dying to ask Amy all sorts of questions but wisely waited until they sat down to have their meal. Since Amy had all but taken over the kitchen, Eileen laid the table with plates and cutlery and two linen serviettes. It was nice to have someone to eat with, but this felt quite unreal.

'There, get that down you,' Amy told her, spooning the fish onto the plates. It had been cooked with the hard-boiled egg, flour, milk and a pinch of curry powder and baked with breadcrumbs.

Tasting it, Eileen was surprised. 'This is delicious, Amy. I have to admit, when I cook fish it comes out all rubbery.'

'Oh, you're overcooking it, then. Fish needs a light touch. This dish, well, it's the Worcester sauce what makes it special, like.'

The Brown Betty was just as good. It was mostly breadcrumbs but made very tasty by baking them with golden syrup, apples and spices. It was a good way of disguising apples past their best. In fact, Eileen smiled to herself, the apples she had left in a bowl were wizened and she'd wondered whether to eat them or present them to the pig kept in the back court at the end of the tenement row.

'How did you find my address?' she asked, as they scraped their plates to get the last dribbles of golden syrup onto their spoons. It was what she'd been dying to ask since Amy had arrived on the doorstep.

'Norman gave me Robert's address and I went there first. Not to the house or nothing, but I walked round the local shops, and someone knew Agnes and she was right chatty and said Agnes's daughter had moved up from Devon to Glasgow. She even remembered the name of your street but not the number or anything else useful. So I came up here and I met a gentleman who says he lives at the top of the last tenement and when I described you he told me where your flat was. Said we were like two peas in a pod, so he did, and he knew immediately that I was your cousin, or perhaps your sister.' Amy laughed.

Eileen was trying to take all this in. The gentleman had to be Leo Mearns. And wasn't it odd that Amy hadn't gone to visit Eileen's parents?

'Why didn't you ring the bell when you went to my parents'?'

'Because your dad and mine... they didn't get on, see. There was a falling-out. Robert was jealous of Norman because he'd done better, got away from their father, a domineering bully, and gone south. Made his fortune in London instead. Norman done good for himself.'

'Why do you call your dad by his Christian name?' Eileen couldn't help asking.

Amy shrugged. 'We're not close. He don't mind. I call my mother Pearl and not Mum, neither.'

'So you're from London. Which part?'

Finding out about Amy was beginning to feel like trying to get the proverbial blood from a stone. She wasn't exactly forthcoming. In fact, the more she spoke, the more of a mystery she became, and the more queries Eileen had.

'Tottenham. You won't know it, I'm sure. But I'm Tottenham born and bred.'

'And why...?' Eileen trailed off.

'More Brown Betty? Won't do to have leftovers. Waste not, want not, as my old gran would say.'

Eileen had to wait until they had a second helping of the sweet pudding before she could ask more. Amy shovelled hers down, patting her stomach with a satisfied sigh when it was gone.

'What happened to your face? It looks painful,' Eileen said, when she had finished her own portion and put the spoon down in the middle of her empty plate just as Agnes had taught her was good manners.

A dull flush gave Amy's pasty skin a little colour momentarily before it faded away, leaving the livid side of her face even more purple than before.

'Oh, it's nuffink. I walked into a door, silly me. I've always been clumsy; you can ask Pearl. She'd tell you.'

Since Eileen had never met Pearl or known of her existence until an hour ago, this was unlikely to happen. She had to take Amy's word for it. But there was something she definitely wanted to know and no polite way to ask.

'Why are you here, Amy?'

'I had to get out of London, didn't I. I've… I've had enough of all them doodlebugs. It's all very well trying to ignore them and carrying on like everything is normal until one comes across and flattens yet more houses and kills little kids and housewives. It gets on the nerves after a while, makes you all shaky.'

Eileen had heard about the doodlebugs attacking London on the news when she listened to the wireless. This July and August, they had been thick and fast across the capital, creating havoc and damage on a city that was already full of rubble and demolished buildings from the London blitz. The unmanned missiles came at all hours of the day as people went about their daily business, with an unmistakable sound. When it cut out suddenly, that was the danger as the bomb landed.

'And since a few weeks ago, there's been something else. The government says it's defective gas mains blowing up, but the explosions are several times a day. Does that sound like gas mains to you? We call them "flying gas mains", but officially they don't exist.'

'How awful. I've not heard about those.'

'And you won't, neither. It's all hushed up, ain't it.' Amy pursed her lips and stared at Eileen. 'I'd like to stay with you, if you'll have me.'

Poor Amy. No wonder she was white and ill-looking if her nerves were shredded by the rockets and explosions, no one knowing quite where the next bomb would land. It was enough to make anyone flee London if they had another place to go. Of course she'd take her cousin in; it was the right thing to do. And, as her enthusiasm for the decision grew, Eileen realised she'd have the company of another young woman her own age in the flat.

'There isn't much space, mind,' she said as she showed Amy the other room. 'I've got the bed, but there's a bed recess here where you can sleep and if you want privacy, you can pull the wee cupboard doors across. I've got spare sheets and blankets. It'll be cosy for you. You can store your suitcase under my bed if you like.'

Amy frowned at the bed recess and glanced across to the rest of the room. Eileen had done her best to make it comfortable, bright and cheerful.

'I could share the bed with you as it's a double. Top to toe, like when you're kids.'

'No, I wouldn't like that. Sorry. You'll have to use the recess. Or there's one in the kitchen that's got curtains if you don't like the wooden slats,' Eileen stuttered.

She didn't want to be rude, but there was a limit. She didn't fancy sharing her bed with a girl she didn't know. Or anyone, for that matter. Growing up as an only child, she'd never had to share a bed. She knew most people had to. There was no choice with large families in small tenement flats.

Amy shrugged. 'I'll take the recess in this room then. And I'll put my clothes with yours in the wardrobe. I don't have many.'

Eileen had imagined Amy would keep her clothes in the suitcase under Eileen's bed but perhaps that was selfish. Only… she did have a lot of clothes already in her wardrobe so there wasn't much space left for another person's. She hid a sigh. Although it was going to be lovely having company, she hadn't realised how difficult it was to share. Hadn't she always wanted a sister? She had to try harder.

'Of course,' she said warmly. 'Take some of my clothes hangers. And you can put your underwear and nighties in the drawers with mine.'

On impulse, she reached over and hugged Amy. 'I'm so glad you're here. I didn't know there was another branch to my family apart from my mum's sister and her daughter. I'm pleased to get to know you.'

Amy stiffened and then returned the hug briefly. 'Yeah, me too. I'll just get meself sorted in 'ere and you can make us a nice pot of tea.'

Eileen smiled. She turned at the door and looked back at Amy.

'You can stay as long as you need. I think we'll get along with each other just fine.'

—

Amy trailed her finger lazily along the surfaces in the bedroom. Yes, it would do very well. Cousin Eileen was as trusting as a newborn. She wouldn't last a day in the part of Tottenham where Amy had grown up. Yes, she'd landed on her feet here all right.

As long as her past didn't catch up with her.

Chapter Five

'Maybe you'd like to come for your dinner one day?' Morag said.

'I'd like that very much.' Eileen smiled.

The women were on their morning break from the sewing machines. Eileen and Morag had gravitated to each other as a group of them stood outside looking over at the Green, some of them taking the opportunity to smoke a quick ciggie. Eileen enjoyed Morag's company, and it seemed this was reciprocated.

'It'll not be that grand, I'll warn you now. My lodgers like plain fare, nothing fancy, and so does George. That's my husband.'

Eileen heard the pride in Morag's voice when she spoke about George.

'Have you been married long?' she asked.

'We celebrated our fourth anniversary last week. George took me to the pictures and bought me flowers.'

'He sounds like a perfect husband,' Eileen said warmly.

Did she imagine the slightest hesitation before Morag nodded?

'Have you got a fella?' Morag said quickly as the bell went for them to return to work.

As they trooped back in to the sewing machines, Eileen told her about Jimmy. She felt Morag had become a proper friend now that they were arranging to meet outside of work and she felt a warm glow of contentment.

She was tired but still feeling happy as she turned the key in her flat door that evening. There was a delicious aroma of mince and tatties. Her stomach grumbled. In the weeks since Amy had arrived, she'd got used to her evening meal being made.

'That smells good,' she shouted through to the kitchen. She put her handbag onto her bed and changed out of her working clothes. Lint and cotton thread clung to them. She liked to have a clean blouse and skirt for her evenings at home. She frowned as she searched her wardrobe. Where was her brown skirt? She slid her tartan wool skirt on instead, buttoned it at the waist and put on her blue blouse. A quick brush of her hair and she felt refreshed.

'What's cooking?' she said, going into the kitchen. She came to a standstill. 'Oh!'

'Do you like it?' Amy sounded defiant as she fluffed up her hair.

Eileen was speechless. It was like looking in a mirror. Gone were Amy's mousey-brown locks. Now her hair was bleached blonde, just like Eileen's. And her locks weren't straggling; they were now luscious curls.

'You had your hair done. It's... it's very nice.' What else could she say?

But it wasn't just Amy's hair that had changed. She had painted her lips carmine red and shaped her brows. After staying in Eileen's flat all these weeks, her complexion was a healthy pink, and she'd put on a little weight, which gave her figure attractive curves.

'Is that my...?'

'Yes, it's your skirt. I knew you wouldn't mind if I borrowed it. I like brown; it's my favourite colour.

Reminds me of the trees near my home in Tottenham. Great big oaks they are, and the bark is just this shade. Why don't you sit down? I'm just about to serve up. Mince and potatoes, I know you like that, and I've made a rice pudding for afters.'

Eileen was distracted by the solid helping of mince and tatties that Amy slid in front of her and the rice pudding looked sweet and filling in its dish on the iron trivet on the table. It struck her that Amy had made herself indispensable, but she shook that rather unkind thought from her mind. She wasn't sure she wanted Amy borrowing her clothes without asking. But wasn't that what sisters did? And cousins. She'd always wanted a sister, and God had given her Amy. She had no right to complain. But Eileen had a sneaking sense that once in a while, just occasionally, it might be nice to have her flat to herself.

'Have you looked for a job again?' she asked tentatively.

Last time she'd hinted that Amy get a job, her cousin had been upset and accused Eileen of wanting to get rid of her. Eileen had been frightened that Amy would leave and hadn't asked again. Until now. Suddenly she wanted Amy to be occupied with something other than Eileen's clothes and making meals from their rations.

It was unnerving glancing at her. It might have been Eileen herself scraping her plate to get the last forkful of mashed potato and skim of mince. Although Eileen thought Amy's table manners let her down. Agnes would never have allowed her daughter to gobble so quickly. She was a believer in putting your fork and knife down between bites to aid digestion and to be polite.

'I can ask at Greenbank if you like,' Eileen persisted.

Amy shook her head, making her new curls bounce. 'No thank you. I'll find something myself. As it happens,

I might have something soon enough. I heard one of the local women is starting a nursery so that other women can leave their kids and go to work. I might help with the children. I love kids.'

'That's wonderful news,' Eileen said enthusiastically, trying to hide her relief. 'After all, getting your hair done can't have been cheap. You'll need cash coming in.'

'I've got a bit put by. I'm paying my way, ain't I? Give you something for rent, buy half the food. You oughtn't to have any complaints.'

Amy stood up abruptly and stomped over to the range. She picked up the griddle and slammed it down on the surface, making Eileen wince and pray it wasn't damaged. Amy shook out flour into a mixing bowl for scones.

'I'm not complaining, Amy,' Eileen said. 'You know I love having you stay. I just think you'll be happier when you've got something to do during the day. It must get boring on your own when I'm out.'

'I'm never bored. I like being in the flat.'

'The nursery sounds interesting. I didn't know you love kids.' Eileen made an effort to ignore Amy's sullen face.

'Why would you?'

'You haven't told me much about yourself except where you're from. Do you want kids someday? Jimmy and I want to have a family once the war's over.'

'If I could, I'd have a big family, maybe six children. Four girls and two boys,' Amy said dreamily. 'I'd have a girl first cos then she could help with the little 'uns. If the boy came first then...' She stopped.

Eileen couldn't see her cousin's face. All she saw were Amy's hunched shoulders over the mixing bowl and the flick of the wooden spoon in the scone mixture.

'If the boy came first?' she prompted.

'It don't matter. 'Ere, will I make little scones or big 'uns?'

'I don't mind. Whatever you think's best. Are you all right?' Eileen asked with concern.

'Course I am. Why wouldn't I be? Listen, you get on with your sewing and stuff, leave me to bake these and wash up. Put the wireless on. I could do with a tune.'

Eileen paused. She put out her hand towards Amy but then drew it back slowly. It didn't seem like the other girl wanted sympathy for whatever she was feeling. Perhaps she didn't like Eileen meddling in her plans. She'd get work when she did. Eileen shrugged. Amy could sort it herself.

'I'm popping out for a wee while. Back soon,' Eileen said, taking her coat from the coat stand in the tiny hallway.

'Where are you going?'

'To see if my friend Jeannie is in.'

'Thought you said she was away on a farm?'

'Aye, she was, but I'm hoping she might be back now.'

Eileen could tell Amy was hoping to be asked to come too, but she wanted to see Jeannie on her own. Besides, Amy had never met Jeannie, only heard about her from Eileen.

'I won't be long.' She smiled and slipped out of the flat.

After all, she couldn't discuss Amy with Jeannie if her cousin was there. Was it wrong of her to feel uncomfortable with Amy's new look? Eileen's blonde curls were Mother Nature's gift, while Amy had managed similar with hair bleach and curling iron. Perhaps borrowing Eileen's clothes was nothing more than making ends meet. After all, who had the money to buy new outfits and the coupons to do so? Agnes always said that copying was a sign of flattery. She ought to feel pleased then that Amy liked her so much.

While all these thoughts tumbled around her head, she had reached number four and clattered up the steps to knock on the door. Mary answered it and insisted she come in.

'Come and have a cup of tea with us. Away into the parlour.'

Eileen felt relieved. 'Are they back, then?'

But there was only Harry in the neat parlour. Eileen hid her disappointment with a polite smile. She liked Harry and knew that Jeannie was very fond of her stepfather but there was no sound of the children. Mary brought in a tray with a teapot and cups and a plate of shortbread. She poured them all a cup. The tea was a good, strong brew. Although she'd had her meal, Eileen managed a finger of the crumbly shortbread.

'You're looking for Jeannie,' Mary said.

'Aye, I was hoping to have a wee chat with her.' Eileen brushed a crumb from her lips.

'They're not back, love. They're still on the farm with Jeannie's aunt and uncle.'

'But she's been away for ages. She said they were going for a few days, and that was three weeks ago.' Eileen tried not to wail.

'It got complicated,' Mary said with a shake of her head. 'Martha, my cousin, came down with the flu and then Bob and Flora caught it, so Jeannie was nursing them all.'

'I didn't know that. Are they all right?'

She had a sudden terror that she would lose her best friend. Or that her best friend might lose her baby.

Influenza could be dangerous or fatal, she knew that. After the Great War, Agnes had lost a sister to it.

'Och, they're on the mend but Jeannie doesn't feel it's right for her to leave now.'

'And her job at Fearnmore? What will happen with that?' Surely Miss McGrory would insist that Jeannie come back.

'They'll keep it open for her if she wants it. I had a notion she may stay on the farm and help out. Her letters hinted at it.'

'Oh.' Eileen was deflated.

'Was there something in particular you wanted to ask her? Can I help instead?' Mary asked, filling Eileen's teacup again and giving her a sympathetic glance.

Maybe she could discuss her problem with Mary instead. She didn't even know if she had a problem with Amy or not. She needed someone else's perspective. Someone to tell her she was being daft. She opened her mouth to explain when Harry shifted in his armchair and put his cup down. It looked dainty in his big, workworn hand with the calluses from gardening in his beloved allotment. He coughed apologetically at Eileen.

'Now, Mary dear, you know what Doctor Graham told you. You've to rest and not take on too much. This war has worn folk down and we don't want that to happen to you.'

Eileen flushed. She hadn't realised Mary was ill. How awful that she was intruding, she thought to herself. She stood up carefully.

'I'm so sorry. I shouldn't have bothered you.'

'Och, you've not bothered us one wee bit. You know we love you as if you're our own and you're always welcome. Harry's making a mountain out of the proverbial molehill. I'm fine, whatever Doctor Graham says.'

Eileen wasn't so sure. Now that she looked carefully, Jeannie's mother did have lines of strain around her eyes and mouth that she hadn't noticed before. If the doctor was telling her to rest, then it wasn't for Eileen to add to Mary's burdens. They were all tired. Tired of this endless war and hunger when the rations pinched and everything being grubby and faded and irreplaceable.

Mary saw her to the door. There was concern in her motherly gaze as she hugged Eileen.

'Are you sure you don't want to tell me something?' she said kindly.

Eileen shook her head. 'It's nothing really, Mary. I'll catch up with Jeannie when she comes home or write her a letter. Please take care of yourself.'

She kissed Mary's soft cheek as she returned the hug. She loved them. Sometimes she wished they were her family. Heading back up to number eight, she thought she was no further forward. Amy was a mystery. That was for certain. She wouldn't write to Jeannie about it, she decided. She was making a fuss out of nothing. Jeannie would only tell her so.

—

The following Monday, Eileen and Morag both had a day off. Morag was as good as her word, inviting Eileen to dinner at midday. Eileen took special care with her appearance, wearing her blue blouse and the brown skirt, which she found in the bed recess where Amy slept. It was slightly crumpled but she smoothed it out with a damp iron that morning before getting dressed. Amy had gone out to see about the nursery and Eileen found herself enjoying the peace and quiet in her flat.

She took a bus over to Bridgeton, looking out the smeared window at the city as they drove past brick air raid shelters, shops with criss-cross-taped windows and sandbags against doors. Men and women in different uniforms strode along the pavements intent on getting somewhere important quickly. Mothers with small children dawdled with prams, gossiping. The barrage balloons at Glasgow Green glinted brightly in the October light. How awful, Eileen thought, she was so used to it all that it felt quite normal.

Morag's house turned out to be a sandstone building set beside the more familiar tenements and not too far from a large cinema that Eileen stared at with interest. It wasn't one she'd been to before, but she bet that was where George had taken her new friend to the pictures for their anniversary celebration. Instead of roses in the tiny front garden, there were cabbages and leeks growing.

An elderly gentleman opened the door, taking Eileen aback.

'Hello. Is Morag… Mrs Kincaid in, please?'

'Thank you, Mr McLeod, I'll take it from here.' Morag appeared and waved Eileen in.

The old man tottered away into the house, leaning on a wooden stick. Eileen remembered that Morag had briefly mentioned lodgers. She stepped into a long, carpeted hallway with a polished wood staircase leading upstairs. The house smelled of beeswax and carbolic soap. The scents were homely and put her at ease.

'I have two lodgers,' Morag said, as Eileen followed her along the hall. 'That's Mr McLeod and Miss Linton is upstairs having a wee lie-down. As Mr McLeod is in the parlour, should we go into the kitchen to talk while I get the dinner ready?'

'That sounds perfect,' Eileen said. 'Does George come home for his dinner?'

Morag gestured to a chair beside the kitchen table for Eileen to sit on. 'Och, it's a pity but you won't get to meet him. He used to come home for his dinner, but it's got very busy at the shipyards, so I don't see him until teatime most days. He's trying for promotion, so he has to put in the hours as he says.'

Eileen got the impression that Morag wasn't pleased by that, but she didn't feel she knew the other girl well enough to pry.

'What a lovely home you have,' she said cheerfully.

She was surprised that a young couple like George and Morag would live in such a grand house. Eileen had been lucky to grow up in a modest home on the west side of Glasgow. She knew it was probably because she was an only child, so Robert and Agnes had a bit more money than their friends with several children. And her father had had a good job as an engineer before ill health forced him to retire early.

'George inherited it from his parents along with all the furnishings,' Morag told her. 'It's not decorated the way I'd like it, but George wants it to stay the way it was when he grew up. I'd love to paint this kitchen yellow and have silk butterflies sewn onto the curtains and buy new chairs that are a wee bit more comfortable than that upright Victorian monstrosity you're sitting on. But there we are. I mustn't grumble. We're well off compared to most folk around here.'

'It must be hard work doing your shift and then cooking for your lodgers too.'

'Aye and cleaning their rooms and making sure Mr McLeod gets his newspapers and that Miss Linton finds her false teeth, which she's forever losing, and keeping George cheerful when he hates his job.' Morag's hand flew to her mouth. 'Sorry, I shouldn't have said all that.'

'Do you have anyone to help?'

Morag shook her head. 'My mum and dad live nearby, but they're elderly. I'm an only child and a late baby.'

'Oh, I'm an only child too,' Eileen said, feeling pleased they had that in common.

'Do you live with your parents while Jimmy's away fighting?' Morag asked.

Now it was Eileen's turn to shake her head. 'I live with my cousin. Or rather she lives with me.'

'Will Jimmy mind sharing you?' Morag grinned.

Eileen hadn't thought about that. She couldn't imagine Jimmy coming home anytime soon so it hadn't occurred to her that Amy might still be there when he did.

'I wrote to tell him about Amy. She turned up unexpectedly, you see, from London, and needed a place to stay. I haven't had any letters back but that's not unusual. No doubt I'll get a big pack of them soon, tied up with string. It's been seven weeks since he wrote the last one.'

Jimmy would be glad for her, that she had company in Amy. Oh, but she missed him so much. If only a letter would arrive. It was like she was constantly holding her breath, waiting. When a letter did come, her shoulders dropped, and she never realised how much tension she held in her body between hearing from him.

Morag laid out the dinner on the dining room table and wouldn't hear of Eileen helping.

'You're my guest,' she said. 'You sit right here and be a lady of leisure until it's ready. After all, you've worked the last seven days in a row.'

So had Morag, but Eileen didn't argue. It was clear that Morag was proud of her house and hospitality. Eileen was impressed when she went through. She didn't know anyone else who had a separate dining room in their home. It was a dark, gloomy room with ceramic figurines on the mantelpiece over a tiled fireplace, but still, it was a change from eating in a kitchen with a hot range and steaming pans nearby.

Morag winked when she saw Eileen's glance at the furnishings. 'My in-laws again. This room hasn't changed since before George was a baby.'

Mr McLeod shuffled in and tucked his napkin into his collar. 'Is it fish today, Mrs Kincaid?'

'Fish for tea, Mr McLeod. For dinner, it's National Loaf, home-grown cabbage and a wee bit of bacon between us.'

Morag went upstairs to tell her other lodger that dinner was served. Eileen sat with Mr McLeod in a silence that wasn't altogether uncomfortable, but she was glad to hear Morag's footsteps coming back into the room.

'Miss Linton isn't feeling well so she won't be down to join us. Can I slice you some bread?' Morag said.

After the meal, Mr McLeod went back into the parlour and Morag beckoned to Eileen.

'You like to sew, don't you? Come and see what you make of these.'

Eileen followed her upstairs to a chest on the landing. It was made of thick, dark wood with carvings showing scenes of farmers and cows. Morag lifted its lid, and she saw folded blankets. She smelled naphthalene and saw the mothballs tucked among the fabric. Morag lifted the top blanket and pulled out a linen bag.

'What is it?' Eileen asked curiously.

Morag opened the bag and took out four tiny outfits. There was a blue sailor suit and a pink dress, a pale yellow shirt and, finally, a long white christening robe.

'They're beautiful,' Eileen said as Morag passed them to her. 'Did you make these?'

Morag nodded, looking pleased.

'Are you...?'

'Oh, no. I'm not pregnant. But I'm... prepared, shall we say.' She laughed, but Eileen caught a hint of sadness in Morag's brown eyes.

'The stitching is perfect. Your talents are wasted sewing army blankets, that's for sure. I hope you and George get your wish very soon. What a lucky baby Kincaid he or she will be.'

'Aye, well, if George has *his* wish, there'll be no baby for a very long while.'

'Oh, Morag. I don't know what to say.' Eileen stroked the soft folds of the christening robe and glanced up awkwardly.

'There is nothing to be said. I shouldn't have spoken but somehow, Eileen, I feel like I can tell you anything.'

'It won't go any further, I promise. Anyway, I've no one to tell.'

'That cousin of yours?' Morag joked feebly, taking the tiny clothes and folding them before sliding them back into the linen bag.

'Not Amy,' Eileen assured her.

'Are the two of you not close, then? I thought, her living with you and all, that you'd be like sisters.'

'She only moved in a few weeks ago. We're still getting to know one another,' Eileen replied quickly.

'Aye, it takes time, I'm sure. As my mum says, blood's thicker than water, and family's the most important tie there is. Has Amy got family in London? Och, that's a silly question, isn't it. If she had family, she'd be staying with them.'

'She mentioned her mum and dad. Come to think of it, she never said whether she lived with them or not. But you're right. Why did she come to Glasgow if she stayed with them? It doesn't make sense.'

I must ask her, Eileen thought. *I know hardly anything about Amy and it's been almost a month. What on earth do we talk about?* Frowning, she realised they chatted about cooking, or Amy did, and that personal questions were deflected or ignored.

—

Morag's words rang in her ears as she walked into the city centre. She was right. Family was important and she had to try harder with Amy. She still didn't know her cousin's background growing up and asking about her Uncle Norman hadn't brought forth any family stories. It was disappointing.

I'll buy her a wee treat, Eileen thought, glancing in at the shop windows with their empty displays and promises of goods returning after the war.

What would Amy like? She sighed. That was the problem. She had absolutely no idea. She passed a tea shop and decided to have a cup of tea while she mulled it over. She wasn't going home empty-handed.

She queued at the counter behind two women who were loudly bemoaning the number of clothes coupons it took to buy a winter coat. The taller one paid and they moved away to a table with the waitress promising to bring their order as soon as possible.

'What are ye havin', hen?' The waitress's face was weary, and she made no effort to look cheerful.

'A cup of tea and a scone, please.'

'That'll be tuppence.'

Eileen opened her bag for her purse, but it wasn't there. Flustered, she dug around in the bag disbelievingly.

'I've lost my purse,' she said.

'Is that right?' the waitress said sceptically, taking the scone back off the plate and pushing it onto the shelf under the glass counter.

Eileen felt her face burn. It felt as if all the customers in the crowded tea shop were watching her.

'I'll pay for the young lady's tea and scone along with the same for myself, please.'

The smooth voice came from behind her. She turned to see Leo Mearns tipping his homburg politely to her.

'Oh, I can't let you do that, Mr Mearns,' she protested.

She didn't want to be in his debt. But it was too late. With a long-suffering sigh, the waitress tipped the scone onto its plate again and added another. Leo Mearns paid and then escorted Eileen to a table at the far wall, his guiding touch on her elbow making her want to recoil. Of course, she couldn't. Not in public with people already staring at the little drama that had livened up their day.

'What a delight it is to bump into you.' He took the homburg and carefully laid it on the chair next to him.

She saw his oiled hair flattened against a balding pink scalp and gave an inward shudder. She managed a polite smile.

'Thank you. I must have dropped my purse or left it at home.'

'I do hope you find it. How are you, Miss Boyle, or may I call you Eileen? You look as pretty as a picture. It has quite brightened my day, meeting you.'

She wriggled on her chair, wondering how quickly she could find a reason to leave. His lingering glance took in her legs and she stopped moving them.

'How is Mrs Mearns? I hope she is feeling better.'

It would do no harm to remind him he had a wife. He returned her sweetened smile, and she had an awful sense that he was toying with her, playing a game.

'Ah, poor Alice. If anything, she's a little worse. She can't leave her house and can only bear a short visit. It leaves me with time to spare.'

'Don't you have a job for the war effort?' Eileen asked rudely.

'Indeed, I do. I'm a guard on the railways. It's a busy job but they give me time off for good behaviour. That's my little joke, of course.' He paused as if to allow her to laugh.

Eileen ate her scone as fast as she could. It tasted like sawdust, choking her throat until she coughed. She swallowed some tea, horribly conscious that it was all paid for by the man sitting opposite, who was staring at her as if he wanted to eat her.

She grabbed her bag and stood up. 'Thank you for the tea. I have to go.'

Her shoulder blades prickled as she walked to the door without looking back. She was annoyed to find her hands trembling as she passed the steamed-up window. Out of the corner of her eye, she could see his dark outline, the homburg hat back in place.

Leo Mearns lingered over his tea. It had been a lucky chance, glimpsing Eileen as he walked around the city centre looking for some items on Alice's shopping list. He visited her every day as a dutiful husband should. But Alice was no fun. Losing the baby had changed her. She hardly bothered to dress nicely or wash her hair. He had hired a nurse to help, and the woman had assured him that Mrs Mearns would get better. He didn't care. He had lost interest in Alice.

Miss Eileen Boyle was another matter entirely. He hummed as his fingers touched the leather purse in his coat pocket. It had been a simple matter to lift it from her open bag. She hadn't noticed a thing. His misspent youth had come in handy, the pickpocketing simply a thrill in those days and not a necessity. After all, he came from a well-off family. No one had suspected a boy like that. It was the risk that was enjoyable.

Chapter Six

It was another month before a letter arrived for Eileen. With a whoop of delight, she tore it open and then frowned. It wasn't Jimmy's handwriting. This letter was written by someone with a round curling script. She read it quickly and covered her mouth with her hand to stifle a cry.

'Bad news, is it?' Amy asked, from her perch on the bed recess.

It was a dark Monday afternoon, and rain was hitting the window panes as if someone was throwing buckets of water at them. The letter had been put on Eileen's bed by Amy and she'd found it when she went to change her clothes after arriving home from her shift.

'Yes, mostly bad. It's Jimmy. He's been injured, which is the bad news, and he's back in Glasgow at the Cowglen military hospital, which is the good news. Please God let him be all right.'

'He's not going to want me 'ere if he comes home and you two get married,' Amy remarked.

'Oh, I'm sure that's not true,' Eileen said distractedly, still preoccupied with the letter and worried about Jimmy.

'Course it is,' Amy said scornfully. 'There ain't room to swing a cat in 'ere. Stands to reason, don't it. He'll want you and this flat to hisself.'

She frowned and jumped down lightly to the floor. Her fingers tapped on her chin as she stalked the bedroom. Eileen read the letter again as if she could strain more information from it by doing so. Amy snapped her fingers suddenly.

'I can sleep in the kitchen. There's the bed recess in there. That old red curtain will give me privacy. I don't mind moving, honest.'

Amy spoke as if she was doing Eileen a favour. If she wasn't busy fretting about Jimmy, Eileen would've been irritated with her cousin.

'Can we discuss it later? I have to go round to Jimmy's mother and see if she's had a letter, and if not, tell her the news.'

Eileen put on her coat as she spoke and didn't notice Amy's sour expression. When she turned, Amy smiled.

'Course. You hurry on. I'll make the tea. Your favourite, mince and tatties. Isn't that what you call it up here? I suppose without me, you'd be eating bread and jam every day.'

'Thanks. I might be a wee while but you can leave it in the oven for me if I'm late.'

'Ungrateful cow,' Amy whispered to Eileen's retreating back as the door to the flat closed.

—

Mary clasped Eileen's hand as the bus drove along a tree-fringed road on Glasgow's south side. There was a woodland on the crest of the low hill and a patchwork of fields where the large Pollok Estate adjoined Cowglen. Somewhere close by, the White Cart Water flowed, and a tributary split off into the Brock Burn, the rivers crossed by old stone bridges and then almost lost among the city streets. The trees were bare of leaves so late in the year and the grass looked dull and brown. The sky was pewter-grey, threatening yet more rain and inside the bus with its misted windows, the passengers were bulky with winter coats and hats.

'Tell me again what the nurse said,' Mary asked.

'Well, she wrote the letter on Jimmy's behalf. He has bandages over his eyes…' Eileen swallowed and took in a breath before she continued. She had to be brave. As brave as Mary, who was now patting Eileen's hand in sympathy.

'A shell exploded, and Jimmy was blown clear off his feet and landed badly, you see,' she went on. 'That's what she wrote anyway.'

'Are you all right, love?' Mary asked.

'I'm worried, as you must be too,' Eileen said. 'But we have to go in cheerful, don't we. We can't let Jimmy sense how frightened we are for him.'

'Did the letter say if he's improving?'

Eileen shook her head. She didn't remind Mary that she'd already read the letter. They were both in shock, she thought. They couldn't take it in that the man they both loved was in a military hospital and goodness knew how he really was.

'I suppose the nurse didn't want to get our hopes up or make promises she couldn't keep.'

'Aye, but he's going to get better. We'll make sure of that,' Mary said firmly.

Mary's attitude fortified Eileen and she knew she had to be strong too. The bus dropped them at the hospital entrance. There were copses of trees on either side of the path and in the near distance a tall water tower.

'It's enormous. So many buildings,' Eileen marvelled.

A Jeep passed them on the entrance road, and they heard American accents in the air before they saw the GI uniforms. Beyond the hospital and office buildings, Eileen glimpsed an army camp with barbed wire and tall gates and vehicles.

They found their way to the main reception and were escorted by a nurse to the ward where Jimmy was. The nurse was chatty as she walked briskly along the polished linoleum floor. She didn't seem to notice the smells of carbolic and blood and other nastier aromas, but Eileen's nostrils stung. Mary hurried to keep up with the young nurse's fast gait.

'The American Army Medical Corps is based here, you see. That's why you'll hear so many American accents. There are some wards that are kept off-limits, though. That's the ones where they treat the German sailors, injured at sea.' Her voice hardened at that. 'We have to treat them just the same as our own brave lads. But it's difficult when you know they caused all the wounds we're healing in the rest of the hospital. Here we go, Mrs Dougal. Your husband is in here, fourth bed down on the right. You can have ten minutes. No longer or Matron will have my guts for garters.'

Eileen didn't correct her. She might not be Jimmy's wife yet, but she still hoped to be. Whatever injuries he had come home with, she promised him silently that they'd cope, and she'd help him recover. She glanced at Mary. The strain showed in her tired face. Eileen linked her arm with Mary's and drew the older woman gently with her into the ward. The men who were able to sit up in their beds stared curiously and some called a greeting.

Jimmy was lying down in his hospital bed with the sheet and blanket drawn up to his neck. His face was hardly visible under the padded bandages over his eyes. Mary stifled a sob and Eileen felt her own eyes prickle with unshed tears. This wouldn't do, she reminded herself. They had to stay cheerful for Jimmy. It wouldn't do his recovery any good at all to find two weeping women at his bedside.

'Jimmy. It's your Sheena. I'm here with your mammy,' she said softly as they sat on two chairs placed by the bed.

'Sheena? Is it really you, ma wee doll?' Jimmy's voice was gravelly, either with injury or emotion.

He struggled to free his arms from the blanket and reached in the direction of her voice. Now Eileen was crying. Hot, silent tears rolled down her cheeks and dripped off her chin. Mary fumbled in her handbag and passed over a clean cotton handkerchief. Her own eyes were shiny.

'Aye, I'm here,' Eileen repeated, taking his hot hand in hers.

'And Mammy?'

'Aye, son, I'm here and all. Give me your other hand to hold so I know you're real.'

They sat joined as three for a moment without speaking until Eileen could bear it no longer. She had to know.

'Are you badly injured?'

Jimmy's laugh turned into a cough, alarming her.

'Don't speak if it hurts,' she begged.

'I'd never talk at all if I took that attitude,' Jimmy said with another small laugh. 'I'm on the mend, so they say. I don't remember much about it, to be honest. There was a very loud noise and next thing I knew I was on other side of the street, upside down and back to front. The medics picked me up and stretchered me out to an ambulance.

Eventually they got me on a boat back to Blighty and I spent a few weeks in a hospital on the south coast of England. Then I heard I was being transferred up here.'

Eileen gazed at her fiancé. The sheet and blanket were turned down where Jimmy had pushed them away to get his arms free. It seemed as if his whole upper body was swathed in bandages.

'Did you get my letters?' Jimmy asked. 'Nurse Collins said she'd write them for me.'

'I got mine, but your mammy didn't get hers.'

'It doesn't matter, son. What matters now is that you get better. You have to rest and do what the doctor tells you,' Mary said.

'No chance of doing anything else,' came the doleful reply.

Jimmy tired quickly and Eileen and Mary tried to soothe and cheer him with stories of home, how Dennis was growing up and what Jeannie's letters described about life on the farm with Isa and Bob and their aunt and uncle. His smiles encouraged them, and his fingers curled lovingly around Eileen's.

'I'll give you two a wee moment together,' Mary said kindly, and, despite their protests, she walked quietly out of the ward.

'Sheena, I wish I could see your beautiful face,' Jimmy murmured. 'I can imagine it, though, as if I really could. I've gazed at your photograph so many times while I've been in the army camps and in transit that I wore the paper thin.'

'Darling, you will see me soon, I'm certain of it,' Eileen said, trembling with emotion. 'I want to lie down beside you and hold you so very tight until I make you better. Oh, Jimmy, I can't bear that you're injured but I'm so very glad that you're here and not over there in Europe in the midst of the fighting. Is that selfish of me?'

'Well, if it's selfish, that makes the two of us,' Jimmy replied, pressing her fingers with more urgency. 'I wouldn't want to be anywhere else but with you, Sheena. You're my heart, my everything.'

'Are you in pain?' she whispered, as he moved restlessly in the bed.

'A wee bit, but better since you're here,' came the reply.

'I wish I could take it all away. I'd take it on myself if I could,' Eileen cried.

Jimmy's lopsided smile was worth it, but his grip on her fingers soon loosened and his mouth went slack. For a horrible moment, she thought he had gone but then there was a rattling snore and she realised he'd fallen asleep.

'You shouldn't be here; my patient needs his rest,' a sharp voice said.

Eileen looked up into the steely glare of a stern-faced nurse. She glanced back down at Jimmy before gathering her bag up to leave. The nurse stood there as if guarding Jimmy and Eileen knew she couldn't linger any further. She nodded and rose from her chair. As she hurried out of the ward, a white-coated doctor caught her at the door.

'Mrs Dougal? I'd like to give you a quick update on your husband.'

'Yes, please,' Eileen said as Mary joined her from where she'd been waiting against the corridor wall outside the ward. 'This is my… mother-in-law, Jimmy's mum.' She hadn't the energy to correct the doctor's assumption about her marital status and she knew Mary wouldn't mind.

The women stood side by side, gaining comfort from each other as they faced the tired-looking doctor.

'You have my sympathies. It must have come as a shock to discover Mr Dougal's whereabouts. He was very sick when he arrived, and I won't lie, he is still poorly, but if his wounds continue to heal, then we will consider sending him to a convalescent home for soldiers.'

'Oh, but that's good news, isn't it?' Eileen smiled, and Mary's body, so close beside her, seemed to relax at the doctor's words.

'Let's take it a day at a time,' he said kindly. He gave them a brief nod and disappeared into the ward.

'I don't care that he didn't answer that,' Eileen told Mary as they walked to the hospital exit. 'It is good news. I just know it is.'

They were quiet on the journey home in the bus, each occupied with their own thoughts as the vehicle bumped and swerved on the badly maintained roads. Mary hugged her as they parted on Kiltie Street.

'We'll visit him again soon. It won't be long before you two have tied the knot and settled in a wee flat together.'

'I hope so.' Eileen had a dreadful notion that they might heal Jimmy's wounds and send him back to the fighting, but she didn't voice it to his mother. They would have to wait and see.

She felt quite weary as she went up the stone steps to number eight and her own top-floor flat. Her neighbour was out sweeping the landing, and it took all her reserves to make polite conversation about the awful weather and lack of coal before she could take her leave to put the key in her front door and push it open.

She was surprised to find Amy lounging in the bedroom on Eileen's bed, flicking through a copy of *Woman's Own*.

'Aren't you at the nursery helping out?'

'Oh, they didn't need me today. There's a bad cold going the rounds so half the kids weren't there.'

Eileen waited for Amy to ask after Jimmy, but her cousin's head was bent over her magazine. How did she afford to buy it? It wasn't Eileen's place to ask, of course, but she couldn't help wondering where Amy's money came from for the lipstick, face powder, hairdos and other items she managed to get her hands on. It wasn't as if she had a proper job. And even a 'proper job' like Eileen's at the factory didn't pay well enough for fancy things. If you could get them in any case.

'Jimmy's on the mend,' she said, when Amy didn't ask. 'He's still poorly but if his wounds continue to heal, then the doctor said he can go to a convalescent home for soldiers.'

'When will he come home?' Amy asked, rolling over to lie on her side, one arm propping up her head so she could see Eileen.

'I don't know. They didn't say.'

Did Amy care about Jimmy at all or was she simply concerned about where she'd live if, and when, Eileen's fiancé came home and they got married? Eileen wondered.

'You must've got a scare, seeing him like that,' Amy said.

'It was a wee bit frightening,' Eileen agreed, glad that her cousin was showing some sympathy and interest. 'But he's tough. They call him Lucky Jim as he's had some scrapes and always comes out on top.'

'Is that right?' Amy seemed impressed.

'Shall I make the meal this evening? Give you a break from cooking?' Eileen said warmly.

Amy jumped up smartly. 'No need for that. I like doing it. Besides, if you cook, we'll be eating burned toast and marg.'

Eileen laughed to show she could take a joke. After all, Amy was right. She was a terrible cook. But it felt as if it was Amy's kitchen these days and that Eileen didn't belong in half of her own flat. Which was silly. She tried to shake the feeling off. She ought to be grateful. She watched Amy walk off into the other room. It seemed as if she even walked the same way as Eileen these days.

'You had a visitor while you were out,' Amy shouted from the kitchen.

'Who was it, then?' Eileen went to the kitchen door and stood looking in at the back of Amy's blonde head as she clattered pans and lifted down a ladle from the hook on the wall.

'It was that nice Mr Mearns. Quite a charmer, ain't he? I let him in and gave him a cuppa. Very chatty he was, all about his poor wife and his inheritance. Lovely manners, a real gentleman.'

'Be careful... I don't trust that man,' Eileen warned.

'Why on earth? Cos he's a different class from us?' Amy said derisively.

'No, it's not that. He gives me the shivers, that's all.'

'Well, he don't give me the collywobbles, shivers, or what have you. He was very nice to me, gave me compliments and said I was far too good to be 'ere when I was pretty enough for the stage.'

Eileen rolled her eyes. *Dearie me*, Eileen thought. Amy had been taken in all right by his gloss and fancy ways.

No, there was something... bad about him. Eileen could feel it.

'Just watch yourself with him. Promise me,' she said.

Now it was Amy's turn to roll her eyes, and, unlike Eileen, she didn't bother to hide it. 'You want to live a little. Life's short, and we need to take our chances.'

'I'm quite happy with my life. Especially now that Jimmy's home. If he's invalided out or maybe on an army desk job somewhere, we can get married and set up home. I'll be perfectly content with my lot when that happens.' Eileen smiled dreamily.

She stared at the old black-and-white diamond-patterned linoleum, not really seeing it but rather imagining her and Jimmy waltzing. For some reason, she was in a long green ballgown, and he had a bow tie and dinner suit just like Fred Astaire, with his hair slicked back and a charming grin. As her eyes focused on the lino, Eileen screamed and pointed.

'A mouse. There's a mouse right there! Oh no, it's over there, watch your feet.'

She jumped onto a kitchen chair while Amy grabbed the brush and tried to thump the offending rodent while laughing. The mouse scampered off and disappeared behind the cupboard on the wall. Amy bent over, gasping with amusement, only kept upright by the long brush handle.

'A mouse, ooh, a bloody great mouse. It's the size of a cat, I reckon. Save me, Amy.' Amy mimicked Eileen, getting her voice absolutely right.

'Och, you're terrible, mocking me like that. I'm feart of mice, so I am. How do you do that?' Eileen said, eyebrows raised in amazement.

'It's a little talent I have. I can mimic most folk,' Amy said. ' 'Ere, who's this?'

She waddled across the floor, supporting her lower back with one hand and with a pained expression on her face.

'Aye, ma lumbago's givin' me gyp, so it is, the day.'

Eileen smiled with amusement. 'That's Mrs Heaney, the butcher's wife. You've got her spot on. You could go on the stage, you're so good.'

'Turns out you and Mr Mearns have something in common after all; you both agree on that point,' Amy replied cheekily.

-

'Who is she, Mum?'

Eileen had gone to visit her parents as soon as she'd got time off. Now she was sitting in Agnes's kitchen because Robert was asleep in his armchair in the parlour. Agnes was wearing her green and purple Women's Institute uniform. She hadn't been home long before Eileen arrived.

'She's your cousin. Robert's brother, Norman's daughter. I'm sorry we never told you about her, but your father had his reasons. It was unlikely we'd ever see Norman or his family, so it didn't seem important to Dad to tell you.'

'I know that much, although I wish you had told me about my uncle and that I had more relatives than just my aunt and Linda.' Eileen tried to hide any bitterness in her voice. It was just another example of how, at times, she felt left out of her own family. Much as she loved her father, she didn't agree with some of his decisions, including this one. 'Amy's very tight-lipped about her family. She's hardly said a thing about them since she arrived. I feel as if she's hiding something.'

'You're being dramatic,' Agnes said with a shake of her head. 'What could she have to hide? You said she was escaping the doodlebugs in London. Poor girl, of course she would come north.'

'But why not stay with you and Dad or at least visit you?' Eileen asked.

'Norman probably told her that Robert has been unwell. Your father always writes at Christmas, although he very rarely gets a reply. Or perhaps she thought she wouldn't be welcome because the brothers aren't close.'

'What about Pearl, Amy's mother? What's she like?' Eileen persisted.

Agnes frowned. 'I never met Pearl, and I only ever met Norman once, before the argument that caused the rift. It was about Pearl, you see. Robert was the elder brother, and he knew she was no good for Norman. She was a showgirl, the worst kind. Kicking up her legs and showing her underwear on the stage for all and sundry to see. It wasn't respectable. Your father told Norman that and there was a terrible argument. Norman declared his intention to marry her, and Robert told him if he did that then he wasn't welcome in the house. Your uncle packed his bags and headed down to London. That's where Pearl hailed from. He'd met her when he was down there looking for work.'

Eileen's eyes widened. She wasn't sure whether to feel shocked about Pearl or intrigued that she had had such an occupation. Her brow creased. 'Amy told me that Dad was jealous of Norman because he'd done better than him and made his fortune in London.'

Agnes gave a humourless laugh. 'Norman was a travelling salesman. And not a very good one at that.'

'Why did she lie?'

'I expect she didn't want to tell you the truth. She was ashamed of her parents' behaviour,' Agnes said drily. 'It's only been in the last few years that Robert has been in contact with Norman and as I said, he almost never gets a reply, but we have to assume that he gets all the letters. I persuaded your father to write to his only brother as they're both getting on in years. His parents were both dead by the time the brothers fell out, but I told Robert that they would be turning in their graves to know that the family was split.'

Eileen hesitated. 'What was Grandfather Boyle like?'

'Goodness, why on earth do you want to know that?' Agnes shook her head. 'He was a nice old man, very kind to children and dogs and had a long white beard in his latter days.'

'So he wasn't a...' Eileen tried to remember Amy's words. 'Domineering bully? That wasn't why Norman left?'

Agnes looked taken aback. 'Not at all. Besides, he and your grandmother had both passed on by the time Norman left. What makes you say that?'

'It doesn't matter. Thanks, Mum. You've been a big help.'

Eileen was left feeling more confused than before as she helped Agnes tidy the room, set the fire and prepare a small meal for her father. Why had Amy lied? What was she hiding?

Back in Kiltie Street, Amy enjoyed having the flat to herself.

It was lovely and quiet. She didn't expect Eileen back until after tea. There wasn't much left of their rations for the week, but she wasn't hungry so a cuppa and a bit of bread and dripping and she was as happy as Larry, as the saying went. She'd worked at the local crèche that morning, helping with the babies and toddlers. She loved it and it was far better than working her fingers to the bone in a factory like her cousin Eileen did. It was still war work, letting other women away to do their bit making bombs or what have you.

She felt a prickle between her shoulder blades. Getting up, she went over and peered out the window from behind the curtain. There was no one on the street. She was jumpy, that was all. Still, she was unnerved for a moment.

'No one knows you're 'ere, girl. Relax,' she murmured to herself, letting the curtain fabric drop.

Besides, she had other problems to sort out, such as Eileen's plans of marriage and home-making. It would be very inconvenient if Jimmy was to move into the flat.

Somehow, she had to stop that.

Chapter Seven

'You look very glamorous.' Eileen smiled.

Amy had acquired a new hat. She turned this way and that in front of the cracked mirror in the bedroom, admiring herself. It was black velvet with multi-coloured silk flowers at the front. Amy fluffed her bleached blonde curls around it.

'You want to set it back a wee bit, though; the flowers are shading your face.'

Amy smiled back but didn't adjust her hat. She frowned at her shabby winter coat, which was a dull grey wool with horn buttons. 'Me hat shows up me clothes.'

'Unless you've got fourteen clothes coupons spare, you'll have to make do,' Eileen sighed wistfully.

Her own winter coat was showing its age with shiny patches at the elbows and hems. But buying new was out of the question with the clothes rationing and prices. She wondered, not for the first time, how Amy could afford a new hat, even if hats were off-ration.

'What was it you worked as in London again?' she asked.

Amy pulled on her boots, scuffed and worn down at the heel, and grimaced at them. 'I worked in a shop.'

'A clothes shop? Like a fancy boutique?' Eileen said, thinking of Amy's love of finery.

'Mmm... yes, that's right. It was. It was a clothes shop selling all sorts of lovely stuff.'

Had Amy told her that before? Eileen couldn't remember.

''Ere, we'd best stop gabbing and get a move on else we'll miss the whole bloomin' thing,' Amy cried.

The cousins were going to George Square to see the standing-down parade of the Home Guard. Following the success of the D-Day landings in France and the Allies' drive towards Germany, the government had decided that defence against invasion was no longer needed.

It was early December, and the weather was cold, damp and foggy, but that hadn't stopped a huge crowd gathering to watch the parade of men in their Home Guard uniforms marching with their weapons along the streets and through the famous central square of the city. A band played military music at the front and people clapped to the rhythm of the beat. Eileen felt herself caught up in the atmosphere. Everyone was cheerful, laughing and enjoying the pomp and ceremony, the live music and the impressive marching troops. The Home Guard was mostly made up of older men, but there were younger faces, boys too young to fight and those whose medical histories made active service impossible. They deserved the applause, she thought proudly. They'd been prepared to fight the enemy in the streets and houses to the death if necessary. How brave they were.

Beside her, Amy seemed twitchy. She was staring over at something. Eileen followed her gaze but only saw the back and shoulders of a well-built man wearing a working man's jacket and cap. As if feeling their gaze, he turned, and Amy shrank back behind Eileen.

'What's the matter?' Eileen said, turning to her, brows knitted in confusion.

Amy looked beyond her, and her expression was relieved. When Eileen glanced back at the big man, he'd stopped looking in their direction and pushed his way on through the throng of onlookers.

'Did you recognise him?'

'Course not. Don't be daft. I don't know anyone 'ere, do I. Just you.' Amy pushed her hat forward until the flowers almost touched the bridge of her nose.

'You're as jumpy as a cat on hot tiles,' Eileen said. 'Is everything all right?'

'I told you, I'm fine,' Amy snapped.

Eileen shrugged, a little bit hurt. She concentrated on enjoying the parade and decided to ignore Amy until her mood improved.

'Eileen! Eileen, is that you?'

She turned to find Morag beaming, her cheeks pink with the cold, and her arm tightly hooked into that of a very handsome young man.

'Fancy finding you here, in among all this lot.' Morag grinned. 'Can I introduce my husband, George. George, this is Eileen, my friend from the factory I've told you about.'

Eileen's heart warmed at being described like that. Morag had told George about her. That was lovely.

'Pleased to meet you, George.' She shook his hand, noticing his fair hair, firm, squared jaw and brown eyes. Morag was a lucky woman. They were a good match, she decided, as Morag was very attractive too.

'And this is my cousin Amy.' Eileen turned politely to find that Amy had vanished.

'An invisible cousin?' George joked feebly.

'I've lost her in the crowd. Never mind, I'll catch her up in a wee minute. So, are you enjoying the parade?' Eileen asked with a smile.

'Och, it's wonderful, isn't it, George?' Morag said, glancing up at her husband.

Eileen felt as if George wasn't quite as enamoured of the whole thing as his wife, but he patted Morag's arm and said yes, he was having a good time.

'It's freezing. Reminds you that Christmas isn't far off. Only another twenty-two days to go. Will you go to your parents' for it?' Morag asked Eileen.

Eileen tucked her cold fingers into her pockets, realising the fog was quite icy. She nodded.

'Yes, I'm expected to go home. Part of me would like to stay in my wee flat and make it cosy for Christmas but my mother would never let me hear the end of it. She'd be so upset if I didn't spend it with them. Besides, Jimmy is still in the hospital, so it won't be festive in the flat without him.'

'Is he getting better?' Morag asked, hugging into George's side, as if for comfort. Perhaps she was glad that he wasn't in a military hospital fighting an infection in a shoulder wound.

'Aye, he's on the mend, or so they keep telling me. I don't know why it's taking so long. They have these wonder medicines now to fix an infection. Jimmy's tough. I know he'll be all right.'

'Come round to ours for a hot drink,' Morag said impulsively. 'We're heading home as soon as the parade finishes, aren't we, George.'

A frown wrinkled George's forehead before he smoothed his features, but Eileen was sure he didn't want guests.

'It's a kind offer and I'd love to, but I really must find Amy. I'll see you tomorrow bright and early for the first shift.'

Eileen hugged Morag and was glad to feel the other girl's embrace. It was so nice to have a friend, and one who had 'no side to her', as the Glasgow expression went. Morag was simple and friendly and honest. Unlike Amy, who was a very complicated creature indeed. Eileen waved to them both and turned back into the crowd. She made her way along the nearest street, past the air raid shelters, looking for a higher vantage point to see if she could spot the black velvet hat and its colourful silk flowers.

'Eileen.' Amy grabbed her arm and pulled her in beside a stall selling hot pies. There was a delicious aroma of meat, gravy and pastry.

'Where did you go?'

'I came to get us a pie each. Here you go. Mind the grease don't get on your coat.'

'That's a generous thought, thank you.' Eileen took the proffered pie in its wrapping of newspaper. She wasn't particularly hungry as they'd had their dinner before coming out, but she was pleased that Amy had been so kind as to think of her. 'I met Morag. The girl I know from the factory. I wanted to introduce you, but you'd disappeared like a puff of smoke.'

'Is that right?' Amy mumbled through a mouthful of flaky pastry. 'Come along, let's see the last of the marching. Bring your pie.'

Eileen followed Amy's slight figure back into the main street, trying not to get bumped by elbows, umbrellas and wide hats, when an uneasy thought struck her. Had Amy really gone for pies, or had she wanted to avoid Morag and George?

—

Hopes of a swift end to the war vanished with the German breakthrough in the Ardennes in the middle of December. Everyone was sick and weary of war, and rationing and shortages were worse than ever. Eileen went out, wrapped up well against the rain and cold, with the intention of going to the shops to queue for meat and then tea and then vegetables. Luckily, the main street had all the shops she needed and anything extra she could get in Franny's Emporium, where Jeannie and her sister Kathy had once worked before the war. She sighed heavily in anticipation of waiting with her bag for whatever scrawny cut of meat Mr Heaney would offer. He kept the best for his special customers, everyone knew that. And Eileen wasn't one of them.

'Away you go. Shoo, nasty creature!' her downstairs neighbour bellowed as she came downstairs, and she saw his leg kick out and a dirty white cat shot away down the steps.

'Everything all right, Mr Downey?' she asked, knowing the old man had a temper and there was often shouting to be heard from the Downeys' flat as he berated his wife.

'Aye, just a flea-bitten tom cat trying its luck. Keeps coming in whenever the wife leaves the door open. I've told her to close it, but she never learns. Bloody crittur stole a sausage.'

Eileen hid a smile. It was terrible, she knew that. Food was in short supply and strictly to be kept for human consumption. In fact, at the beginning of the war, people had been encouraged to have their pets put down as it was believed there wouldn't be enough to feed them. Clearly, the white cat was a survivor.

'Is it a stray, then?' she asked.

'It's not owned by anyone around here. Looking to take it in, are ye, hen?' he sneered.

'I might just do that, Mr Downey. Excuse me, I must get going.'

She had no intention of doing any such thing, but the man's tone and expression grated on her. She went down the steps, sure that the cat must be long gone, but there it was, sitting on the pavement, licking its paw, the sausage having vanished. Eileen crouched down and put out her hand tentatively. She wasn't used to cats and didn't know if it might bite or scratch her. But it came towards her in a friendly fashion, tail up, and pushed its cheek against her fingers. Its fur felt soft and damp from the drizzling rain, but it was purring.

'You're very naughty, stealing from Mr Downey like that,' she murmured. 'Still, I expect he deserved it; he's probably kicked you before now. How about coming up for a wee saucer of milk? The Ministry of Food won't approve but, do you know, at this moment, I don't really care.'

Carefully, she scooped the cat up. It was light and bony and Eileen reckoned it hadn't had a decent meal in a while.

'Come on, Snowy. That suits you fine. You're a wee bit grubby but if you'll let me wash you, I bet you're a beautiful white cat under all that grime.'

She chuckled and her spirits rose. The cat's fur tickled her nose, making her sneeze and laugh all at once. It was as if she'd found a new friend. Snowy couldn't replace

Jimmy, of course, or fix the hole of wanting him home safe and well, but she felt less alone with the purring creature, and goodness knows, Snowy was a simpler, less complex creature than her cousin Amy, at any rate. She forgot about the food shopping and took the cat inside to find a saucer and a blanket and a flake of soap for her new companion.

—

'How's about we go to the cinema?' George said that Saturday, coming out from behind his newspaper to grin at her.

Morag put down the breakfast dishes and the dishcloth. 'What's on?'

'You're spoiled for choice. Everything from *Christmas Holiday* at the New Savoy to *Sing, Neighbour, Sing* at the Playhouse. Actually...' His head disappeared behind the newspaper sheets again for a moment before reappearing, 'I count ten different films we can go and see.'

'I could do with something to cheer me up, what with that awful news about the Germans attacking in Belgium. I'm scared they're going to win the war, George.'

There was a wobble in Morag's voice, and she picked up the dishcloth again. Scrubbing dried egg off the dishes might take her mind off things.

'Now, now,' George soothed, coming up behind her and kissing her neck. 'Look, let's splash out. Forget the cinema. There's a pantomime on this afternoon, matinee performance at the Pavilion Theatre. It's *Babes in the Wood* with Jack Anthony. You like him, don't you? What do you say?'

'Oh, George, that's a wonderful idea.'

Morag kissed him. He could be so thoughtful sometimes. And she knew what it cost him to spend any extra cash when he wanted to save for their future. She heard him whistling as he went out of the room. She picked up the paper from the table and flicked through to see the films. Not that she wanted to see them now that the pantomime was on offer. Still, it didn't do any harm to check as they were bound to go to the cinema at some point in the following weeks.

Glancing down, she saw a small item under *Theatre Notices* and above *Articles Wanted*. The articles in question were a fine mix of carpets, rugs, bicycles and furniture and usually she liked to check them and see if there was anything useful for sale. She lived in hope of persuading George to change some items in the house. But today, her gaze was fixed on the item entitled *Personal*. She read it again.

> Wanted, couple to adopt girl, aged 7 months.
> Replies to the District Council Office,
> Bearsden.

A familiar longing rippled through her like an ache. If George didn't want their own child, would he let them adopt? As soon as she thought it, she knew she was being fanciful. It was the expense of a child he didn't want and so it didn't matter if it was their own or an adopted infant. And he would have to share her with a child when he insisted he liked it just as a couple.

Morag sank into the chair as a sudden realisation hit her. She rubbed her stomach, and a slow, unbelieving smile covered her face. She was late. Her monthly visitor, as her mother always coyly referred to it, was due over two weeks ago. With the rush to get ready for Christmas, she hadn't noticed. When had it happened? George was usually so careful. But there had been that night when they had both drunk some sherry. She had been a wee bit tipsy, and so had he, and they had got carried away in their love-making so that he hadn't stopped quickly enough. She hadn't thought on it, believing once wasn't enough to make a baby.

She jumped up, ready to call to George, but then sat again. No, she wouldn't tell him right away. She wanted to savour it all to herself. If she was honest, it was because she didn't want him to spoil her precious news. She couldn't bear to see his expression or hear his reaction. Not yet. Not for a while.

'I'll tell him on Christmas Day,' she whispered to herself. She thought it could be an extra special gift, just for him. *He'll come round to it*, she thought. *And maybe, just maybe, he'll be as delighted as I am.*

—

The Pavilion Theatre was in Renfield Street in the busy heart of Glasgow city centre. Morag gripped George's arm in excitement as they stood in the queue and finally streamed into the grand entrance hall with everyone else. Her gaze took in the mahogany fittings and the majestic staircase adorned with white and gold mosaics.

'We have been before, darling.' George chuckled at her expression.

'I know, but not very often, and och, it's an amazing place. I can't wait for the panto to begin, can you?'

Morag's heart was dancing, not only because of the lovely setting and anticipation of the pantomime but because of her wonderful secret. She imagined her baby, nestled in her tummy, and wondered whimsically if it could hear the music and chatter and laughter all around. George's brown eyes were twinkling as if her good mood was infectious.

'I love you,' she whispered close to his ear, catching his scent of wool coat, tobacco and Macassar hair oil.

'I love you too. You look beautiful this evening. Sometimes, I can't believe my luck that you're mine.'

He stole a kiss, and they exchanged smiles as George led the way to their tip-up seats, which were a gorgeous red plush velvet, just as sumptuous as the rest of the theatre. The pantomime was as good as she hoped and, of course, Jack Anthony was marvellous in the starring role of *Babes in the Wood*. She almost cried when the children were tempted into the forest and captured by the witch. She was sure it was because motherhood, hovering on her horizon, made her protective of her baby and fearful of harms that could befall it or other children.

—

'Miss Linton, tea is ready,' Morag shouted up the stairs.

She knew she ought to go up and politely knock on the old lady's door, but she felt bone-weary today. Maybe it was the run-up to Christmas that did it. Buying, storing and planning festive food on top of everyday life was extra work, along with trying to make gifts without the recipients finding out. It was only two weeks until the big day but in that moment she wished it was all done, and they could carry blithely on into January. She and George didn't bother much with New Year, sharing a sherry or beer and playing cards until the ships' horns blew on the Clyde and they kissed and celebrated in bed. Not for them the carousing that went on into the small hours and the drunkenness of the neighbours or going to parties in the tenement blocks nearby. As George pointed out, if they accepted invitations, they'd have to invite people back and put on their own party, and that would cost money.

'Did you mention tea, Mrs Kincaid?' Mr McLeod said, coming out of the dining room.

His napkin hung from his neck like a dapper cravat. As usual he was dressed in an ancient blue suit with matching waistcoat and a fob watch on a gold chain tucked into the waistcoat pocket. A neatly folded handkerchief topped his breast pocket, and his tie was a darker shade of blue with a frayed edge where the silk had given up.

'It's late today,' he remarked.

'I'm sorry about that, Mr McLeod, I really am, but I think we should wait for Miss Linton. Why don't you go back into the dining room, and I'll serve up in a wee moment. I'll run up and chap on her door.'

There was no reply to Morag's gentle knocking, so she hammered more loudly in case her lodger was asleep. She was concerned that Miss Linton was missing too many meals lately. She was a tiny lady to begin with so there wasn't much margin for missing her nourishment, in Morag's opinion.

When there was still no answer, Morag turned the handle and pushed the door open cautiously.

'Miss Linton? It's teatime. I've made a lovely savoury tripe casserole with sheep's kidney and calf liver to build you up. I'm sorry to barge in on you like this but I've been calling, and you haven't answered.'

In the dim light cast through the window, on what was a particularly dull and dreary winter's day, she saw the shape of her lodger under the counterpane. There was a glass full of water beside the bed with a set of pink and white false teeth in it. Miss Linton's hair looked like spun silk.

'Hello?' Morag hesitated, her hand raised, then, with a shrug, she shook the old woman gently on the shoulder. But something was wrong. She was cold and stiff.

Almost immediately, she knew that Miss Linton had passed away. She ran to the top of the stairs, all sense of weariness replaced with a fast-beating heart and alertness as if she'd drunk three cups of proper coffee.

'George!' she cried. 'Will you come up here right now.'

After that, everything was a blur. The shock and grief muddled Morag's recollection of the day, but she remembered the main events: the doctor had to be called out to officially pronounce Miss Linton dead. There was discussion over whether there were any next of kin, but Morag didn't know. Miss Linton had never had any visitors to the house in the two years she'd stayed with them. In between answering the doctor's questions, she managed to serve up tepid tripe casserole to Mr McLeod, followed by a rice pudding with a congealed surface. He clicked his teeth at the sight of it, but she noticed it didn't stop him polishing off a good portion.

The undertakers came at short notice to remove the body, and Morag shuddered. *Poor Miss Linton*, she thought to herself repeatedly. She hadn't been well, but she'd never complained. And now she was gone. When she went upstairs later that evening, she forced herself to go into the old lady's room. The counterpane lay on the floor, trampled. The cotton sheets still held the impression of her body, and the scent of the sweet powder that Miss Linton loved hung in the air. All that, Morag managed to take in calmly. Her glance landed on the set of false teeth, waiting hopefully in their glass of water, and suddenly she was crying. Her body shook with the wails.

George rushed in, looking surprised.

'Hey, hey, what's the matter?' He wrapped her in his arms and rocked them both until her sobs subsided and she sniffled.

'What is it, tell me,' he murmured, kissing her hair.

Morag pulled away, her eyes sore and swollen, and no doubt red-rimmed. 'What do you mean, *what is it?* Someone died, George. In our house! Aren't you at all upset?'

'Well, of course I am,' he said, not sounding it in the least. 'It's a terrible thing to happen. Especially coming up to Christmas.' He tapped his chin and walked around the room, his feet making the floorboards creak. 'In fact, it's the worst time of year for it to happen. No one's going to be moving lodgings until the new year at the earliest. What, darling?'

So he *had* noticed her expression. Morag was appalled with him. 'I'm sad about Miss Linton, who was a lovely old lady, full of cheeriness and never a complaint. And you're thinking about missing out on the rent payments?!'

He had the grace to flush. 'I'm sad too. But we must be practical. There will be a dent in our incomings for a few weeks at least. Christmas is expensive and there's no sign yet of a promotion for me.'

'I'm not listening to you for another second,' Morag snapped.

She stormed downstairs, ignoring Mr McLeod's interested stare as she passed him on his way to the parlour. She'd stay in the kitchen and avoid him and George, she thought angrily. She sat at the kitchen table with a pot of tea. In the other room, she heard the two men talking and then the sound of the wireless being tuned in to a channel. Soon there was canned laughter as *It's That Man Again* came on.

Later, at bedtime, she put on her nightdress and watched George in his striped blue and white pyjamas neatly fold his trousers on top of the chair.

'I'm sorry I shouted at you earlier,' she said, remembering that the old advice for a happy marriage was never to go to bed on an argument. 'I was upset about Miss Linton, and you were right. We will miss the money coming in.'

'I forgive you, darling. It must have been a terrible shock finding her like that. No wonder you were hysterical,' he replied gently.

Hardly hysterical, Morag thought but kept her mouth shut. One argument had been quite enough for the day.

'We'll need to advertise immediately for another lodger even if we don't expect any replies until January,' George said. He looked at her expectantly.

'I'll write up some cards and pop them into the shops and post office tomorrow,' Morag agreed with a yawn.

—

She had a late shift the next day, which meant she could spend the morning writing out the cards once she had made the breakfast and run down the road to get Mr McLeod his newspaper. He usually tottered along to get his own, but today, he complained of stiff joints. He hadn't mentioned Miss Linton's demise, but Morag wondered if he was more upset than he let on. She saw George off early with a kiss. He looked smart and business-like with his hair smoothed down, and she felt a pang of tenderness for him. Surely they'd promote him soon?

She put on her wool coat and beret and placed the cards into her handbag. It was a dry, grey day and bitterly cold. She hurried along the London Road and past what the locals called 'the Bridgeton Umbrella'. It was actually an iron-cast bandstand right at the crossroads in the centre of the area and Morag liked it for its bright red roof and clock tower. Besides, when it rained, it gave a good shelter, as its nickname suggested. She passed Millers' Linoleum Stores and waved to the owner. George had at least given permission to replace the worn lino from his parents' house when they moved in and they had spent many an hour in there debating how much and which pattern before buying.

She left a card in the post office window. It had been where Mr McLeod had found his way to them three years ago and she crossed her fingers that it would be lucky again. Then she went along the road, popping into any likely shops and asking if they'd be so kind as to take a card.

Mrs Corrie, who owned the baker's shop on the main street, greeted her kindly when she reached the head of the queue, which was surprisingly short that morning. The Corries' bakery was where she bought the National Loaves and pies for her and George and the lodgers, so the owner knew her well.

'What can I do you for today, hen?'

'While I'm here, I'll take one of your meat pies, Mrs Corrie, please. Would you mind if I put one of these cards in your window? Only we're looking for a new lodger.'

'No bother, pop it over there with the other advertising cards. Did your lodger move out, then?'

'No, she... passed away yesterday. It was an awful shock. She was such a sweet lady.' Morag felt her lip tremble and hoped she wasn't going to cry in front of Mrs Corrie.

'Och, that's terrible, so it is,' Mrs Corrie said sympathetically. 'Been with you long, had she?'

'Aye, a couple of years.' Instinctively, Morag's fingers cradled her stomach through her wool coat, thinking of her baby and the cycle of life and death that made the world go round. She felt blessed with good luck at falling pregnant but at the same time devastated by Miss Linton's death. What a topsy-turvy thing life was. She almost said it out loud but stopped herself. George must be the first to know about their baby and until she told him on Christmas Day, it was her lovely secret to keep.

'Well, you take care, dear. It is upsetting, even if she wasn't a blood relative.' Mrs Corrie patted Morag's arm. 'And put your card up there. We've a lot of people come into our shop so someone's bound to take notice of it.'

'Thank you. George is keen for us to find a new lodger as soon as we can. We need the rent, especially this time of year.'

Behind her, she was suddenly aware that someone else had entered the shop. Glancing back, she saw a tall man, broad in the shoulder. He touched his cap brim politely when he saw her look.

'I couldn't help overhearing you, missus. Happens I might be looking for a place. Can I see it?'

Mrs Corrie smiled and went back behind the counter to serve another two women who bustled in with stuffed shopping bags, their collars turned up against the weather and their hats pulled down over cold ears.

Morag handed over the card, a little flustered without knowing why. His fingers briefly touched hers and she felt their roughness. He was a working man. His clothes told her that even before the feel of calloused fingers. He had a flat cap and an old tweed jacket over black trousers with faded knees. His hobnail boots had seen a few winters too, she reckoned. She wasn't sure if he could afford their rent. And what would George make of him, she wondered. Close up, he was younger than she'd first thought. Possibly of an age with her and George.

He turned the white card in his hands as if memorising it. 'I'm in a cheap hotel and paid up to the end of the month.'

He took off his cap and scratched his head thoughtfully. Morag noticed he had a thick head of black hair, roughly cut.

'We'd like a lodger who's going to be staying for a while,' she said.

'That might be me, but it depends…'

'I'm not sure it'll suit, to be honest,' Morag cut in.

George would be annoyed if he heard her. Hadn't they both agreed they wanted someone as soon as possible? So why was she putting him off? She didn't know.

'We'll see,' he said, staring at her for a moment before grinning. 'Mind if I keep this?'

She could hardly say no. Morag nodded tightly. When he had gone, she took another card from her handbag and tucked it in with the other advertisements in the window. There was no harm in doing that. Especially as he was uncertain. *It depends*… on what? She shook her head. No, it would be better to have another woman apply, or an older man with whom Mr McLeod would enjoy conversing about the state of the war.

Mrs Corrie, free of customers, came over. 'You've met our Ricky then.' She chuckled.

'Oh, you know him?' Morag said, startled.

Mrs Corrie shook her head. 'I wouldn't say that. Only he introduced himself as Ricky Smith a few weeks ago and comes in regularly for a meat pie.'

'What does he work as? You'd think he'd be in the forces, a big man like that.'

'He could be in a reserved occupation, plenty of those on the shipyards,' Mrs Corrie pointed out. 'I don't know, hen. He hasn't shared that much with me. Although he likes a chat, that one. He was asking me all about Glasgow and the local area. With that thick accent, you can tell he's from London. I can hardly make him out sometimes.'

'What does he ask? You don't think he's a spy, do you? I read in the papers about fifth columnists passing secrets back to the Nazis. Isn't that why they took the names off the railway stations and the street signs?' Morag clutched her handbag.

Mrs Corrie looked worried. 'But he's very clearly English. I can't imagine he's working for the Germans. Besides, he says he's looking for someone. That's why he's here. He told me he goes out every day to a different part of the city to try and find them.'

'Who is it?' Morag asked.

'I've no idea. I did ask the other day when we were chatting, but we got on to other topics and now that I think about it, he didn't answer.'

'He doesn't sound like a spy,' Morag said, more to settle Mrs Corrie's nerves than because she was convinced. 'Anyway, I doubt he'll want lodgings if he finds whoever he's searching for before the end of December.'

'Did you leave your number on the card?'

'Aye, the post office telephone number and my address. I hope we get someone soon although with Christmas on the horizon it might suit better if we don't hear anything until after Boxing Day.'

'Good luck with it. Ricky might be in touch, you never know. Glasgow's a big city. What are the chances he'll find his person in another month, or ever? Folk manage to disappear all the while, and with a war on, it's even easier.' Mrs Corrie waved to her and hurried back behind the counter as the shop door opened to admit a customer.

Morag thought Mrs Corrie was right as she walked up the road to the house to get ready for her shift. Glasgow was the largest city in Scotland. How was it possible to find anyone if you didn't know their address or where they worked? Who was he looking for in any case? Her thoughts turned to fixing a meal for Mr McLeod before getting herself across the Green to Greenbank, and she soon forgot about Ricky Smith.

Chapter Eight

On Christmas morning, Eileen went to visit Jimmy at Cowglen hospital. She knew Mary and Harry had been in the day before, but she wanted time with him all on her own.

The nurses had made an effort to put up some festive cheer with paper chains made from scraps of old paper and painted newspaper. There was a small fir tree inside the entrance with red glass baubles and Eileen wondered where they had got it. Christmas trees were like hens' teeth to find these days.

Jimmy was quiet and barely had a smile, although he held her hand as she sat on the chair as close to the bedside as she could get.

'Happy Christmas, darling,' she said and kissed his forehead, the bandages over his eyes brushing her lips.

Jimmy's jaw tightened. 'When am I getting out of here? Have they told you? Cos they've not told me a thing.'

Eileen shook her head and then realised he couldn't see her do it. 'I can ask again.'

'Och, don't bother. I'll be the last to know. They're always fiddling about with my eyes or my shoulder or some bit of me,' he said gloomily.

'I'm sorry I've not been in for a while, but I've been doing extra shifts lately to make up a wee bit of money for Christmas. This will cheer you up. Me and Amy went to this parade in George Square a couple of weeks ago. It was so special, Jimmy. You'd have liked it, so you would. All those Home Guard soldiers marching and a band playing with the pipes and drums. It was grand, so it was. Just grand.'

Eileen injected as much cheer into her voice as possible, determined to make up for Jimmy's sullen mood. It was hard work, and she felt her own mood slide down. When *was* he coming home? There seemed to be no sign of improvement in his condition. The doctors and nurses were tight-lipped when she asked. Private Dougal had an infection in his shoulder and leg. He couldn't be moved until they were healed. She hadn't dared to ask about his eyes. Why were they still covered with swathes of bandages? She was frightened that he was blind. It must have crossed his mind too, but they had never discussed it. That also disturbed her. They were going to be married, and a man and wife shouldn't have secrets or worries they didn't share. And yet, somehow, she couldn't bring herself to start that conversation.

He grunted and Eileen chattered on, describing the crowds and meeting Morag and the taste of the hot pies that Amy had bought. She trailed off. A one-way conversation was hard. She racked her brains for other ideas. Anything that might spark an interest in Jimmy.

'We've had an awful infestation of mice in the flat,' she told him. 'Your mum says it's because they want shelter in autumn from the damp and the cold weather. At first it was the one wee mouse coming in and out of a hole in the skirting board in the kitchen. Then we noticed another hole in the bedroom skirting and that mouse had a family. I was that worried about it. Them leaving droppings and dirt and a funny smell. But you'll never guess what happened…'

'They multiplied and chucked the both of youse oot the hoose.' Jimmy chuckled.

Eileen laughed. Now they were making progress. He was intrigued, or so she hoped.

'This wee white cat appeared one day. He was hanging around in the close, annoying my neighbours, but he was a stray, and they didn't want him. So I took him in and I call him Snowy. And Snowy has got rid of the mouse problem.'

She'd forgotten how rich Jimmy's laughter was. She was glad she was the cause of it.

'I love you, Jimmy Dougal,' she said fiercely, feeling the roughness of his fingers under hers.

'And I love you, Eileen Sheena Boyle,' came the reply. 'Whatever happens, that'll never change, my darling.'

'All that's going to happen is you're going to get well and come home to me. We'll get married and be together forever.'

And I'm not giving up on you, she added silently, when he didn't answer.

—

'Where is Amy?' Agnes peered past Eileen's shoulder.

'Happy Christmas, Mum. Amy's poorly so she stayed at home.' Eileen pecked Agnes's dry cheek.

Agnes huffed and waved her into the house. In the pre-war years, the Boyle home was overheated but now there was a damp chill in the air caused by lack of coal. Eileen took her coat off reluctantly and hung it on the hook in the hallway. She wished she'd dressed more warmly. She also wished that Amy had come with her. If today was anything like previous Christmases, it would be quiet and dull. Amy would have livened it up, if only by being a novelty. But she had claimed a head cold and decided to stay in bed.

'Your father is in the parlour. Go and say hello. I couldn't get a turkey this year, but the butcher kept a breast of pork for me, and I've rolled and tied it, braised it and stuffed it. I daresay we won't notice the lack of turkey once I've served it up with sprouts and potatoes.'

Robert was snoring in front of a tiny smoking fire so Eileen went into the kitchen to see if she could help. The table was set for dinner with Agnes's best crockery and napkins, and it made Eileen want to cry for some reason. There they were in the middle of a terrible war and yet the celebrations still mattered. It was worth setting out the best china and folded napkins and making a meal that might be small because food was rationed, or simply unavailable – like turkey or chicken – but made the Christmas celebration special.

Agnes came in and tied on her apron. 'The extra rations from the government are as good as a gift. All that marg and meat have all gone into making this meal special.'

'It looks lovely, Mum,' Eileen said with a smile.

It almost felt like normal Christmases as the three Boyles sat down to their dinner. There was no Christmas tree in the house as Robert and Agnes felt it was not Christian. Like most families in Scotland, Christmas was not seen as important compared to Hogmanay and New Year and Eileen knew that Jeannie's family didn't celebrate Christmas Day at all, keeping their presents and good meal for New Year. Christmas Day wasn't even a public holiday in Scotland.

After the meal, eaten mostly in silence as Eileen's parents thought it bad manners to chat and eat at the same time, they moved through to the parlour and the sluggish fire. Eileen poked the ashes to liven the flames and, watched by her mother's sharp gaze, added a little slack and a newspaper taper, to get the fire going.

They exchanged small gifts wrapped in newspaper as colourful wrapping paper was impossible to find. Eileen gave her father a tie that she'd bought in the second-hand market in the city centre, which he seemed pleased with. For Agnes, she had sewn a lavender bag with a ribbon hook, using lavender from a couple of little pouches she'd had tucked between her clothes for a few years. Luckily, there was still some scent, and she'd freshened it up with a drop of water, which had worked well. In return, Agnes handed over a small package of home-made peppermint creams.

'That's where the extra sugar ration went,' she remarked when Eileen thanked them both. 'You can share them with Amy.'

At three p.m., they gathered round the wireless to listen to the King's speech, a plate with a small slice of fruit cake on their knees. It was cake from the previous Christmas, carefully put aside by Agnes, and Eileen realised her mum hadn't been as optimistic as some that the war would end before the festive season and so had made the effort to squirrel some seasonal food aside.

'…I wish you, from my heart, a happy Christmas; and, for the coming year, a full measure of that courage and faith in God, which alone enables us to bear old sorrows and face new trials, until the day when the Christmas message – peace on earth and goodwill towards men – finally comes true.'

Eileen's eyes prickled with tears at the emotional message sounding straight from the King's heart, and, glancing at her parents, she saw that Agnes and Robert's eyes were shiny too. She imagined families all round Britain, listening to the wireless and having the same reaction. It was true, they really were all in it together and had to carry on, whatever happened, in the hope of better days.

She picked up the tiny glass of sherry beside her and raised it in a hand that trembled slightly. 'To our loved ones and absent friends.'

She thought of Jimmy, in his hospital bed or perhaps walking round the ward to the common room, helped by another patient or a nurse as he couldn't see. Her heart ached for him. How brave he was. And how much she longed for him to come home.

'To absent friends,' Agnes and Robert murmured too.

'And talking of absent friends, your father had an unexpected letter,' Agnes said.

'From my brother, Norman,' Robert said as Eileen raised her eyebrows in query. 'Though your mother didn't need to mention it. It's a private matter.'

The hurt hit her right in the chest. *Every time*, she thought. *I never learn. I know they love me, but they form a unit of two and I'm always on the outside. I can't get close no matter how much I wish to.*

'He's my family too,' she said quietly. 'My uncle, whom I've never met.'

'Not much of a word from him in the last twenty-five years and now he writes a proper letter,' Robert mused.

'He's getting older. We all are. Time's running out to make amends and mend bridges,' Agnes said.

'What does he say, Dad?'

Robert took a moment to pack his pipe with tobacco and set it alight until the thick, aromatic smoke curled up above his head.

'He wishes us a merry Christmas and asks if we've seen Amy.'

'You'd have met her today if she wasn't feeling poorly.' Eileen sipped her sherry.

Agnes shook her head. 'Your father thinks I'm being fanciful, but the way I read it, it's as if Norman wonders if Amy is here in Glasgow at all.'

They listened to a beautiful carol service from Norwich Cathedral and at eight p.m. there was *Christmas Night at Eight* with Arthur Askey, Gert and Daisy, and Barbara Mullen, which made them laugh. Eileen had to leave to get her bus home before the final *Christmas Cabaret*.

'Merry Christmas. Don't get up, I'll let myself out,' she said.

She put on her winter coat, beret and gloves and looked in again at the parlour. Her parents sat either side of the wireless in their armchairs. The fire blazed a little higher, flames curling gold and red with a satisfying crackle and hiss. The plates, with a few cake crumbs, sat on the small table along with the empty sherry glasses. Agnes hummed along to the music and Robert's head nodded as he slumbered. His pipe, propped against the sherry glass, exuded little smoke trails.

All the way home in the freezing-cold bus, Eileen wondered why Norman had written. It made her feel anxious for him worrying about where his daughter was. She wished she knew more about Amy and her side of the family. Eileen's own father wasn't very forthcoming on the subject and Amy never mentioned them at all. She bit her lip, musing. Perhaps she was making too much of it, especially on Christmas Day. She rubbed her gloved fingers together to get a little warmth and tried to forget about it all as they arrived at the bus stop.

—

Amy hopped out of bed as soon as Eileen had left. She danced through the flat, glad to have it to herself. She'd faked a cold coming on and had had to spend an annoying hour in her bed recess, under the covers, pretending to be sick. She had no intention of spending Christmas Day with Eileen's parents. They might be her aunt and uncle, but she bet it'd be a dull afternoon and evening.

She rummaged through Eileen's wardrobe and chose a midnight blue velvet dress that was definitely pre-war in its style and the amount of material. It had ruches and folds in the skirt and the bodice was pretty with a sculpted neckline. It suited her blonde curls, and she painted her lips carmine, smacking them in pretend kisses in the mirror. Snowy stared at her with large amber eyes from his perch on the windowsill before losing interest and folding himself into sleep.

She tuned the wireless until she found Christmas songs. Then she pulled up the corner of her mattress to find a bottle of stout she'd bought a few weeks before. There was also a box of mince pies that Bessie, the woman running the children's crèche, had given her to share with Eileen. Too bad Eileen wasn't there.

Amy hummed along to the wireless as she slugged directly from the bottle and ate a deliciously crumbly mince pie. She kicked her feet up, glad of the freedom to be herself. She'd had an awful fright that day at the parade, thinking that *he* had found her. A tall, broad-shouldered man who, from the back, looked just like Ricky. Her heart was in her mouth when he turned. And the relief when she realised it wasn't him, well, it was marvellous. By then, of course, she'd hidden in the pie shop, having seen a couple intent on reaching Eileen. She didn't care for too many people to know who she was. It was easier to pretend she was buying pies.

She almost didn't hear the knock on the door. Tiptoeing across, she pressed her ear to the wood, but it was hard to hear anything. With a sigh, she opened the door. Leo Mearns stood there, a smile quivering his moustache and a box of violet creams in his hand.

'A merry Christmas and a wee gift for you,' he said, pushing the box of sweets towards her and walking into the flat.

'And very welcome it is,' Amy said, her mouth watering at the sight of the delicate crystallised violet petals on top of the creamy chocolates. 'I ain't… I mean, I've never tasted one of these before.'

'Then you must have one immediately,' Leo Mearns said. 'Here, let me.'

He opened the box. Greedily, Amy took a chocolate and popped it into her mouth.

'Mmm, it's delicious. 'Ere, do you want a cuppa?'

Leo's gaze flickered round the room. 'Where is your delectable cousin? I brought these for her too.'

Amy laughed. 'Not your lucky day. Eileen's off visiting her mum and dad. I'm 'ere, though. I'm sure we can have a nice chat, can't we?'

He hesitated. Amy twirled, feeling the full skirt lift and expose her legs. His dark eyes widened, and his smile broadened. She moistened her lips and flicked a blonde curl back into place.

'Would you like to see my home?' he said. 'I have five rooms at the top of tenement number one in the street.'

'Don't seem quite decent. Me being a single girl and you a gentleman on his own.' Amy injected a bit of reluctance into her tone. It didn't do to look too keen.

'Oh, my dear. We won't be alone. Goodness, no. I live with my spinster sisters. It will be quite respectable.' His wolfish grin was at odds with his words and Amy thought his dark eyes were curiously flat, not a window to the soul at all.

'Very well, I'd love to. Let me get me coat on. You can leave them choccies right there.'

It took only a few minutes to walk along to number one Kiltie Street, but Amy made sure that her hat was tilted to shade her face. People would think it was Eileen walking alongside Mr Mearns. They were both smartly dressed, even if her coat and boots were a little shabby with the lovely dress. His astrakhan coat was as handsome as ever and she found a man in a homburg classy. The men she'd grown up with wore flat caps.

A bitter-faced woman in a brown dress that sucked colour from her skin opened the door at the top of number one Kiltie Street. She didn't speak to them despite Leo's polite greeting.

'This is my sister Ada. She'll bring us a pot of tea and perhaps a slice of cake if there is one.'

Amy almost gasped out loud at the furnishings and size of Leo's home. He led the way to a parlour. Amy had never seen one so full of furniture and knick-knacks and cushions. A pale woman in her fifties sat on the couch knitting beside a good fire in a wide hearth. The wireless in a large, polished walnut case was playing Christmas carols.

'This is my sister Sarah. Sarah, this is our neighbour Amy Boyle. We'll need the room, thank you.'

Sarah nodded obediently, picked up her knitting and slid past them.

'Your sisters don't have much to say for themselves,' Amy remarked.

'They know which side their bread is buttered on. I'm very good to them. If it wasn't for me, they'd be out in the street. My mother, rest her soul, left her inheritance entirely to me as her only son.'

'Really?' Amy smiled. 'Lucky for you.' She slid her arm into Leo's and beamed up at him.

'This was Mother's favourite room. I've left it all as she liked it. My wife, Alice, wanted to redecorate but I refused to let her.'

The mention of Leo's wife made Amy chew her lip. Still, Alice wasn't here, was she. And Amy was. She grinned and patted the couch beside her.

'Come and tell me more. I'd love to hear about your old mum.'

'She married well to my father, Arnold, and they moved in the best circles of people of course, moving up in class. When he died she came back here and bought this property. I grew up here and now I own it.' There was a note of triumph in his voice.

'Can I see round the place?' Amy asked.

'It would be my pleasure.'

He stood up and took her hand as she rose from the couch. Amy let him. She smiled encouragingly as he told her about the value of some of the ornaments, the ormolu clock on the mantelpiece and the walnut wireless case. She didn't really care about the details, but he was obviously out to impress her, which was flattering. He was well off, that was crystal clear. So she nodded and smiled in all the right places while her sharp gaze took in the high-ceilinged hallway with its thick carpet and the spotless kitchen where Ada scowled at her when Leo wasn't watching.

'And this is my bedroom. It used to be Mother's,' Leo said proudly, flinging open the door to a large room.

Amy stayed in the hallway and peeked in. It too was fussily decorated and more like a woman's bedroom than a man's. She guessed he hadn't changed anything. The bed dominated the room in solid oak with a maroon quilt and a soft blanket folded at the end. The curtains matched the colour of the quilt, and she could see they were made of quality, thick velvet that hung in perfect drapes due to the weight of the material. A dressing table, chair, bedside cabinet and dark wood wardrobe completed the bedroom, while two shelves running along the wall were crammed with ornaments and another ormolu clock.

'Shall we go in?' Leo said, and his dark eyes flickered over her body.

'Another day perhaps,' Amy said sweetly.

She disentangled her hand from his, which felt damp and warm, but made sure to give it a little squeeze and let her fingertips trail on his palm. He coughed and stroked his moustache.

'Bloomin' heck, is that the time? I'll have to go; I expect Eileen will be back and looking for her Christmas meal,' she lied.

Amy hummed as she sauntered back along Kiltie Street, her hat drawn down and her coat collar up. The neighbours could make of it what they wanted. Eileen Boyle visiting Leo Mearns was bound to get the gossips stirred up. And Leo could turn out to be quite useful, she was sure. She just had to keep him sweet.

It took all Morag's willpower not to share her news with George until Christmas Day. In the intervening days she'd persuaded herself that he would be ecstatic too.

'I'll tell him in the afternoon, once Mum and Dad have gone and Mr McLeod has his nap,' she murmured.

'What's that, dear?' her mother said, coming into the kitchen where Morag was basting the pork leg she had managed to get from the butcher.

'Nothing, Mum. I was talking out loud to myself, wondering how long it'll take this pork to cook.'

'Och, surely you know by now. You've been married long enough. I hope you're feeding George well. A wife must look after her husband first and foremost and put herself second.' Mollie frowned.

Morag nodded. 'I know, you're right and I do make the best meals I can with the rations but it's not easy. Here, Mum, do you mind doing the apple sauce while I steam up the pudding?'

'I hope you like it. Your dad and I couldn't think of a better gift, and I have a wee stash of plum puds from a few years ago.' Mollie took a knife and began to peel the apples.

'It's perfect, thanks.' Morag kissed her mother's cheek and Mollie looked pleased.

'Of course, once you and George start a family, I'll be giving you a larger pudding each year,' Mollie said with a hopeful glance at her daughter.

Morag had to bite her lip. It wouldn't do to share her news with her mother before George was told. Her parents kept hinting about 'weans' and 'leaving it too late' and other nuggets of advice, which was why George didn't like inviting them over very often.

After the meal, they sat in the parlour and exchanged presents. It had been difficult to find anything in the shops to buy. The gifts were all wrapped in old newspapers, and they hadn't been able to get a tree. Morag had made paper chains and painted them; these were now draped over the paintings on the walls and on the sideboard. In the end, she'd made coconut cookies and put them in jam jars. Each jam jar had a ribbon round it, taken from an old dress, and she thought them quite pretty. In return, she got a warm, knitted scarf from her parents, an embroidered handkerchief from Mr McLeod and a necklace made from tiny, coloured stones from George. She knew he'd got it from the local pawn shop because she had seen him going in there recently, but she didn't care; it was a beautiful piece of jewellery. She could hardly wait for her parents to go and for Mr McLeod to take his nap.

'You won't stay for another wee cup of tea?' she asked politely as George helped them into their coats and passed them their hats.

She was relieved when they shook their heads. They lived close by and headed off along the dark road with a wave. She could hear Mr McLeod's snores when they stepped back into the warmth of the hall and closed the front door.

'George, I've got something to tell you. Come into the dining room in case Mr McLeod wakes up,' Morag said.

'I'll wager the old codger will be asleep now until he smells the bedtime cocoa.' George laughed, following her into the room where the aromas of their Christmas meal still lingered.

Morag folded her arms, then let them drop loose and finally stood behind one of the dining room chairs, her hands on top of its back frame, the feel of the smooth, polished wood cool to her touch.

'What is it, darling? You're being quite mysterious.'

'We're having a baby,' Morag blurted out.

His smile froze. His hand swept through his carefully oiled hair, displacing strands, which stuck out. He shook his head disbelievingly.

'Are you certain?' he said.

'I'm late with my monthlies and this morning I felt a wee bit sick at the smell of the pork cooking. Say something, George. Tell me you're happy.'

'I don't understand... we were so careful.' He stared at her.

'It was that night when we shared the half bottle of sherry. It was stronger than I realised. Are you happy? I know we didn't plan for a family for a couple of years yet but we're having a baby whether we planned it or not.' She hated the desperation in her voice.

'You did this on purpose,' George shouted. 'You knew I didn't want children, but you went ahead and did it anyway!'

Morag recoiled, stunned and hurt. It was as if he'd slapped her.

'It was an accident,' she cried.

'How convenient,' George snapped. 'So you get what you wanted and to hell with our plans to make a good life for ourselves.'

'Did you mean that?' Morag made herself ask even though she was shaking both in shock and anger. 'That you don't want children ever? Even though we agreed to wait a couple of years and have them?'

'You don't get to ask that,' he said coldly. 'Not now, when you've ruined everything. I'm going to bed.'

He stalked away, leaving her to follow him. Where else was she to go? They got ready for bed in silence, the horrible argument still simmering in the air between them. When they got into the bed, instead of the usual kisses and cuddles, they lay rigidly with a strip of air between them. Morag couldn't bear to touch him. How could he be like that? He blamed her. Yet he was the liar. He'd promised a family in a couple of years' time, but he hadn't meant it at all. He simply wanted her to stop yearning for what she was never going to have. She'd never felt so bleak.

She curled protectively over her stomach and wished, with all her heart, that they were both excited about their wee baby. Still, life wasn't all perfect, was it? She had enough love for both of them to shower on their unborn child. Hopefully, one day George would feel it too.

—

In the middle of the night, Morag woke up with stomach cramps. She stumbled from the bed and ran along the corridor to the bathroom.

It's a tummy bug, it has to be, she thought, afraid to look.

When she dared to glance down, she saw her nightdress streaked with blood and the water in the toilet was red with it too. She sat and cried for a long while, alone in the dark, before mopping her eyes and taking a deep, deep breath in. She'd never be sure if she had been briefly pregnant or whether her period was simply late.

Stumbling back into the bedroom, she switched on the lamp. George gave a groan and sat up, his hair and face rumpled with sleep. Morag took a fresh nightgown and underwear from the chest of drawers and changed quietly, slipping in a pad.

'I've lost the baby,' she said quietly.

A brief expression of relief flew across his face before he hid it with concern. If she hadn't been watching him closely she wouldn't have seen it.

'I'm so sorry, darling, and I'm sorry we argued. Come here and I'll kiss it all away. You poor thing, does it hurt? It's for the best, you'll see. We weren't ready to be parents. In a few years we'll try properly, won't we? We'll have our own little baby, but it wasn't to be, not now.'

She let him hold her. She felt numb and icy cold as if her body wasn't working. As she listened to him, she felt the iciness creep up into her heart. That evening they had spent at the Pavilion Theatre she had said she loved him and meant it. Now, she hated him for being so relieved. He was being nice and kind now that it had all turned out the way he wanted it. She *hated* him.

Chapter Nine

January came in bitterly cold. Women, hurrying past each other in Kiltie Street and muffled up in hats and scarves, said it was the coldest winter they could remember, even worse than the previous year. There was frost on the inside of the windows, and waking up in the mornings, Eileen could see her breath, like white smoke, as she jumped out with bare feet onto the threadbare carpet and washed and dressed as quickly as possible. The coal rationing made it impossible to keep more than a small fire going in the kitchen range and the fireplace in the bedroom was not lit at all. To save fuel, she and Amy had made a hay box.

It was Amy's idea. She'd waved the Ministry of Food's *Food Without Fuel* pamphlet at Eileen.

'Instead of griping about 'aving no coal to keep the range lit, we oughta make a hay box just like what it says 'ere.'

'Let me see.' Eileen grabbed the pamphlet and scanned it. 'We don't have a box with a hinged lid, and we don't have nearly enough newspaper; they say it needs three or four of them. Or a supply of dry sweet hay.'

Amy winked. 'Don't we?'

She beckoned Eileen with a curl of her fingers and Eileen found herself following Amy out into the chilly close. At their door was a packing case and a tied bag, slightly dusty.

'Go on, then, 'ave a look. Open it up,' Amy encouraged with a grin.

Eileen smelled the straw before she finished untying the knot. She stared up at Amy. 'How did you manage to get this?'

'I wheedled it out of a boy I'm pally with. Works for the greengrocer down on Maryhill Road. The packing case came from old Heaney, the butcher. He was throwing it out and I found it in the lane at the side of the shop.'

Eileen opened her mouth to say she doubted Mr Heaney was getting rid of it and that he was probably storing stuff in the lane and would be livid when he found out it had been stolen, but slowly she closed her lips. Amy looked so excited she didn't want to spoil the mood. Instead, she nodded.

'You've thought this through. What a marvellous idea. I was going to use our old newspapers as tapers for the fire but maybe we can spare a couple for this.'

They kneeled on the kitchen floor while Amy read out the instructions. The packing case had to be lined with the newspapers to a thickness of fifteen layers of paper and fastened in place with drawing pins, which, thankfully, Eileen had. Next, they pressed down a good five-inch layer of the hay on the bottom of the case. The sweet, dusty fragrance reminded her of summer days as a child, growing up in a house next to fields on the edge of the city. The stubble, left after the farmer had harvested the crops, had smelled exactly like this.

'This will cook stew or porridge,' Amy announced, eyes narrowed as she focused on the printed words. 'Heat up the food to boiling, put it in the box and it'll keep cooking all day or night.'

'Right. We can try it with porridge first. I'll stir in the oatmeal and water,' Eileen said, getting up to fetch a pan.

'And we need an old pillowcase. Says we 'ave to make a small straw mattress for the top of the box to keep the heat in all round.'

Eileen felt a real sense of achievement as she and Amy stood proudly and gazed at the completed hay box with its straw mattress stuffed over the top of the porridge pan and the rest of the straw tuckedin.

Amy giggled. 'Looks like the home of a zoo animal, don't it?'

Eileen laughed too and impulsively grabbed Amy and hugged her. It was so lovely to make something together. It had been fun as well as useful and at that moment she felt they were closer than ever. Amy hugged her then pushed Eileen back so she looked her right in the eye.

'You couldn't 'ave done that without me. You need me. Don't forget that,' she said fiercely.

Lying in bed later, Eileen mulled it over. She could hear Amy's soft snores emanating from behind the wooden doors of the inset bed. Had Amy only wanted to make the hay box to make a point? Was she really so insecure she believed Eileen would make her leave the flat? Her thoughts flitted to Jimmy. If they got married and lived here, it would be cramped, but Amy was welcome to stay. Surely Jimmy wouldn't mind that. They could hardly send her back to London and the awful rockets that were blasting the capital. Perhaps she ought to reassure Amy of that… she drifted off to sleep dreaming of Jimmy.

'Bloody 'ell, it's brass monkeys in 'ere,' Amy exclaimed, pulling back the doors of the inset bed and shivering the next morning. 'I'm tempted to stay in bed today.'

'Aren't they expecting you at the nursery?' Eileen said with a frown. Honestly, she wouldn't put it past Amy to take the day off.

Amy laughed. 'Your face is a treat. I'm kidding you on. I'll get up in a moment once you've heated the water for a bowl to wash in. It's your turn, innit?'

Eileen was dressed by now. She had to admit, it was her turn to fill the jug so they could hastily scrub themselves. She longed for a bath, but they only managed to fill it once a week and set it before the range for a bit of luxurious warmth. Even with the six-inch waterline rule, that was a lot of water to heat and a lot of effort. She glanced up longingly at the tin bath tub as she hurried into the kitchen. It hung from a hook on the wall. Never mind, she'd stoke up the range and get the kettle on. Her foot trod on something soft, and she squealed, leaping back and banging her back on the door handle.

Snowy jumped up onto the table and stared at her. Eileen took the dead mouse gingerly and dropped it into the bin.

'I know you're doing your job, but I wish you'd take them outside. Or eat them. Waste not, want not as the slogan goes.'

Snowy licked his paw, yawned and stretched.

'You shouldn't be on the table either,' Eileen warned.

She ought to scoot him off, but she hadn't the heart. He was a good wee mouser and another bit of company and life around the flat. She missed Jeannie, her friendship, good humour and practical advice. She was glad that Amy was living with her, but their friendship hadn't developed the way Eileen had hoped. How could it when her cousin was still a mystery and didn't share her past or her thoughts easily? She wanted Amy to be as close as a sister but there was a distance she couldn't seem to broach. As if Amy was pushing her back with an invisible yard brush. Och, she was being fanciful.

'There we go, one jug of hot water. I'll pour it into the bowl, and you can have the first use… oh…'

Amy was not only dressed but had her coat and hat on. 'I'll see you later. Got to rush.'

Eileen stared after her, the jug clutched in her hand as the front door slammed behind Amy. She put it down, went over to the window and drew back the curtain just enough to see down onto the street. She was interested to see which way Amy went. If she went to the left, that was the way out of Kiltie Street and along to the main street where the women held their little nursery. She watched and, a moment later, saw the top of Amy's ridiculous black velvet hat, the flowers bobbing. Amy stood there and Eileen held her breath. Then, her cousin took a jaunty step to the right as if she had no cares in the world.

With a gasp, Eileen dropped the curtain. The brazen cheek of her! There was only one place Amy could be going as Kiltie Street in that direction was a dead end. Leo Mearns had his fancy flat in the first tenement. Amy had to be visiting him before she went to work. If indeed she went to work at all. Eileen shook her head, appalled. She had tried to warn Amy against him; she didn't trust him one little bit. And what about Amy's reputation? There was no doubt she'd be seen by the neighbours, many of whom liked a juicy slice of gossip to cheer up their days.

She didn't have time to dwell on Amy's behaviour that morning because she was going to visit Jimmy, it being her day off at Greenbank. As she washed and re-dressed, she thought that the only brightness in these dark, short days was that Jimmy had finally been transferred from the military hospital to a convalescent home. She had the instructions from his nurse at Cowglen, who had kindly written them down. Overtoun House was situated on the hillside overlooking the town of Dumbarton. Eileen took the train and then a bus before walking the last long stretch along a steeply upward country lane, her feet slipping on the icy stones and her way fringed by tall trees whose bare branches clutched at the air. Her first view of the house was stunning. It was like a fairy-tale castle with a tower and turrets, the grey stone blending in with a pewter sky and the woodland around it. She wondered who owned it and whether they were upset when the government commandeered it for the war effort.

She felt she ought to find a servants' entrance instead of boldly going inside the main door. There were painted friezes on the entrance passage, and once inside, straight ahead, a massive carved oak fireplace with smoky, crackling logs.

Soldiers wandered about everywhere, and the nursing staff seemed less harried than those at Cowglen. Somewhere, someone was playing the piano and the gentle melodies drifted in the air alongside the cigarette smoke. Loud guffaws of laughter erupted from a room off to the right, and glancing in, hoping to see Jimmy, she glimpsed wide bay windows looking out onto a lawn. The ceiling was painted with pictures of women in billowing robes of blue with angels surrounding them, and there was beautiful white decorative plasterwork all over the ceiling and walls. Eileen gaped. She imagined wealthy women in evening dresses sipping drinks before the war in the beautiful setting. Now the room was empty of fancy furniture and crammed with chairs and a darts board, and, ah, there was the piano and a soldier, missing an ear, rippling his fingers over the keys with a passion.

'Excuse me,' Eileen said as a nurse with red hair and freckles went past. 'I'm looking for Private Jimmy Dougal. I'm his fiancée.'

'He'll be glad to see you,' the nurse said, then blushed a bright pink. 'I'm sorry, he can't see you, but he'll be glad you're here, is what I meant.'

Her Irish accent put Eileen at ease. There were plenty of Irish families living around Kiltie Street and she loved their sense of humour and good-natured approach to life.

'I thought he was better and that's why he's here?' Eileen said, dismayed.

'He's better, of course, and his wounds have healed, but his sight hasn't come back. The doctor says there's no medical reason and he should be able to see so it's likely hysteria and it'll come back in its own good time. Oh, I've said too much. My mother is always telling me, "Aoife Margaret Mary, you talk too much for your own good." And she's right. You'll need to ask the doctor himself, so you will. It's not for me to say…'

'But…?' Eileen persisted. She'd rather talk to the freckled red-haired Aoife with her expressive, friendly face than a doctor who would talk down to her or confuse her with medical expressions.

'Well… my tuppence worth, if you like… in this case, I'd agree with the doctors. They don't get it right sometimes, between you and me, but in Jimmy's case, I truly believe his sight will come back when he's ready.'

'And how do I help him be ready?' Eileen said.

But Aoife Margaret Mary shrugged with a sweet smile and patted Eileen on the back. 'I don't know. Sure, if I did, would I not make a fortune giving these poor men back their sight? Your Jimmy's not the only one here who's blind, colleen. Now I must rush. I hope it works out for the both of you, I really do. He's upstairs on the first floor. Go back out and past the fireplace; the stairs are on the left.'

Eileen went up the stairs not knowing what to expect. The room on the left as she stepped onto the first floor was full of beds and each one had a man either sleeping under the blankets or sitting on top of it reading or playing cards. How sad that Jimmy could do neither. He was standing at the large window as if staring out at the grand gardens.

'Jimmy, it's me,' she called softly, trying to ignore all the interested looks from the other men.

'Hey, Lucky Jim, your sweetheart's here. Wanna take your stick and walk the young lady to the common room?' An American soldier grinned at Eileen and nodded to a walking stick beside one of the beds.

She smiled gratefully and took the stick over to Jimmy. She was desperate to kiss him, but she wasn't going to provide a show for the others. Besides, when he turned round, his expression was serious. She was relieved to see that the bandages over his eyes were gone and his shoulder and hip likewise. He was dressed in trousers and a shirt with a knitted tank top over it and she wondered whose clothes they were.

'Sheena, is that you? Come on, we'll take Charlie's advice and get out of here.'

She guided the stick into his hand and led him slowly out of the room. There was no one in the next room and she thought it must be the common room as there were some chairs and a table with ashtrays on it.

'Shall we sit down?' she asked. 'Here, let me help you.'

'I can manage,' Jimmy snapped, shaking off her hand.

Eileen gulped. There was an awful silence, and she didn't try to fill it. Jimmy felt for the chair and sat carefully, his stick gripped so hard that she saw the white of his knuckles. She had to remember how hard this was for him. Only, she wanted to help him, but she didn't know what to do.

'I'm sorry, darling. I shouldn't have shouted at you. I get… frustrated… that I can't look after myself. Someone has to help me walk and eat and go to the bathroom.' He blew out a heavy breath and shook his head.

'Let me help you,' Eileen cried, taking his hand and stroking it. 'I want to. As soon as they say you can leave here, let's get married and stay in my flat and be happy together.'

Even as she said it, she wondered how he was going to manage four flights of stone stairs up and down to the flat. How would he get about without crashing into things or, worse, burning himself on the kitchen range? Absurdly, her mind flew to the hay box that sat on the kitchen floor. They'd have to move it so he didn't trip over it. Amy would be mad at that.

'You don't want to marry a cripple like me. I'm no use to you, darling. Not to you or anyone in this state.'

'Don't say that, Jimmy,' she cried. 'I love you and I know you love me too. We've been engaged for nearly five years. Of course we'll get married.'

His answer was a stony silence.

The whole visit had been a disaster. Eileen was numb. She stood outside on the narrow stone bridge in Overtoun House's grounds watching the river far below. The white water frothed as it tumbled down the rocks on its way to the sea. There was a view of the Clyde through the treetops, but she barely noticed it in her misery. Jimmy wouldn't discuss their future at all. Their conversation had been stilted and they'd ended up discussing the weather and Eileen's Christmas instead of anything remotely intimate. They hadn't kissed either. Eileen didn't want to try, afraid of rejection. And Jimmy didn't attempt it. He'd mumbled goodbye when she left, and guiltily, she was relieved to go.

Above Overtoun House, in the opposite direction to the town and sea, were the grey cliffs of Lang Craigs. They looked forbidding in the dull winter light. Eileen shivered, turned up her collar and began to walk out of the estate and back down the icy lane.

She got off the train in the centre of Glasgow. She was meeting Morag, who had a half-day shift. In her bag she had a late Christmas present for her friend. From the old clothes in the suitcase that Frankie had left her, she'd found material to make an apron. She'd already adapted one of the blouses from the suitcase to fit Amy's slim figure and her cousin had been thrilled with it and that had inspired her to make further use of the suitcase contents. Goodness, if she didn't have her love for sewing to keep her spirits up and fill her spare hours, she didn't know what she'd do.

Morag arrived, out of breath, into the café with its steamed-up windows. It was blessedly warm inside compared to the frosty air outside. Eileen still had her coat on and buttoned up, though. It wasn't *that* warm. The lack of fuel was clearly affecting the local businesses too.

'Sorry, sorry,' Morag said, sliding into the seat opposite. 'The supervisor kept us late today. The quota had dipped because some of the girls are off sick with that flu that's going around. How are you? How's Jimmy? I know you said were visiting with him today.'

'Och, it didn't go well. I'm at a loss to know what to do,' Eileen replied. 'He's improving but his sight hasn't come back even though apparently there's nothing seriously wrong with his eyes. I don't really understand it.'

'Did they say when it will come back?'

Eileen shook her head. 'It's almost as if they're blaming him. As if it's his fault he can't see. And it's not his fault. How can it be when he wants to come home as much as his family and me want it too.'

'Oh, that's awful, Eileen. I'm so sorry. I hope he recovers soon for both your sakes.'

The waitress came over to take their order and Eileen waited until they had both chosen bread and soup before she gave Morag her gift.

'Don't get too excited; it's a late Christmas present.'

'Och, it's beautiful. Thank you. Just what I need. My apron is so old I can't get the dirty marks out of it. I'll enjoy using this, and when I do, I'll think of you.' Morag smiled. 'I didn't get you a Christmas present, I'm afraid. I was so upset about my lodger that I rather forgot to do a bunch of things I meant to do.'

'Don't worry about getting me anything, I don't mind at all,' Eileen assured her.

She glanced at Morag with concern. There was a brittle quality to her friend's smiles and the skin under her eyes looked bruised as if she had had little sleep. The war had ground many people down, especially women, who bore the brunt of keeping the home fires burning, working and cooking and looking after family with no time to rest. Was it simply that? Eileen felt there was something more to it, but did she dare to ask? It wasn't as if they had been firm friends for years.

She hesitated, but when Morag looked down at her soup, her face was so sad that Eileen knew she had to ask.

'What's the matter? Are you all right yourself?'

'Yes, of course,' Morag said brightly. Then her shoulders sagged, and she sighed. 'Actually, I'm not at all right, if I'm honest.'

She stared about the small café, but it was mostly empty apart from a couple in the other corner who were out of listening distance.

'Do you want to tell me?' Eileen asked gently.

'It's George.' Morag made a wry face. 'He's hardly at home these days.'

'Everyone's working long shifts now. Isn't that normal?'

'No, it's more than that. We had a terrible row and now, instead of coming home for meals, most days he goes to the working men's club in Bridgeton. He can get a pie and beer there and read the journals and I know it's a good place to learn and have company and George does want to better himself, but... he should be at home with his wife. People will talk.'

'A row?' Eileen picked out the important part of what her friend was saying. The words had poured out of Morag, almost tumbling over each other.

Morag picked up her spoon, stirred the vegetable soup and then laid the spoon down again with a raw sigh.

'I told you George doesn't want children. At any rate, not now while we're saving. Well, at Christmas, I thought... I *knew*... I was pregnant. Not far on, a month, and then... I lost it. It was horrible. But before I lost it, George was furious. He blamed me for getting pregnant and we had the worst argument ever. Oh, Eileen. He was so angry. I've never seen him like that. And I hated him. I did. My own husband, whom I promised to love, honour and obey.' Morag let out a sob. 'And the awful thing is, I haven't truly forgiven him.'

Eileen got out of her chair, never minding the waitress's nosy stare from behind the counter, and hugged Morag.

'There, there,' she murmured as if Morag was a child needing comfort. She waited, crouched there until the shaking stopped and Morag relaxed before she took her chair again.

'Have some soup before it gets cold,' she coaxed. 'It'll do you good.'

They took spoonfuls of the thick lentils and carrots. Eileen didn't know what to say to truly comfort Morag. She wasn't married and couldn't imagine Jimmy acting like George had done. Jimmy had always made it plain he wanted children, having grown up with four younger siblings himself. Eileen hadn't much liked George when she met him, but she knew deep down that Morag loved him, so it was important they found their way back to each other. But how?

'I shouldn't have told you,' Morag murmured. 'Please forget what I said.'

'It's safe with me, I promise. Friends keep each other's secrets.'

Eileen walked home from the bus stop with a heavy heart. As she thought about how unhappy Morag had seemed, Eileen knew she wasn't much better. Her worries about Jimmy were swimming in her mind. She kept hearing his words ringing in her ears: '*You don't want to marry a cripple like me.*' As if she cared what state he was in. She was in love with him, whatever his health. But how was she to persuade him? She was no closer to an answer as she let herself into the flat and hung her coat on the hook in the hall. There was a letter on the floor where the post had been delivered, so she picked it up. She recognised the handwriting as her mother's. Inside, instead of a letter from Agnes, there was another envelope with *Amy* written on it. How very strange. Eileen had a sudden strong urge to know who had written to her cousin and what they imparted. She was tempted to steam Amy's envelope open. After all, the covering envelope had been addressed to her.

'It's cabbage for tea,' Amy said, emerging from the kitchen with her cheeks flushed from cooking. 'I couldn't get any meat at Heaney's; he said to come tomorrow early.'

'Here, this is for you.' Eileen passed her the letter. 'I guess someone didn't know you were here and wrote to my parents' address, hoping to catch you there.'

Amy slipped it into her apron pocket. 'Ta, I'll read it later.'

How could Amy casually put it in her pocket and carry on making cabbage and mash without wanting to read it immediately? Her cousin gave nothing away. It was infuriating.

By the evening, Eileen had forgotten about the letter because her throat was sore, and her nose was tickly. She sneezed into her hanky and felt her head throb.

'You don't sound too jolly,' Amy remarked, reaching over to feel Eileen's forehead. 'You're burning up. I'll bring you a cuppa.'

'Thanks, I don't feel too great. I think I've caught that flu off Morag. She's not sick but the factory's rife with it.'

'Best thing for it is bed,' Amy said wisely.

—

Eileen was sick with the flu for the next week and off work. Her supervisor was very understanding, Amy reported, having gone over to Glasgow Green to let them know.

'I feel like I'm letting them down.' Eileen coughed. She lay in her bed, exhausted. 'Worst of all, I want to see Jimmy, but I can't go in this state.'

'I'll go if you like.' Amy shrugged casually. 'If you think he'd like a visitor.'

'Thanks, Amy. That's kind of you. Mary will be visiting every week, but she doesn't go every day either, what with her housework and the travelling distance. Would you mind?'

Amy didn't mind at all. In fact, it was the perfect excuse. She was at once restless and bored in the flat, so desperate for something novel to do. She was also curious about Jimmy and wanted to meet him. More particularly, she wanted to know if he was the sort of man to throw her out of the flat once he married Eileen and moved in. Eileen had mentioned that they wouldn't live with Mary and Harry as there wasn't enough room once Jeannie and her other brother and sister came home. Amy was settled here and had no intention of moving. At least, not unless she had to. Pearl's letter had thrown a spanner into her plans.

She had opened the letter in the privacy of her inset bed, the bedroom door firmly closed so Eileen couldn't see her. She was annoyed. She'd told her mother not to write. It was too risky. But Pearl had, anyway. She unfolded it with an impatient sigh. Her impatience gave way to a rising dread as she read it.

> *Amy,*
> *I know you said don't write but you will want to hear this. Ricky's gone. He came round here looking for you weeks ago and I haven't seen him since. I didn't tell him the most important thing. You know what I mean. But I had to tell him where you are, so I said you was in Glasgow but not your uncle's address. He threatened to punch my lights out otherwise. Be careful.*
> *Pearl*

Her sixth sense had known Ricky was in Glasgow. That feeling of being watched at the parade had been real. She had dodged him by disappearing into the crowd to the pie shop, probably. Luckily, Pearl didn't know Eileen's address, so she couldn't give away Kiltie Street and Amy's hideout. And Amy had never mentioned the Boyles' address to Ricky. He wasn't interested in her relatives. The question, then, was where, exactly, would her husband start searching for her?

—

Amy gaped as she stared up at the turrets of Overtoun House. *Bloomin' heck, it's a proper castle*, she thought. She walked in through the front door with no one stopping her and enquiring of a soldier on crutches, found that

Jimmy Dougal was upstairs. She enjoyed the admiring glances and a few whistles as she sashayed up the staircase with its lion rampant woven into the ironwork below the bannisters. She looked nice, she knew that. She couldn't fault Eileen's dress sense, having borrowed her blue dress with its pretty embroidered pockets and pearly buttons. Her coat was folded over her arm, and she'd removed her hat so that her blonde curls showed nicely.

'Which one's Jimmy?' she whispered to the first man she saw in the bright lounge, knowing it wasn't him for he was about eighteen and looked as if he had yet to shave.

The young patient pointed across the room to a man sitting on the edge of a bed and Amy smiled her thanks. She took a good look before she went over. He was nice looking in a gaunt sort of way, with fair hair and grey eyes. She could see why Eileen was attracted to him. She smiled brightly as she approached.

'I can see you, darling. It's a bloody miracle but I can see your lovely hair and your dress. I've always liked that blue dress. And your perfume. I'd know you anywhere by that scent. Sit down here with me, doll, and tell me what's happening outside.' Jimmy chuckled.

Amy froze. It took a moment for her to realise that Jimmy's sight may have come back but it wasn't perfect. He was squinting at her through narrowed eyes. Amy had borrowed some of Eileen's precious perfume as well as her dress and she realised that with her dyed hair, he'd mistaken her for her cousin. Her brain ran through the possibilities in double-quick time with the option of telling the truth dismissed almost immediately.

She was a good mimic and Eileen's voice was easy to copy.

'Darling, I can't believe it. You're not blind any more. I'm so happy.' She moved to sit beside him on the bed and took his hand. His grip was tight and warm, and she felt the pressure of his fingertips curl onto her palm.

'Aye, I'm on the mend. Soon there'll be no stopping me. Maybe I'm Lucky Jim after all.' He laughed. 'We can set a date once I'm home, if you like. I'm sorry I was so down on your last visit, my lovely girl. I do want to marry you, Sheena. You know that. You and me… we're meant to be.'

That was the last thing Amy wanted to hear. Where did that leave her? Out on her ear, is what. And with Ricky no doubt hell-bent on revenge after what she'd done, she couldn't be out in Glasgow looking for a place to stay, nor could she go home to London, where he knew all her old haunts. No, the best solution was to stay in Kiltie Street. And that meant no wedding for Eileen.

She modulated her voice again, getting that Glasgow accent just right and adding in that quintessential warmth that Eileen injected into her voice with no apparent effort.

'Aye, we're meant to be, darling, but… you don't mind if we have a long engagement, do you?'

'Five years isn't long enough for you?' Jimmy laughed again but there was a slight strain to it.

'Och, I know we've promised ourselves that long, but… it's this war. I can't get my mind onto weddings when there's so much uncertainty and it's hard every day just getting through. You understand, don't you, darling?'

His shoulders went down but he managed a grin. 'We'll take it at your pace, dear. If you want to go slow, that's fine by me. I'll stay with Mammy and Harry until you're ready.'

Relief washed over her. If Jimmy's spirits had sunk a bit, Amy's had soared. She'd managed it all very well.

There was no harm done, was there? Eileen would be disappointed when she next visited, and Jimmy didn't press her on a wedding date, but she'd live. In fact, Amy had done her a favour. It wasn't much fun getting married during a war, what with rationing and whatnot. It wouldn't have been much of a celebration. She also guessed that her cousin wouldn't pursue the matter if Jimmy didn't. Eileen was far too soft for that. No, this had all worked out perfectly.

She had to sit for a while longer, bored, while Jimmy told her of his plans for after the war, which seemed to consist of being demobbed and finding a trade since he'd been a professional soldier before the war started and as a result, had few other skills. He'd kept hold of her hand and Amy quite liked it. She hadn't been touched in so long. Not since Ricky, and his touch hadn't always been kind. That blow to her cheek had been the last straw and she'd turned up in Kiltie Street with a purpling bruise as a reminder of why she'd had to leave.

'…and a wee house somewhere for us to start a family,' Jimmy said softly.

Amy stifled a yawn. 'Goodness, is that the time? I'll need to go. Amy will wonder where I've got to.' A nice touch and a good excuse.

'She still living there with you? How's that working out?' His voice had a sharper tone.

'I love her living with me. I'd miss her dreadfully if she left,' Amy said with an inward grin.

'Maybe she'll move back down south. Besides, I'll make sure you're not lonely once I'm out of here. Give me a kiss, darling.'

'I'll kiss you next time. I've got a bit of a cold now, and I don't want to pass that on to you; otherwise, they might keep you in,' Amy said quickly.

She left smartly, waving once at the door, but he didn't wave back, and she reckoned his sight wasn't good enough to see it. Not yet. But soon he'd be back in Kiltie Street and living only a couple of doors down. It was something to consider.

—

Back in Kiltie Street, Eileen felt a little better. She'd eaten the soup Amy had left and felt good enough to get out of bed and totter about, wrapped in a blanket for warmth. As she passed the inset bed, she brushed past the cupboard door and a sheet of paper slid out and sailed gently to the floor. Picking it up to replace it, Eileen saw it was Amy's letter. She hesitated. It was wrong to read it. She knew that. But Amy never gave anything away. Wasn't it only right for Eileen to know a wee bit about her? With a guilty lurch of her stomach, Eileen unfolded the sheet of paper and began to read it. Every word confused her more than the last.

Eileen didn't know what to make of the letter. Pearl was Amy's mother. She still thought it odd that Amy didn't call her 'Mum' and that Pearl didn't sign herself as that either. Clearly, they weren't close, but they were close enough for Pearl to warn her about 'Ricky'. Who was Ricky? Was he a boyfriend or lover? Whoever he was, he could be violent, and he was looking for Amy. What was 'the most important thing' that Ricky mustn't know? For a short letter, it was packed with mystery.

Eileen shook her head, perplexed. Her cousin had received this letter over a week ago and yet she'd given no sign of being afraid or anxious. Had it really made no impact on her? If Eileen had got this letter, she'd have been terrified to find out someone was after her. And why was he so desperate to find Amy?

She folded the sheet of paper carefully and put it back on Amy's bed before shutting the door across. She had to hope that Amy wouldn't notice its position had changed because Eileen wasn't ready to challenge her about it. Amy had a stubborn streak and was likely to clam up. Eileen decided to be patient. Perhaps Amy would confide in her.

Chapter Ten

Two weeks passed, and Amy had not mentioned the letter at all. It wasn't for want of Eileen trying.

'Are you all right?' she asked casually, the day after reading its contents.

Amy had raised her eyebrows. 'What do you mean? I ain't got your flu, if that's what you're getting at. I just don't have a shift at the nursery, is all. So don't go badgering me to get up and get doing something useful. Them kids 'ave got Sunday school instead.'

'I'm not complaining about you sitting reading a magazine. You looked a wee bit worried, that's all. Is something bothering you?' Eileen improvised quickly.

Amy shook her head. 'Not a thing, thank you. Life's just tickety-boo.'

Looking at Amy, lying on Eileen's own bed, her feet crossed and flicking through the latest issue of *Woman's Own*, she decided that Amy was not only an excellent mimic but a good little actress too. There were no signs of nerves. It was as if the strain of the war and Ricky didn't exist.

'What are you staring at?' Amy said rudely as Eileen hesitated at the bedroom door.

'Nothing,' Eileen replied, turning away and feeling stung.

She was only trying to help. What if Ricky turned up? Amy was slightly built and no match for a man bent on punching someone's lights out, as Pearl had so graphically described. Was Amy in danger? If only Amy was a different sort of person, open and easy to chat with. Short of admitting to reading her personal letter, there was little Eileen could do. She imagined saying, *Amy, I read your letter, the one from your mum, so what's the important thing Ricky mustn't know, and who is Ricky anyway?* She didn't need much imagination to know that Amy would be angry at Eileen prying into her business. Much as Amy could be annoying, Eileen didn't want to lose her friendship. The flat would be very lonely if there was a cold atmosphere between them.

She put on her coat and took her bag. 'I'm away to the shops. I'll see you later.'

The pavement outside the tenements was thick with glittering frost and her breath came out in little white puffs. She smiled at one of the neighbours as she passed and was taken aback when the woman glared at her.

'I'm sorry, have I offended you in some way?' Eileen asked, gripping the handle of her bag tightly. She hardly knew the woman so was sure she hadn't done anything to offend.

Her neighbour sniffed. 'Well, if you don't know, maybe someone needs to tell you then. Only, round here, we don't go consorting with married men.'

'I don't know what you mean,' Eileen said faintly. Only she did know and cursed Amy.

'You and Mr Mearns. It's not right. He's got a wife who's sick and you're his fancy piece. It's disgusting!' The woman brushed past her, her shoulders rigid and head held high.

Eileen was left standing on the frozen pavement, her mouth open in dismay. She wanted to shout out that it wasn't her, it was Amy, and that she agreed, it wasn't right at all. But she couldn't do that. It wasn't fair to Amy. She'd have to have a strong word with her, though. Eileen's reputation was in tatters and that wasn't fair. Oh, how she missed Jeannie and her common sense. She'd know what to do and how to put people right. Her feet crunched on the icy surfaces as she headed glumly to the main street. Only when she reached it did she find an answer that made her step forward more confidently. There was one way to stop the gossips. She and Jimmy had to get married as soon as possible.

On her next visit to Overtoun House, she decided to broach the subject with Jimmy. She hadn't visited in three weeks because of being ill and she was desperate to see him. As she boarded the bus that would take her to the bottom of the hill, Eileen remembered her last visit. It had been so awkward. He had protested that she shouldn't marry him because he was no use to anyone. She hadn't been able to persuade him that she loved him, all of him, in good health or bad. But this time, she was determined to show him that she meant it.

She walked into the room where Jimmy was living, her steps filled with trepidation, but she needn't have worried – immy's radiant expression greeted her.

'Sheena, they're letting me go. I'm being discharged, darling. Isn't that wonderful news?' Jimmy beamed as he came towards her.

'Oh, Jimmy. That's marvellous, so it is. Just marvellous.'

Eileen hugged him tightly and felt his strong embrace around her. He smelled of Player's cigarettes and tar soap and simply Jimmy. She felt a surge of desire and was surprised. Recently, she'd felt nothing but tenderness and love for him. Now, she felt his body length against hers and wanted him. She drew back, conscious of the other recuperating soldiers watching them.

'I can see perfectly,' Jimmy said. 'Thank the good Lord for that. I'm fine, so I am.'

'Will the army want you back?' Eileen asked, a swift dread replacing the desire that had spread through her bloodstream.

Jimmy shook his head. 'I'm no' that fine. I failed my recent medical. They say there's no guarantee I won't go blind again, and one arm's been left weak after the infection.'

'I don't care. I'm glad they don't want you,' Eileen cried.

'Aye, me too, dear. I've done my bit fighting Hitler on the front. I'll find some other way to serve.'

Eileen wondered what exactly a soldier like Jimmy could do with a dicky arm and uncertain sight, but she wasn't going to spoil the moment by saying it out loud.

'We'll get married, won't we, my love?' she said, instead.

He drew back with a frown. 'I thought you wanted a long engagement?'

'Sure, haven't we been engaged for five years already. Isn't that long enough?' Eileen countered with a wavering smile. 'Don't you want to marry me?'

'Of course I do... It's just... I thought you... Never mind. Let's do it. Let's get married. I can't wait until you're Mrs Dougal.'

Eileen giggled as he tried to sweep her off her feet and she staggered a little as his arm failed him. They sank down onto the bed together, sitting on its edge and ignoring the other patients in the room who pretended to play cards or push chess pieces around while glancing at the couple discreetly.

'Last time you were in, you said you wanted to wait and not set a date,' Jimmy said cautiously.

'No, I didn't. I wanted to get married, and you said you were no use to anyone and wouldn't discuss it,' Eileen protested.

'Och, in any case, let's do it. I feel much stronger and what's the use in waiting. This war could go on for another year or forever. We must make use of the time we've got.'

If that sounded like the darker, gloomier side of Jimmy speaking, Eileen chose to ignore it and focus on the positive. They were getting married. A thrill ran through her. She couldn't wait to tell Amy.

-

'You see, Mrs Kincaid, it's quite simple. The Soviets are advancing from the east and the British and Americans from the west. It's described here as Germany – the common enemy – lying between the jaws of a gigantic vice. We've got them on the run. It won't be long before it's all over.' The newspaper rustled as the old man peered at the print.

'I wish I was as certain as you are, Mr McLeod,' Morag sighed. 'I can't help feeling there's a ways to go yet.'

'Och, nonsense. Look here at the main headline. "Huge German Losses: Soviet On Gulf of Danzig". And if we read further down... "Moscow last night gave details of the staggering losses inflicted on the enemy since Stalin launched his great winter offensive on 12 January".'

Mr McLeod sounded so chipper that Morag didn't have the heart to argue but she didn't feel confident that the war would end. In fact, after more than five years of conflict, she could hardly imagine peacetime any more. It didn't help that she and George were barely speaking to each other. If her mother was there, she'd have told Morag it was up to her to mend her marriage. 'It's your job to keep your husband happy,' she'd said to Morag on her wedding day. 'It doesn't matter whether you think he's right or wrong. He's the master of your house and you should obey him and have his meal on the table for when he comes home from work. That's the key to a good marriage.'

'Poor little mites,' Mr McLeod said, breaking into her thoughts. 'Says here the first party of five hundred children from the liberated part of Holland is expected to arrive in Britain early in February.'

Morag's heart squeezed. Poor little mites indeed. Who knew what horrors they had experienced under the Nazis. Perhaps George was right. It was not a good time to bring a child into the world when there was such evil around. But she didn't believe that no matter how hard she tried. She still wanted her own wee baby to love and cherish.

'Mr Kincaid was out early again,' Mr McLeod remarked, sipping his morning Camp coffee and smoothing the paper on his knee.

'He's awfully busy at the yard so he likes to get away sharpish. More coffee?'

'A wee drop more, please. The yard's been busier since Christmas, so it would seem from Mr Kincaid's hours. He isn't home for his tea most nights either. To be honest, I find myself missing Miss Linton for some company at the wireless in the evening.'

Morag was saved from having to answer this by the doorbell ringing.

'Sorry, I'd better see who that is,' she called, rushing away into the hall and then standing for a moment to take a deep breath and adjust her floral housecoat. She patted her dark hair into place, set a polite smile to her lips and opened the door.

A tall, broad figure stood there, and it took her a moment to recognise him.

'Good morning. I'm here about the room. Is it still available?' Ricky Smith took off his hat and grinned.

Morag felt a sense of unease, although she couldn't say why. In fact, she ought to be glad that this man was here about the room to let, although she had had her doubts about him when they met in Mrs Corrie's bakery. They could do with the money. It might make George happier, she thought suddenly. It might fix what was wrong between them. He worried so much about their finances.

'Yes it is. Please come in.'

She stepped back to let him by and for a moment he seemed to dominate the space, lingering too closely to her before smiling and walking into the hall to glance about.

'Very nice indeed,' he said.

'In the baker's shop you said you were in a hotel paid up until the end of December. Where have you been staying since then?'

He stared at her thoughtfully before giving a bellow of laughter. 'Fancy you remembering that. Well, the last few weeks I've been here and there and now I'd like a proper place to stay. I can pay a month's rent upfront.'

Morag couldn't argue with that. She imagined George's delight when he saw the money. Perhaps Ricky Smith moving in as a lodger was a good thing that would make her and George close again. She hadn't forgiven her husband, but it was time to mend her marriage, she knew.

'I'll show you the room.' She smiled politely.

She led the way upstairs to what had been Miss Linton's room, conscious of him following close behind. Her legs felt naked despite the lisle stockings, and she resisted an impulse to tuck stray curls behind her ears. All Miss Linton's belongings had gone, and the room felt quite bare apart from the bed, wardrobe and chair.

'It's not a big space but our previous lodger was very happy here. The rent is three shillings a week and we have our meals downstairs in the dining room. You're welcome to use the parlour in the evenings to listen to the wireless or write letters. We have another lodger, Mr McLeod, who likes a bit of company.'

He went over to look out the window. It wasn't much of a view unless you liked factories and tenements, but Morag always felt secure surrounded by other buildings, knowing there were plenty of neighbours and workers in the busy Bridgeton area.

'Very nice.' Ricky Smith nodded. 'I'll take it.'

'Will you be here long?' Morag asked. 'We prefer a long-term lodger.'

Even as she said it, she knew she was lying. She didn't want this man here for months or years. George might prefer the constancy of money coming in, but there was something unsettling about Ricky Smith.

He shrugged then offered a lazy smile. 'I really can't say. But you'll be the first to know, Mrs Kincaid, when I decide to move on. That I can assure you.'

Morag had the distinct impression that he was mocking her. She paused for a moment but returned his smile, trying to remain business-like.

'Very good, Mr Smith. I'll leave you to get settled in, then. Dinner's at twelve and tea is served at six p.m. Hot meals when possible but I work shifts at a factory so sometimes it'll be a cold collation.'

Downstairs, she took a duster and flicked at the ornaments in the parlour. Mr McLeod coughed.

'Not working today?' he said.

'I've got a late shift, so I'll be able to make your dinner, and I'll leave a hot meal in the oven for tea. We've got our new lodger, so you'll have someone to talk to if Mr Kincaid is busy.'

Although, she couldn't imagine what Mr McLeod and Ricky Smith would possibly have in common. She hoped she hadn't made a terrible mistake in taking him in.

—

'Marry in haste and repent at leisure.' Agnes sniffed.

Eileen twisted so she could check the back of her gown. Yes, her hem was straight. She had spent her evenings since January sewing for her trousseau. Her wedding dress was pale blue crepe, sweeping her calves with the flare of the skirt, and had taken her ages to stitch perfectly. She had sewn a matching short jacket with long sleeves. The silver shoes were borrowed from Agnes and her hat was a wedding gift from her parents: a natural straw Breton hat dyed navy blue to complement her outfit. It sat back from her blonde curls, which she'd washed and set for her big day.

'It's hardly in haste,' she said to her mother. 'Jimmy and I've waited long enough. I want you and Dad to be happy for me. Please?'

'All we want is your happiness,' Agnes said. 'Are you sure he's right for you?'

'I love him, Mum,' Eileen said simply.

Agnes nodded. She put her arms awkwardly round her daughter and gave her a short hug. For anyone else, it might seem meagre, but Eileen knew how difficult it was for her mum to show affection. She hugged her then laughed and moved back.

'I mustn't get my dress crushed.'

Agnes took her handkerchief out and mopped her eyes. 'No, that wouldn't do. You look lovely. Dad and I, we're very proud of you.'

There was a knock on the door followed by Jeannie rushing in, baby Flora balanced on her hip.

'Sorry to interrupt, Mrs Boyle, but it's nearly time to go to the church.' Jeannie turned to notice her friend. 'Oh, Eileen, you'd best open our present now. It's from me and Bill. He said he's really sorry he can't be here but there's no leave approved just now and he's in the thick of it.' Jeannie thrust a newspaper-wrapped gift at her.

Eileen held it tentatively. She didn't want to get newsprint all over her hands or on her dress and she still had her gloves to slide on.

'You've already given me the eggs. I thought that was your wedding gift?'

Jeannie had arrived back for the wedding the previous day and come round to the flat where she'd been introduced to Amy and given Eileen six eggs 'for her wedding breakfast'.

'Och, that was from Aunt Martha and Uncle Angus. They don't have the same problems with rationing on the farm as we do in the city. Actually, this is sort of from Uncle Angus too, but I did the stitching. Go on, open it up.'

Eileen unwrapped the newspaper to discover a small fur stole.

'It's beautiful, thank you both so much.' She wrapped the stole over her shoulders and smiled at her reflection in the mirror.

'It's made from rabbit fur. Uncle Angus shoots the wee buggers when they come for the crops, but they make a tasty stew and a fine lady's furs.' Jeannie laughed, looking pleased at Eileen's delight.

'Are you back for good?' Eileen asked hopefully.

It was wonderful to have her best friend beside her even if it seemed as if Amy's nose was put out of joint because of it. Amy had been markedly quiet since Jeannie's arrival and no amount of jollying or trying to include her in the wedding preparations had softened her up.

'Sorry, hen, but no. I'm here for your celebration and then back to the farm. It's the weans, you see. Isa and Bob love it there and so does Flora. I'm trying to persuade Mammy to send Dennis too. It's healthy and away from trouble and there's plenty of good food.'

'Girls, we ought to go,' Agnes said, handing Eileen her silk gloves. They had been Agnes's own wedding accessories.

'I'm nervous; why am I nervous when it's Jimmy I'm marrying, and I want it so much?' Eileen cried, clasping Agnes and Jeannie's hands.

'Wedding nerves are quite normal,' Agnes said calmly, guiding her daughter out of the flat bedroom. 'But if we don't go right now, there'll be no wedding. Come along.'

'Where's Amy?' Eileen said.

'You go on with your mum and I'll fetch her out from the kitchen,' Jeannie said. 'We're lucky it's a dry day for walking up to the church. No one owns a motor car, and even if they did, petrol rationing rules mean there'd be no fuel to drive it anyway.'

—

Amy sulked in the kitchen. She heard the laughter of the other three women and scowled. Eileen had ignored her since that Jeannie had arrived. Even though Amy was Eileen's cousin, and family ought to mean something. And after all the things she'd done for Eileen too, all those meals she'd cooked, constructing the hay box and whatnot. Eileen would be lost without her.

'What's with the long face?' Jeannie appeared. 'Lost a shilling and found a penny? It's time to go so let's smile for Eileen; it's her big day and we're here to support her.'

Amy trudged after Jeannie and made a face behind her back. There was a small stream of neighbours heading along Kiltie Street towards the church with friendly calls to Eileen and her mother and friends. There were white puffs from their frozen breath and a few snowflakes drifted down to adorn the women's hats from the February air. Grumpily, Amy pulled her own hat down over her ears to avoid being talked to.

Eileen was getting Jimmy, which was what she wanted. But what did Amy want? She crunched over the light snow on the pavement, staring at her feet to avoid everyone. She needed to wait out the war in Glasgow, avoiding her husband. She rubbed her bare finger with her thumb. Perhaps she shouldn't have taken off her wedding ring. She'd have more respect if everyone knew she was a married woman. But then there'd be questions about where her husband was and more lies to be told or she'd feel their disapproval at leaving him.

Her musings had to stop as they reached the church and were ushered into the pews for the ceremony. Amy had to admit that her cousin looked very pretty in her blue dress and that Jimmy was smart in his suit now he was formally discharged from the army. He had a silver medal on his lapel to show that he had served his country. She felt a pang of envy in the way he looked at Eileen. When had Ricky last looked at her that way? Still, her mouth twisted, Ricky had adored her when they first married, and by the end, he was using her as a punchbag when he felt like it.

The church was bitterly cold, and the wedding guests kept their coats firmly wrapped up and were glad of their hats as a chilly draught blew in from the door. The wintry temperature didn't stop Eileen's rosy blush as the minister pronounced the couple to be man and wife and everybody clapped enthusiastically.

The church hall was equally cold, but no one seemed to care, and as the bodies piled in for the wedding celebrations, it gradually warmed up and coats were shed and hats put to one side. There was a piano in the corner and a stage with faded velvet curtains. Tables and chairs were scattered around, and people began to sit and talk. Two trestle tables were set with food provided by kind neighbours as well as Agnes and Mary. Eileen had been to the local food office to apply for extra rations for the wedding and had told Amy how she'd had to provide information on how many guests, the location and other details in order to be eligible, all under the beady gaze of a clerk.

Amy cast her eye over the food. There were plates of sandwiches with fillings of fish paste, jam or grated cheese. A tray of home-made biscuits sat next to a large, red moulded jelly. Someone had chipped in with a sponge cake that had a thin raspberry jam centre, and there was even a small, cooked ham. Pride of place was given to a very impressive three-tiered cake with white icing. On closer inspection, Amy discovered the cake was in fact made of plaster. On the base, there was a small hatch, and she knew that inside there was probably a tiny fruit cake. Her stomach grumbled. She quite fancied a slice of sweet cake.

A portly man began to play the piano and Jimmy bellowed to everyone to help themselves to food. Amy reached for a plate and napkin, glad to be at the front of the queue.

'How are you, dear?' Her aunt Agnes was at her side, staring at her curiously.

Amy rubbed her face in case she had a smut. She'd only met Agnes and Robert recently when Eileen insisted she visit with her before the wedding. It had been awkward. They asked a lot of questions about her parents and were clearly puzzled as to why Amy was in Glasgow and not in London.

'I'm very well. What a lovely wedding,' Amy said politely, wishing Agnes would get out of the way of the food table.

'It's a pity Norman and Pearl aren't here to see it,' Agnes said.

Amy nodded. She wasn't getting into all the family stuff again. Bloomin' 'eck, the woman never gave up, she pondered.

'Can I get you some sandwiches, Aunt Agnes?' She attempted to divert her attention elsewhere.

Perhaps she could just squeeze past her. To her relief, Agnes turned to the table and Amy was free to grab a plate.

She made sure she was well away from Eileen's mother as she took two biscuits and a slice of ham.

'There you are, Amy. Isn't this wonderful?' Eileen cried, rushing up to her, arm crooked into Jimmy's and pulling him along.

Amy put on a smile. She had to get along with Jimmy if she was to stay living in Kiltie Street. Oh, she could afford to rent a flat all by herself, but it would be very lonely, and Ricky was less likely to find her if it was Eileen or Jimmy's name on the rent book. Besides, she liked Kiltie Street. It was full of possibilities especially now she was friendly with Leo Mearns.

'It's perfectly wonderful,' Amy said. 'Especially your cake.'

'Och, well, it's a pretend one, so it is,' Eileen said, deflating slightly. 'Everyone will get a wee cube of the real cake inside it for luck but there's not enough of it to eat.'

'It'll look real enough on our wedding photos,' Jimmy said, kissing Eileen on the lips and, with a slight bow to Amy, guiding his new wife away to where Jeannie was waving excitedly to them with a plate of wobbly jelly and two spoons. Amy disliked him already. His narrowed grey eyes had looked right through her.

She ate her food while standing, not wanting to join the merry groups at the tables. The piano player belted out 'Don't Sit Under the Apple Tree' and the guests joined in the singing. After a while she went outside for a cigarette, inhaling moodily. When she came back in, Eileen and Jimmy were opening their wedding gifts at another trestle. She hung back until more drinks had been poured and the guests started dancing. Her Uncle Robert was playing the piano now, an old-fashioned melody that had the older couples holding each other closely as they waltzed round the room.

She wandered over to see the gifts. She had given them a teapot cosy and matching egg cosies that she'd bought at a market stall. Someone had gifted a National Savings Certificate. There was a pair of nylon stockings, a bottle of whisky, bottled pears, home-made sweets and a lovely blue and silver powder compact in the shape of a scallop with a small dent showing it was pre-loved. How easy it would be to slip it into her pocket. Who would know? Oh but it was lovely. She wanted it. She reached out her hand.

'Hello.' A voice interrupted her. 'You must be Amy. You're very like Eileen, aren't you?' a dark-haired woman said sharply, her glance flicking from Amy to the compact and back.

Amy's hand fell away. The woman looked familiar, and it took her a moment to place her as Eileen's friend who had been at the parade in George Square with her handsome husband.

'I don't think I've 'ad the pleasure?' Amy said.

'Morag Kincaid. I'm here with my husband, George. People have been very generous, haven't they?' Morag indicated all the presents.

Amy nodded, with a last wistful look at the powder compact.

'I've taken a list for Eileen, so she knows who gave what. For thank-you letters,' Morag said.

She was making it obvious she knew what Amy had intended to do. Amy felt herself flushing. She walked away smartly. She didn't need that old compact anyway. She had enough cash to buy several – and those brand new. She hadn't escaped Ricky empty-handed. She had been scared of him returning to their house that day but that hadn't stopped her from taking time to grab his secret stash of banknotes and coins, her cheek swelling from his punch and her body shaking from fear and anger.

Chapter Eleven

Eileen looked around the church hall at her wedding guests and felt a warmth in her heart for them all. How kind people were, giving them gifts and bringing food for the celebration. She adjusted her cuff, conscious of her lovely skirt and jacket and felt the texture of the crepe material under her fingertips. It was the nicest outfit she owned and if she looked after it carefully, it ought to last for years. The Board of Trade's Make Do and Mend campaign leaflets had plenty of ideas to make clothes last longer and strongly implied that it was your war duty to do so. Hanging clothes carefully with fastenings closed, removing stains immediately, giving them a good brushing and airing in the sun and using a hot iron over a damp cloth to dissuade moths were all useful instructions she intended to follow for her wedding clothes. Every time she wore them in future, she'd remember this wonderful day.

'You're looking serious. Not having second thoughts, are you, darling?' Jimmy asked, a slight frown creasing his brow.

Eileen smiled at her new husband. He looked so handsome in his suit, with his hair slicked back. 'Actually, I was thinking about keeping my clothes nice and other homely things.'

Jimmy laughed and pulled her in for a quick kiss on the mouth. 'I can't wait for us to have our own wee home for those "homely things".'

'You don't mind us starting out in my flat, do you?'

'Mammy would love us to stay with them but I'd rather we had our own place, even if it's poky.'

'It's not that poky,' Eileen protested.

She loved her flat and wanted Jimmy to love it too. It was nice of Mary to want them at number four Kiltie Street, and it was normal for a son to bring his bride back to the family home to live, but once Jeannie, Flora, Isa and Bob came back it would be very cramped, and they'd have to move out then in any case. Eileen liked the idea of them starting together in their own wee flat. After the war, maybe they could get a bigger flat or even a house, if they worked hard. Her imagination failed at that point, because what would Jimmy do for a job?

'It's poky with three in it,' Jimmy said heavily. His gaze swivelled to where Amy stood at the back of the crowd around the piano.

'Oh, Jimmy, you know I can't just throw her out. Amy… well, she's my cousin and she needs me. She's vulnerable in some way. I can't explain it. If I asked her to leave, where would she go?'

'Back to London where you told me her parents live,' Jimmy said. 'I don't understand why she's up here in Glasgow.'

'I told you, she couldn't take the bombing any more. I think she's seen terrible things, and it's affected her,' Eileen said, wanting him to agree with her.

Surely they weren't going to have their first argument as a married couple right here at their wedding reception?

Maybe Jimmy realised that too, because he smiled and took her hand.

'You're a sweet, kind girl as well as the bonniest in Scotland. Did anyone ever tell you that? Come on, Mrs Dougal, let me get you a drink of fruit punch and we'll join our guests and "gie it laldy" at the piano.'

Eileen laughed and let herself be drawn over to the trestle table where Jeannie was pouring generous cups of the fruit punch. The lack of oranges was more than made up for by the small chunks of bruised apples and a large application of whisky by her father on the sly. She glanced over to see if Amy was chatting to anyone. She couldn't explain her protective instinct towards her cousin. There was something about Amy, even before the strange letter came from Pearl, that made Eileen want to look after her. Perhaps it was that she'd arrived on Eileen's doorstep with that bruise blossoming on her cheek. She had looked so alone. Eileen had felt alone for a large portion of her own life, and she didn't want that for anyone else. Thank goodness she had Jimmy now. She'd never be alone again. She leaned into him as they reached Jeannie, and the potent sweet smell of the punch tickled her nose.

Amy was in the piano crowd but not part of it. Eileen noticed she wasn't chatting to those next to her or joining in the singing. As she watched, Amy made her way to the hall entrance, where the door had opened for a late guest. Her heart sank. It was Leo Mearns. He was on his own, no sign of his wife. While Jimmy and Jeannie talked, Eileen saw Amy greet Leo and take his hat and scarf. No one was watching them yet. But soon the gossip would start. A small part of Eileen was glad they'd realise it wasn't her who had been visiting Leo but she was quickly ashamed of that thought.

'Excuse me a minute,' she murmured to Jimmy.

He waved her away good-humouredly and turned back to his sister, who was regaling him with a funny story about Flora. Eileen stepped smartly across the floor to Amy.

'Amy, there you are. I wanted to ask you to help Jeannie with the drinks,' she cried.

If she could separate Amy from Leo Mearns then perhaps no one would notice how Amy had leaped to greet him at the door.

Amy raised her eyebrows. 'Looks like she's doing just fine. She don't need me. Your hubby's helping 'er. See for yerself.'

Sure enough, when Eileen looked back, Jimmy was behind the table with Jeannie, drumming up business with a loud, happy bellow and folk were drifting across from the piano to get their glasses refilled. Jimmy's cheeks were flushed, and she wondered how much punch he'd imbibed. A horrible memory flashed in front of her. Jimmy had served in the British Expeditionary Force and was evacuated from Dunkirk in June 1940, nursing a leg injury. While recuperating, he had gone out dancing one night, brooding and drinking so much that he had ended up punching a man who'd implied he hadn't joined up. In fact, he had continued to drink heavily for a while before being sent back to active duty.

She shook her head. She was being daft. Jimmy was allowed a few drinks on his wedding day. It didn't mean he was a heavy drinker. There was a lot about her new husband that she didn't know. They had fallen in love at first sight and after that had been apart for so long. *I love him and that's all that matters*, she told herself. *As Agnes would say, don't go looking for trouble; it'll find you anyway.*

'Congratulations on your wedding, Mrs Dougal,' Leo Mearns said smoothly. 'You make a beautiful bride.'

He took her hand and kissed it. Eileen had to struggle not to show her revulsion. She wanted to wipe the back of her hand but instead she managed a smile.

'Thank you, Mr Mearns. You're very welcome. Do have a sandwich and a drink,' she said politely.

He hadn't been invited. Not directly. She and Jimmy had put out a general invitation to their Kiltie Street neighbours, but she hadn't expected Leo to come.

'How very kind. And it's Leo. Mr Mearns is far too formal, don't you think? And I'll call you Eileen as we're all friends here. Amy, will you show me the food?'

Eileen was left flabbergasted. Really, what a cheek he had, calling her by her first name without so much as a by-your-leave. There was a call for the bride and groom to take a dance and she was too distracted then to concentrate on Amy and her companion as Jimmy flung her with more enthusiasm than skill round the makeshift dance floor.

-

'How is Mrs Mearns?' Amy asked as she and Leo approached the table, where very little of the wedding feast remained.

Leo's features rearranged themselves into sadness. 'Poor Alice is too sick to leave her house, I'm afraid.'

'What a shame. You must be awful lonely.'

'Less so for seeing you. I declare, you quite match the bride for looks and style.'

Amy touched her curls. 'Can I offer you a drink? The sandwiches have all been scoffed.'

'Let me, my dear.'

Leo stretched across her to reach the jug with its quarter full of liquid. His knuckles briefly skimmed her breasts but so quickly that Amy wasn't sure if it was deliberate.

'I suppose you can't be completely lonely, as you've got your sisters,' she said, trying to keep the conversation going as Leo's black eyes flickered over the wedding guests and seemed to linger on the bride a shade too long.

'Hmm? Oh, my sisters. Yes, well, they don't make for much companionship. Neither Ada nor Sarah had more than a minimum of schooling, so their conversation is not intellectual.'

Didn't he work on the railways as a guard? Amy wondered how much education he needed for that. She hadn't had much schooling either, but she wasn't going to let that get in the way of her aims in life. One of which, she'd decided, was to nab this man and get him to spend some cash on her. She deserved it, she reckoned, because she found him boring. His most interesting aspect was his wealth.

'What do you want to talk about?' Amy said, noticing he'd poured her a larger drink than his own.

'Let's talk about you. Tell me where you're from and about your boyfriends. You must have a dozen, I'm sure.'

Amy tittered coyly. 'Oh, you are a one. Me with a dozen boyfriends. What kind of girl do you think I am? No, I'm a single girl what likes a nice time. I like going to the cinema or the theatre, but best of all, I like a restaurant meal with lovely grub and good company.'

'Is that so?' Leo sipped his punch and put the glass down. 'I know a couple of restaurants still serving decent meals to discerning customers.' He tapped the side of his nose. 'If you know what I mean. I know the right people.' He puffed out his chest importantly.

'Does Alice like a nice meal out?' Amy asked innocently. She couldn't help goading him a little. He was so pompous.

Leo's hand flicked out and caught her wrist. He twisted it slightly and it hurt. Amy let out a little squeal and he let her go. She rubbed her skin.

'I don't like to be reminded of the plight of my poor, dear wife. Shall we agree not to mention Alice in future?'

She shrugged, acting casual. 'Suits me.'

'Drink up, my dear, and let's discuss where we'll go for our meal together.'

'I haven't agreed to go for a meal with you,' Amy said. 'What would people say?'

There she went again. Testing him, seeing what his limit was. She couldn't say why she did it. After all, she wanted him to spend his cash on her.

'It's wartime. People have more important things on their minds than a gentleman taking a pretty girl out for an evening. Oh, and Amy?'

She waited.

'I'm very exclusive. You're my girl and no one else's – if you accept my invitation.'

—

Morag sat watching the dancing. She was only too conscious of George sitting upright on the chair next to her. He hadn't asked her to partner him in the waltz that was taking place.

'Come on, you two, you have to dance.' Eileen laughed, pink-faced, dragging Jimmy with her to stand in front of them.

Morag thought how they must look, stiff and unhappy in the midst of the gaiety of the wedding. She was suddenly embarrassed for both of them and angry, again, at George. He made no effort to be pleasant or endear himself with the wedding guests. He might as well not have bothered accompanying her. In fact, they had had an argument about that before they left.

'They're not my friends,' George had said when Morag reminded him to get ready that morning. 'I don't see why I have to go.'

'I can't go on my own. It will look odd. Everyone who's married will be there as couples.'

'That's not true. Men are away in the forces; there'll be plenty of women on their own,' George retorted.

'Why are you being difficult? Is it so hard to come with me to watch my friend getting married?'

He grumbled under his breath, but she was relieved to see him go upstairs and return wearing his suit and hat. Both Mr McLeod and Ricky Smith were out so neither had to witness the scene.

'I've hardly seen you these past few weeks. It'll be nice to spend time together,' Morag said, injecting a brightness into her voice that she didn't feel.

Mollie's wise words echoed in the back of her mind, about keeping a marriage together. It was the wife who had to work hard at it and the husband who was always right.

'I'm working longer hours. A man's got the right to relax at the working club and have a beer.' George's tone was defensive.

'Of course, dear. I know if you work long hours, management are sure to notice that favourably.'

'Who's getting married?'

He sounded mollified at her reminder of promotion prospects, so she stifled a sigh and told him about Eileen and Jimmy, although she had explained it all twice before; he just hadn't been listening.

'I miss you, George,' Morag said, leaning in and kissing him.

She *did* miss him. She missed the way they used to laugh and joke with each other and the way he kissed her and made love to her. He hadn't touched her in weeks. Not since… not since she'd lost the baby. They hadn't spoken about that night since. All the angry words, the bitterness, it had been swept under the carpet and ignored. Morag knew if she tried to speak about it, some terrible words would gush from her mouth, and she might never regain her relationship, so she kept quiet. What George thought, she had no idea. Was he hurting too?

He returned her kiss, but it was short and passionless. Was it too late for them? She was suddenly afraid. She didn't look at him as she belted her good coat and put her hat on. Where was her handbag? Were her shoes polished? Had she chipped her nail polish? If she kept busy, she didn't have to mull over it all.

Now, here were the newly married couple determined to rouse them and envelop them in their own happiness. She smiled at them.

'You're right. Come along, George. Let's show them how to move.'

She grabbed her husband's arm and pulled him onto the dance floor while Eileen and Jimmy followed them. The music was a lively foxtrot in a space not quite large enough for all the folk who wanted to dance so there were plenty of toes being trodden on and apologies as elbows dug into backs, but everyone was having fun. Even

George for a while. They danced a waltz after the foxtrot and then George led her back to their table. Morag was disappointed. She loved to dance, and her feet tapped the rhythm.

'I don't trust that fellow,' George said abruptly.

'Which fellow?' She stared about her.

'Not here.' He shook his head impatiently. 'Our new lodger.'

'Ricky? Why ever not? He's only been in for a couple of weeks; give him a chance.'

But she knew what he meant. There was something odd about Ricky Smith. He was polite and he paid his rent, but he was evasive when she asked what he did as a living.

'You should've told him it was a week on probation,' George said firmly. 'That way we could've got rid of him.'

'You were the one pressing for a lodger,' Morag reminded him. 'Were we really going to send him away when we need the money?'

'There's plenty of men and women in the forces needing lodgings.'

'No one replied to the cards in the shop windows until Ricky turned up. He's quiet and clean and has enough to pay his rent.'

She wasn't sure why she was all of a sudden defending Ricky, but George's attitude rankled. He had gone on and on about needing a lodger, and now they had one, he wanted rid of him.

'Mr McLeod doesn't like him,' George added.

That was true. Mr McLeod hadn't hidden the fact either. He had told Morag the new lodger wasn't a patch on Miss Linton and had nothing interesting to say for himself.

'That's too bad,' she hissed. 'But it's not Mr McLeod's house, and if he doesn't like it, he can go elsewhere.'

George looked appalled. Morag was ashamed of herself. Of course they wouldn't put poor old Mr McLeod out the door. He was part of their family, part of the furniture, if you like.

'I didn't mean that. You know I didn't,' she said, when George continued to stare at her as if he didn't know her.

'What's wrong with us, George?' she said quietly. 'You're so distant these days. Is it... because of Christmas? Are you sad? I know I am.'

She flinched as his expression hardened. In that moment, he didn't look like the George she loved at all.

'If I'm distant, it's because of you. You've driven me away. I haven't made love to you since Christmas because I can't trust you not to trick me and get yourself pregnant.'

He stood up and walked away, leaving Morag stunned. She sat, gripping her drink, feeling utterly alone.

Chapter Twelve

After the reception at four o'clock, Eileen and Jimmy walked across to Kiltie Street.

'It was lovely of them to clap us out the door,' Eileen said, hugging into her new husband's arm.

'Aye, and a great gulder of a song too.' Jimmy grinned. 'They gave us a great send-off. You don't mind that there's no honeymoon, do you, darling?' He looked at her with concern.

Eileen shook her head. 'We've no money for that, and I'd rather we saved our pennies for our future.'

They stopped outside the stone steps leading up to number eight and Eileen looked up at her window on the fourth floor.

'Here we are, then,' she said, feeling a wee bit nervous.

Jimmy looked left along the short street of tenements. 'It feels a bit odd not to be going into number four and Mammy's kitchen and my old room.'

'Do you mind?' Eileen asked. 'That we're starting our married life in my flat and not with your family? Your mammy did ask us to move in with them and it's traditional after all.'

Jimmy kissed her forehead. 'Naw, there's no space there and Mammy understands that. Sure, we're only down the street and she can pop in easily. Show us up, Mrs Dougal, to our new abode.'

Eileen led the way, wondering when Amy would appear and hoping she had enough tact to stay away for an hour or so. Just until she and Jimmy were settled in.

'It's smaller than your house,' she warned him, unlocking the front door and pushing it open to stand in the small hallway.

She was glad that a scent of beeswax greeted them. It was quite a different welcome from her first view of the flat when it had reeked of old grease and dust. She had worked hard to scrub it clean and keep it that way. Amy helped too. Neither of them liked dirt. Jimmy followed her into the kitchen, and she tried to see it through his eyes. The range was black-leaded and gleaming; there was a rag rug on the floor in front of it that she had made with bright cheerful strips of pink and red. The kitchen table was scrubbed, and the teapot, cups and saucers were laid out. Silently, she thanked Jeannie for that. Above the range, clothes hung from the pulley. The struggle to dry them in the damp February air meant they couldn't be tidied away, even on her wedding day.

The brass taps on the sink glinted in the light coming in from the window, although dusk would soon be on its way. There was a faint smell of coal from the bunker under the shelves, but she didn't mind that; it was comforting and meant they still had a few lumps to feed the range and keep themselves warm over the next wee while.

'Cup of tea?' she said.

'Show me around first.'

'You've seen half already,' Eileen joked. 'It's a room and kitchen. The privy is outside, I'm afraid.'

Although she still had the same iron-framed double bed, she had managed to get a better mattress from a bomb sale and the lumpy pillows were improved by pillowcases she'd sewn from an old bedsheet. The rickety table and chair still stood under the window, but she was used to them. Jimmy shoogled the table and made a wry face.

'Aye, I know,' she said. 'It's old like everything else in here.'

'It'll do.' Jimmy grinned. 'We have to start somewhere.'

At least she had mended the curtains so that the blackout material had no holes, which meant she could light the gas lamp without fear of a penalty fine. Jimmy flicked back the curtain on the recess bed.

'I'll get Amy to move over to the kitchen recess once she's back,' Eileen said hurriedly, when she saw his raised eyebrows.

'Has she not found another place to stay?' he said.

There was a tiny, uncomfortable silence. Eileen knew Jimmy didn't want Amy here, but she was torn between making him happy and caring for her cousin. She couldn't throw Amy out. Snowy chose that moment to jump out from behind the curtain. He stalked over to Jimmy, his tail held high, a curl at the top.

'Ah, so this here's the wee mouser you told me about.' He crouched down to stroke Snowy's back, and a loud purr began.

'He got rid of our mouse problem but if I let him out into the close, he brings back more. I think the neighbours let him in and he has several homes. But he always comes back here.'

'A cat knows where its bread is buttered. So to speak.' He tugged the cat's ear gently.

'Talking of bread and butter, let's have that cuppa,' she said.

The front door creaked open. Amy's footsteps were loud on the lino. Eileen sighed. It would have been so nice to have Jimmy to herself for that first evening. Jeannie had offered to have Amy stay with them so that they could have a honeymoon night alone together, but Eileen hadn't had the heart to ask that of Amy. She had hoped her cousin would be sensitive enough to find a place to stay just for that one night on her own initiative, but it seemed not.

'We haven't met properly,' Jimmy said, holding out his hand to Amy.

Eileen was going to remind him that Amy had visited him in hospital, but then maybe, him being blind at that point, he didn't count it. Amy stared, and Eileen thought she wasn't going to shake his hand, but she did.

'Amy Boyle. I'm sure Eileen's told you all about me.'

Eileen busied herself making tea and pouring it into the cups, hoping that Jimmy and Amy, left alone, would chat and find some common ground. Instead, there was silence. She clattered the cups onto the saucers, wanting noise of any sort.

'Oh, Amy, I can give you a hand to move your bed, if you like?' she said brightly, to fix the strain in the room.

Amy's expression darkened. 'I'll manage it myself, thanks all the same. In fact, I'll do it right now if it's so important.'

'I didn't mean... Och, leave it just now. There's no hurry...'

Amy stomped out of the kitchen, and they heard thumps and crashes in the bedroom. Snowy ran into the kitchen and hid under the table.

'I handled that badly,' Eileen whispered to Jimmy in dismay. 'I never meant she had to do it right away.'

Jimmy shrugged. 'She has to swap it over before this evening; she might as well do it now.'

He didn't know how moody Amy could be. Eileen hated the thought of an atmosphere in her flat. Not on her first night as a married woman in her home. She put her teacup down as Amy brushed past the table with her bundle of bedsheet, pillow and blanket. Jimmy gulped at his cup as if nothing out of the ordinary was happening.

'Och, you make a grand brew, so you do,' he sighed, taking his packet of Player's from his pocket and lighting one up.

Eileen noticed that his fingers shook and the yellow stains on his forefinger and middle finger as he stuck the fag between them and took a long draw. The smoke blew out from his nostrils. It smelled familiar, of Jimmy, of afternoon dances and of the convalescent home. Her shoulders eased down.

'At least I'll be warm in 'ere,' Amy remarked to no one in particular. 'That other recess bed, I'm like a bloody icicle most mornings.'

'Do you want to make new curtains for the recess? I'll help you. These are so thin and faded, I think they'll be better cut and sewn as dresses,' Eileen said.

'If you like.' Amy's tone suggested she didn't care, but Eileen worried she was taking the move from bedroom to kitchen hard. It wasn't as if there was a choice. Not when Eileen and Jimmy were sharing a bed from now on. She blushed at her thoughts. Part of her couldn't wait for them to be husband and wife properly, and part of her was scared. She was almost glad they had to get through a meal and the rest of the evening before they went to bed together.

'She can do it herself,' Jimmy said, pulling Eileen down onto his knee and pressing a kiss to her forehead. 'It's your wedding day all day. You work hard enough the rest of the time.'

Amy glared at him and marched back out of the kitchen.

'You mustn't stir her up,' Eileen murmured. 'It's not fair. She's trying her best.'

'Doesn't appear that way to me.'

'It's hard for all of us, cramped in here and her playing gooseberry to a married couple,' Eileen said.

'She doesn't have to. She can move out.'

'It's not that easy, Jimmy. It isn't. She's my cousin and I feel a responsibility for her. She's far from home and I won't see her having to rent a horrid single end in a dingy part of Glasgow when she knows hardly anyone.'

'All right, all right, doll. I get the message. She can stay for now if it keeps you happy. Gie us another kiss.'

Eileen succumbed to a deeper kiss, tasting cigarettes and black tea, and a thrill ran through her. She stroked his jaw, feeling the stubble, the masculine but familiar shape and strength of his body under hers as she sat on his lap. She was caught on a rising wave of passion when a dry little cough brought her back like a slap.

'Don't mind me,' Amy said sarcastically. She dragged the suitcase and dumped it on the floor under the recess before going back out.

'There's no room in here,' Eileen said before biting her tongue.

'Didn't I tell you so?' Jimmy grinned. 'Here, up you get, and I'll put the suitcase up for the wee blighter.'

'Don't call her that.' Eileen giggled.

Her laughter came from the tension in the flat and the nerves of getting married, but she glanced round and met Amy's stony face and was immediately sorry. Amy turned on her heel, grabbed her coat and slammed out of the front door.

It wasn't long before Jimmy also left to get his box of belongings from Mary and Harry's, leaving Eileen to ponder what they'd have for their meal. Eileen felt guilty for their treatment of Amy. Somehow, she had to bring harmony to the three of them living here. In the meantime, what was there in the kitchen to make a decent meal to impress her husband?

On the shelf, there was a packet of dried egg and a tin of condensed milk. There was no meat on the cold slab as no one had gone shopping that day. It was too late to nip to the butcher's. On the side, wrapped in newspaper, she found a cauliflower with patchy brown florets. Eileen grimaced. It would have to do. She had become so used to Amy cooking for them both that it hadn't entered her mind that Amy would abandon her tonight.

When Jimmy returned, breathing heavily as he entered the flat from the four flights of stairs, and favouring his weak arm, Eileen had the cauliflower boiling in a pan and had found a tiny portion of their weekly ration of cheese. Combining the Cheddar with milk and flour, she'd attempted to make a sauce. If only it wasn't so lumpy.

They sat opposite each other at the table. Jimmy held his knife and fork upright in his fists, expectantly. Eileen hovered over the range. She'd divided the cauliflower onto three plates. Now, she poured the lumpy cheese sauce over the portions. Amy's, she put in the range oven to keep warm. She took the other two plates over to the table, which she had set with her good side plates and glasses.

'What's this?' Jimmy said.

'It's cauliflower cheese. Like your mammy makes.'

'Is there chops or sausages to go with?' Jimmy asked hopefully.

'It's just the cauliflower. There's nothing else.'

Jimmy pushed it around his plate before forking a floret into his mouth. Eileen waited while he chewed.

'Delicious, darling. Very tasty indeed,' he pronounced with a smile.

Eileen took a mouthful. The lumps turned out to be pockets of flour, unmixed, and the cheese was almost untastable. She swallowed and coughed.

'Och, it's horrible,' she wailed. 'I wanted to make you a lovely dinner. It's our first in our own wee home.'

Jimmy was round to her in a flash and put his arms around her. 'It's no' that bad, Eileen. Come on, chin up.'

'No' that bad,' she choked. 'High praise indeed.'

Suddenly, the daftness of it caught her and she giggled. Jimmy began to snigger and then belly laugh and then she was too. She held him tight and felt his body shake. He kissed her and kissed her again and entwined his fingers in her hair.

'Let's go to bed, Mrs Dougal,' Jimmy said. 'I'd pick you up and carry you through, but my arm won't let me.'

'Shouldn't we listen to the wireless first?' Eileen said breathlessly. 'It's still early.'

'Do you want to?' Jimmy stopped in the hallway.

She shook her head. 'Not really. Let's get into bed.'

She felt daring for saying it. Half excited and half scared all over again. But it was her Jimmy, so what was there to be worried about? They hurried into the bedroom and she shut the door. Amy would be back. They'd have to keep the noise down. What a shame to have to think on it.

She didn't look at him as she slipped under the covers and took her clothes off. Her nightdress was under her pillow, so she put it on, fumbling with the buttons. When she was ready, she saw that he had his pyjamas on, and he got into the bed too. How odd it felt to share, the mattress dipping with his weight. She was awkward.

He turned and kissed her gently. 'I love you.'

And then it wasn't awkward any more as their two bodies fitted together, made for each other with tenderness and rising passion. Afterwards, they lay there, slippery with sweat, their heartbeats slowing, their hands entwined.

'We'll get married again after the war,' Jimmy said. 'Do it properly. You'll have a white wedding gown and fresh flowers in your hair. I'll have a decent suit that fits and a shirt that isn't borrowed.'

'We'll have three bridesmaids and two flower girls.' Eileen yawned sleepily. 'And page boys.'

'And a proper honeymoon. Where to? Maybe Blackpool or Aberdeen.'

'For a week, not a day or two,' Eileen said. 'I fancy Blackpool; it's by the sea. Or Scarborough. I saw a picture of it once in a magazine. You can get donkey rides and fish and chips and fresh whelks.'

'You ever eaten a whelk?'

'No, but they sound exotic.'

She yawned again and rolled over onto her side to face him. They heard the sound of the front door opening and closing and footsteps fading. Amy was back.

'I don't want another wedding,' Eileen said. 'I loved this one; it was perfect. I love you.'

'Come here and show me how much you love me.' Jimmy pulled her gently towards him.

The next morning, Morag woke to find the other half of her bed cold and empty. George had left early for work, and she was relieved that she didn't have to speak to him. His stinging words from the wedding rang in her ears. He blamed her for the baby. He accused her of driving him away. She got out of bed, shivering in her thin nightgown, and stared at herself in the dressing table mirror. Her eyes were like two currants in a dough-coloured face. She pinched her cheeks to bring some colour to them. She felt sick. *There's no time to be sick, what with a marriage disintegrating by the day and two lodgers waiting for breakfast, not to mention a shift at the factory, sewing yet more blankets and army uniforms*, she told the pale reflection sternly.

It took all her strength to get dressed. She covered her wool dress with a wrap-over floral apron and slid her feet into her utility shoes with their wooden soles and heels. They were heavy but sturdy and made to last out the war. Finally, she brushed her hair, rolled and pinned it into place. Now she was ready to face the world. Her tiny world, of rations and work, exhaustion and marital misery. With straightened shoulders, Morag went downstairs to the kitchen to boil up the porridge oats for breakfast.

'Any kippers this morning?' Mr McLeod asked, over the top of his newspaper.

Morag set the pot of porridge down on the mat and shook her head. 'Sorry, it's porridge and toast. I couldn't get any kippers as I was at my friend's wedding yesterday, so I didn't have time to shop.'

Mr McLeod's sad expression only made her feel worse. She'd failed him just as she'd failed George, and her factory supervisor, come to think of it. There had been two reprimands over her speed and efficiency lately. It was because no matter how hard she tried to concentrate on the sewing machine, her thoughts kept wavering off onto George and how different their lives might be if her baby had lived. More hopeful and joyous, she believed.

'Here comes trouble,' Mr McLeod murmured and ducked down behind his papers as Ricky Smith walked in.

'Good morning, Mrs Kincaid. You're a sight for sore eyes, I must say. Is that pink roses on your apron?'

Flustered, Morag glanced down. She wore the apron so often she never really saw it any more. He was right. The pattern was of pink roses. Actually, they had at one time been crimson, but too many washings had faded them to a delicate pink.

'Porridge, Mr Smith?' she said, already ladling the oats into bowls for both lodgers and unsure how to answer on the roses.

He grinned at her and his right eye creased in a brief wink that only Morag saw. 'Lovely. I'm starving this morning.'

'Did you sleep well?' Morag asked politely.

His gaze flickered over her, almost calculating and somehow catching her off-kilter. As if he was imagining *her* asleep.

'Very well indeed. Plenty of energy for a busy day ahead.' He emphasised the word 'energy' as if she was to imagine what he might do with all that energy.

'What is it you do, exactly?'

Morag sat at the table with her two lodgers. Her mother, Mollie, said it wasn't appropriate for the landlady to do so, but it was practical. Besides, she didn't want to eat in the kitchen while the lodgers had the use of their dining room. She had always enjoyed breakfast and other meals with Mr McLeod and Miss Linton and their interesting conversations.

Mr McLeod lowered his newspaper to hear Ricky's answer.

'I've got a spot working down the dockside, selling fish as it happens.' He leaned back and rested his head on his crossed arms to Mr McLeod's disapproving glare.

'Oh, I thought when you said you worked on the docks, it was on the ships,' Morag said.

Ricky looked sad. 'Not with my lungs, Mrs Kincaid. Medically unfit for the forces and any heavy lifting. But I want to do my bit for the war effort, and everyone needs to eat, don't they?'

'What about the person you were looking for? Did you ever find them?' Morag asked, emboldened by the fact he was giving out information for the first time.

'How did you know I was looking for someone?' Ricky said, his arms coming down and his head going up, more alert.

'It was something Mrs Corrie said, you know, the lady in the bakery where you bought your meat pies.'

'Loose lips sink ships…'

'Sorry, I shouldn't have asked,' Morag said tightly, gathering up the empty bowls.

'If you are searching for someone, who is it?' Mr McLeod chipped in, unexpectedly. 'You're more likely to find them if you describe them to everyone. Keep it to yourself, you'll never meet up.'

The old man's eyes twinkled with curiosity, and Morag realised how bored he'd become since Miss Linton had passed away. He had no one to bounce ideas off or educate about politics or any other topic that he had cared to share with the kind old lady, who was a wonderful listener. Perhaps there had been a touch of romance between them that had never had the chance to blossom further.

Ricky's large hands tapped the table before he replied. 'It's a big city, Glasgow. I've not found her yet, but I have noticed how many thin girls with light brown hair there are now that I've accosted a few!' He chuckled mirthlessly.

'Who is she?' Mr McLeod asked the blunt question that Morag wanted to ask.

'Is that the time? Must dash.' Ricky jumped up as the grandfather clock in its dark wood case in the corner chimed.

As Morag took the dishes out, he brushed past her in the doorway, and she felt the momentary warmth of his hands on her shoulders as he murmured an apology. The feeling of his touch lingered as she scrubbed up at the sink, but she couldn't place her finger on why.

—

Over in Kiltie Street, Eileen had a slow, luxurious start to the day. It was Sunday, and she had a day off because of her wedding. They might not be away on honeymoon, but she and Jimmy had this precious day together before she had to go back to the factory, and he went out to get work. Snowy slept at the end of the bed, curled up like a white powder puff. Jimmy snored. Eileen stretched her feet out under the covers and wondered if Amy had slept well, tucked up in the recess in the kitchen.

She padded out to put on the kettle. The curtains were drawn and there was no sound from Amy's bed space except a light purr like a cat's. Walking, she felt a slight tenderness between her legs and smiled, remembering last night's love-making. She was a married woman, and she was in love with her husband. She hugged the thought with happiness. She wasn't alone, and that sense of loneliness, so often with her, had vanished like the morning's mist.

'Peasouper gone?' Jimmy appeared and kissed the back of her neck.

'Aye, the air's clear enough. Want some toast?'

He nuzzled her ear. 'I'm not hungry that way. Come back to bed, Sheena.'

She giggled and turned to kiss him, feeling his eager body poking hotly at her through her nightdress. Only too conscious of Amy so close through the red curtain material, she took Jimmy's hand and followed him back to bed. They made love frantically and then more slowly, enjoying discovering each other's bodies.

'I'm going to wash and get dressed and I'll make you a nice breakfast.' She kissed him.

'Not cauliflower?'

She threw a sock at him, and he hid under the covers, pretending to be afraid.

'I'll just have another wee lie-in. Call me when it's ready.'

Eileen hummed under her breath as she fried the tiny strips of bacon from their ration and boiled an egg for them to share. Amy's curtain tweaked back, and her sleepy face appeared.

'You making enough for three?'

Smothering a sigh, knowing it was unfair to expect the flat to themselves, Eileen nodded. 'Aye, five minutes, if you want to get dressed.'

'I wouldn't usually, but with his nibs 'ere, I suppose I oughta.' Amy sounded resentful.

They ate in silence. Eileen was thankful that she hadn't burned the precious bacon or cracked the egg. They had to fill up on National Loaf. One egg didn't go far between three.

'What's that smell?' she said suddenly. 'Something's burning.'

Two faces turned to the range, but Eileen knew she hadn't left any food to scorch. Snowy scampered in, eyes wild and tail big. Three chairs screeched on the linoleum as they all ran through into the bedroom where the mattress was smouldering, and black smoke roiled up.

'Get water!' Jimmy shouted.

Eileen ran back into the kitchen, almost bowling Amy down as she stood staring at the bed.

'Don't just stand there, help me,' Eileen shouted as she filled a pan and rushed back through to fling it on their bed.

The fire was extinguished quickly. Eileen looked in dismay at the sodden bedclothes and the blackened holes in the fabric. The mattress itself was damaged, the springs visible and the stuffing melted in the middle.

'Sorry, doll, I must've dropped my lit fag when I came for my food,' Jimmy said contritely, an arm round Eileen's shoulder.

She was too distressed to comfort him and say it was all right. Because it wasn't all right. His carelessness meant they'd have to buy a new mattress, sheet and blanket when they could hardly afford them. He could've burned down their whole flat. She thought of his yellowed fingers and how she rarely saw him without a cigarette in those fingers or clamped to his mouth.

She was fond of her flat. The thought of it being destroyed, of having to move, was awful. She stepped away from him and pulled at the mattress to get it off the bed frame. Glancing up, thinking about where to dump the smelly stuffing, she saw her cousin.

Amy was smiling smugly.

Chapter Thirteen

The tide of war was turning, and there was a feeling that this had to be the last year of it. The newspaper headlines were full of articles where the Allies were forging forward. That Monday, the *Glasgow Daily Record* proudly announced in its first page column that *Field Marshal Montgomery was at the front today. He watched crack Scots troops, some from Edinburgh and Glasgow, preventing Rundstedt's paratroops making a 'little Cassino' of the Siegfried town of Cleves...*

Below that, a couple of smaller articles gave hope: *Big US Raid Left Berlin Heartless... US Eighth Air Force's 1000-Bomber Raid on Berlin* and *Germany's last known defence line in the east has been shattered by Marshal Konev's forces...*

Strange how far away all the action was happening, yet it influenced all their lives, Eileen mused, folding the papers that morning and leaving them on the table for Jimmy to read when he returned from searching for work. They were very lucky not to be in the thick of it. They had to put up with meagre food rations and long shifts at the factory, but the bombing over Glasgow had stopped a while back, and with the ease-up on blackout and the disbanding of the Home Guard and reduction in air raid wardens, there was a real sense of change and hope.

'What do you need me for?' Amy whined.

Eileen rolled her eyes before turning to her cousin. That air of hope didn't extend to the fourth-floor flat at number four Kiltie Street, where it seemed a small war was beginning to be waged. She hadn't imagined Amy's smug expression after the bedroom fire. Amy had taken a wicked delight in going on about it that day and evening. How they could all have died, how careless it was to drop a fag into the bedclothes, and on and on until Eileen had snapped at her to shut up. As it was unlike Eileen to be unkind, Amy had shut up. Eileen felt needled and on edge. During a restless night's sleep in the bedroom recess, while Jimmy slept on the floor, she resolved to try and fix the situation between Jimmy and Amy. The best way to do so, she reckoned, was by getting Amy out of the flat and occupied.

'My mum asked me to go and help at her WVS centre. They've got a huge pile of clothing come in for folk who need it, evacuees and so on, and they could do with an extra pair of hands to help.'

'That's you sorted, then. If you want to do that on your day off,' Amy said rudely.

'I want you to come too,' Eileen said. She softened her tone. 'Please come, Amy. Mum'll be so pleased. It'll get the job done sooner and afterwards we can go to a British Restaurant and get a nice dinner. What do you say?'

'Oh, very well,' Amy grumbled. 'I'll get me coat and hat. Anything to stop you going on and on at me.'

They trotted down to catch the bus on the main street that would take them out to the western edge of the city and the WVS centre, which wasn't far from where the Boyles lived. There was something comforting in the regular jolting motion as the bus went over potholes and around bomb sites. Their bodies lifted in the leather seats and the flowers on Amy's hat quivered. Eileen stared out the window, enjoying the views of the city. Women, wrapped against the February chill, carried shopping bags and trailed small children with knitted pixie hoods and mittens dangling on strings from their sleeves. A small dog darted out in front of the bus and the driver let out a few ripe words. Eileen was a wee bit shocked, given it was a female bus driver.

'I have got my job in the crèche,' Amy said suddenly. 'I don't need another job in the WVS if that's what you're thinking.'

That was exactly what Eileen was thinking. She hoped, if Amy enjoyed the morning, that she'd volunteer and so be out of the flat every day and therefore out of Jimmy's way.

'You're hardly at the crèche,' she pointed out.

Amy went a bright red. She adjusted her hat and sniffed. 'It ain't on regular like. It depends on the women's shifts. I can't help that, can I?'

Eileen suspected that Amy didn't always turn up when the crèche was running. She was so often at home. Wisely, she didn't argue the point. Instead, she watched a giant Clydesdale horse pulling a cart full of milk bottles up the road and the elderly milkman nimbly lifting the bottles and delivering them into the tenement closes.

—

'Hello, dear. You made it. And Amy too. That's wonderful. We have a huge mountain of clothes and Mrs McGrath is poorly with her lumbago and Mrs McNeil isn't here; her son was killed last week, so we're short of bodies.' Agnes Boyle's hair was sticking out of its usual permed set and her skirt was creased.

'Don't worry, Mum. Amy and I will take over.'

Eileen pressed a kiss to her mother's face, Agnes shrinking back automatically before returning her daughter's embrace. She smiled and led the younger women over to the back of the room.

'You weren't exaggerating,' Eileen said, taken aback at the generosity that showed in the tall pile of clothing, stacked against the wall.

'Believe it or not, there are still families bombed out from the Clydebank blitz with no fixed address and dependent on relatives and friends for somewhere to stay. Those poor people find it hard to make ends meet, never mind clothing themselves and growing children.'

Even Amy was impressed into silence for a moment.

'Well, how about I make you both a cup of tea while you begin to sort things out?' Agnes suggested. She paused. 'It was a lovely wedding, Eileen. Your dad and I enjoyed it very much. Jimmy's our son-in-law now and we're very happy about that.'

'Thanks, Mum. Jimmy was pleased to get to know you both too.'

'What about you, Amy? You must miss your own family,' Agnes said.

Amy shrugged. 'I'm glad I'm up 'ere away from the doodlebugs and what have you, Aunt Agnes. That's the honest truth.'

'But you must worry about your parents.' Agnes's glance went to Amy's fingers. 'Is there a young man in London you might worry about too?'

Amy licked her lips and unbuttoned her coat. 'I'm very thirsty, Aunt Agnes. I'd love a cuppa. Come on, Eileen. Let's tackle this hoard, shall we? Get it all sorted before the families arrive.'

Agnes raised her eyebrows but didn't persist as Amy marched off to the mountain of clothes with Eileen following. There was a not unpleasant smell of wool and mothballs wafting from the clothing and they both exclaimed when they found pretty jackets and girls' dresses among the heap.

'This will suit someone nicely.' Eileen held up a thin grey cotton dress with red embroidered pockets. 'Pity she'll have to wait a few months to wear it. It's too thin for winter.'

'Add this 'ere cardi and a coat and she can wear it right now.' Amy grinned, stretching a brown knitted cardigan against her small chest. 'Look out, 'ere they come.'

Eileen glanced over her shoulder to see a woman holding the hands of a boy and a girl. Another older girl walked beside them. Agnes intercepted, smart in her green and purple WVS uniform. She pointed towards them and the family came across.

'Good morning,' Eileen said brightly. 'What do you have in mind?'

The woman was thin-faced with dark shadows under her eyes. Judging by the ages of the children she was probably in her forties, but she could have passed for twenty years older.

'What have you got, hen?' she said, in a dry, cracked voice. 'We're in need of everything.'

'What about this?' Amy showed her the brown cardigan. 'And there's a dress to go with it.'

She gave these items to the woman and then kneeled in front of the little girl. 'What about you, love? Fancy a pretty dress?' She looked at the child's worn shoes with holes at the toes. 'I reckon I've got a lovely pair of boots what'll fit you an' all.'

Eileen dealt with the woman and found clothes to fit her son. Out of the corner of her eye, she watched in amazement as Amy talked to the little girl and soon had her giggling and trying on the dress and a coat.

'She's a natural with the weans,' the woman remarked wearily. 'Nice to get a wee rest from dealing with them, to be honest. There's five of us living in one room. My man's away in the army and my oldest girl's out every day in the factory, but I could scream for a wee space of my own sometimes. Shouldn't grumble, should I now. Others have got it worse.'

Hearing that, Eileen felt ashamed that she found it hard in her flat with just her, Jimmy and Amy. Here was true hardship, and yet this poor woman still had enough generosity of spirit to pity others worse off than herself.

'Would you like a cup of tea?' she offered, now that the family had taken the clothing gratefully.

She guided them back to Agnes, who looked proud to be pouring tea and offering biscuits.

'She's right, you are a natural,' she said, re-joining Amy, who was folding clothes and sorting them into sizes. 'One day, you'll make a great mum.'

Amy frowned. 'Not me. I'd be a terrible mother.'

'What makes you say that? You had that wee girl eating out of your hand in minutes.'

'I don't deserve to be a mother,' Amy said sharply. 'Leave it, will you.'

Another family arrived and soon they were busy with a growing group of tired mothers with children whose clothes were too small or worn. More than a few children wore plimsolls, frayed and holed and completely unsuitable for the wintery slush on the pavements that day.

'It's an eye-opener to the huge need for help around here,' Eileen said when she, Amy and Agnes were able to stop for a cup of tea. 'I know there's poverty in Glasgow but it's different seeing it up close.'

'Makes you glad to 'ave a roof over your head,' Amy agreed, somewhat pointedly.

'We are very lucky,' Agnes said. 'Now, drink up. I can see another bunch approaching. After that, you're free to go. You've been a big help, thank you. Perhaps you'll come on a regular basis, Amy? Eileen can't because of her factory work but she said you need more hours of war work yourself.'

Amy threw Eileen a dark look. 'We'll see, Aunt Agnes. I'll let you know.'

—

There was a British Restaurant in St Vincent Street in the city centre, conveniently near to the bus stop. It had opened in 1942, the first in Glasgow, and offered a three-course meal for a shilling. They hurried inside, out of the bitterly cold air. The restaurant was in a large hall with white-painted fluted columns holding up the roof.

'Blimey,' Amy breathed.

The tables were covered in cheerful red-and-white-checked oilcloths and almost every table was occupied. At one, there was a group of uniformed soldiers, two men and two women. At another, a woman in a fur coat and matching fur hat spoke fervently to her companion, another woman in a less fancy outfit of wool coat and felt hat, her scarf slung around her neck as it was chilly enough in the huge space. A comfortable fug of grey cigarette smoke laced the air above the diners and there were ripples of laughter and loud voices as the various groups enjoyed eating and chatting together.

Somewhere, a wireless blasted out military tunes, but the music couldn't compete with the chatter or the whoosh of noise from the street when the door opened and closed. Plenty of office workers used the British Restaurant and they were on short breaks. A young woman, high heels click-clacking on the tiles, brushed past them with a murmured apology, glancing at her watch on a delicate wrist. Eileen smiled at her to show they didn't mind.

'My treat,' Amy said, nodding her head to an empty table at the back of the floor.

'Thanks, that's kind. I'm a bit short this week after the wedding.'

Eileen was surprised and touched that Amy was going to pay. She didn't often offer to do so for anything, apart from a contribution towards rent and food in the flat.

Amy rubbed her hands together gleefully. 'I could eat an 'orse; I'm starving. Today's choice is lentil soup, followed by stew and veg with rice pudding and prunes for afters.'

Eileen realised she was quite hungry too and was glad when the waitress brought their meals. They ate in companionable silence until dessert was brought.

'You were so good with those children this morning,' Eileen said. 'What did you mean you don't deserve to be a mother?'

Amy shoved her empty bowl away and shook her head savagely. 'Give over, will you. I don't want to talk about it.'

'Is there something wrong? Can I help?'

'You're such a soft touch, you are,' Amy growled.

'Maybe I am, but I care about you. You're my cousin. I can see something's wrong. Is it because of the letter from Pearl?' Eileen asked, knowing she had to be careful not to let it slip that she knew the whole contents of what had been written.

'That's my business. You didn't oughta go near my letters.'

'It had been posted through the letterbox so I couldn't help but see it when I came home. If there's a problem, you can share it with me. A problem shared is a problem halved, as they say.'

Amy's laugh was like a bark. 'A problem shared is a problem spread about, is what I say.'

Eileen scraped the last of her rice pudding onto her spoon and ate it. 'Well, if you change your mind…'

'If you knew what I've done in me past, you wouldn't be so accommodating,' Amy said bleakly.

'It can't be that bad. We all make mistakes. I'm very fond of you, Amy, and I'm not going to give up on trying to help. Soft touch or not.'

Amy grinned, her miserable expression vanishing. 'You're a good sport, I'll say that for you. I like being with you. I feel… *safe*. Like Snowy does. That's why he's moved in, I guess. Knows he can't be in a better place.'

It was the longest conversation that Eileen felt she'd had with Amy. She sat quite still, hoping not to break the magic and wishing with all her heart that Amy would confide in her.

But the other girl took a deep breath in and out and paused. 'Wonder if they've got any more grub.'

Amy chewed her lip as the bus rattled homewards. Her mind spiralled about Ricky. Where was he now? He wasn't going to let her go so easily. His pride wouldn't let him. Leaving him had been about escaping but also inflicting hurt. She knew he'd be humiliated in front of his friends and neighbours when they discovered his wife had left him. *I'll hunt you down if you leave*, he'd shouted when she threatened to do so. He had two good reasons to come after her. Firstly, she'd taken his stash of saved cash. It wasn't as if she had any money of her own. Ricky had made sure of that. He'd given her a measly amount for 'housekeeping' each week and kept the rest of his wages for himself so he could go down the pub with his mates.

Secondly, she had taken something much more precious. Eileen would never understand if she knew. And Amy couldn't bear to see the disappointment on her cousin's face. She was becoming a soft touch herself when it came to Eileen. What she'd said was true. She did feel safe with Eileen and living in Kiltie Street. Amy wasn't stupid; she knew she had her faults. She could be lazy and selfish. But lately, a better part of her was emerging, and maybe that was because of Eileen's care of her.

Cajoling the little girl today into trying on the clothes had given her such an intense yearning for Alfie it was like a knife in her belly. Ricky had never hit his son, but it was only a matter of time. Alfie was young, but Amy could see it… he'd grow, and he'd challenge his dad one day, and then there'd be a terrible fight. Besides, she saw Alfie's little face fearful when Ricky hit her, and it broke her heart. No, he was better off hidden with Pearl.

Alfie was better off without her.

'Come and see what me and Harry got.' Jimmy greeted them at the door with a grin.

Eileen kissed him, and he squeezed her with his good arm, lifting her up till she squealed. Behind the couple, Amy rolled her eyes and waited.

'Harry got it at the market, cost him next to nothing as he got it off a friend. I paid him a wee bit more, though,' Jimmy said, motioning them through to the bedroom and pointing proudly at a blue-and-white-striped mattress on their iron bedframe.

'Thank goodness for that,' Eileen said. 'I wasn't looking forward to another night in the recess and you on the floor. Well done to Harry.'

If Amy hadn't been there, she'd have suggested to Jimmy that they try the mattress out, there and then. Instead, she held his hand. It was warm and rough and the touch of him sparked a need she had to suppress. Jimmy winked at her as if he knew her thoughts.

'Tonight, darling,' he breathed in her ear.

Amy looked annoyed and stalked away into the kitchen. Eileen sat on the bed with Jimmy. The air still smelled of burned stuffing.

'Good to have a wee moment to ourselves.' Jimmy kissed her cheek.

Amy yelled from the kitchen. 'What's wrong with Snowy?'

Eileen leaped up and pulled Jimmy with her, ignoring his deep sigh. Amy was cuddling a limp Snowy in the kitchen.

'He was all right earlier.' Jimmy frowned. He stroked the cat's ears and murmured to him.

'He's not all right now,' Amy said fiercely, tears in her eyes. 'What do we do?'

'Let's make a wee bed for him,' Eileen suggested, feeling she had to do something as Amy's eyes beseeched her.

She brought a towel and folded it into a box that had held vegetables. Harry had brought it full from the allotment but he wouldn't mind waiting for it back. Normally Snowy disdained a particular place to sleep, moving around depending on where the best sunny or warm spot was. Now, he made no fuss as Jimmy carefully took him from Amy and laid him in the box. They all stared in at him. He was too docile to be well. Despite her worry for Snowy, Eileen couldn't help thinking that for the very first time since Jimmy had moved in, all three of them were in agreement and working together. If only it could be like that all the time.

'Maybe he needs to eat?' Amy said, her glance flicking between Eileen and Jimmy.

Eileen doubted poor Snowy could eat. The cat's eyes were closed, his head low on his front paws and his body rising and falling slowly with each breath.

'He's poorly all right. Do cats get colds? There's no sign of injury on him.'

'How about a nice piece of fish?' Amy said, brightening up. 'That'll do 'im good.'

'We don't have any.' Eileen got up off her knees from beside Snowy's box to get her purse. There was a fishmonger on the main street who sold tins of snoek and chunks of whale meat and other disgusting items, so she didn't often shop there.

'I'll go down the docks,' Jimmy offered. 'There's a man there sells fish but also fish heads and tails cheap. That'll tempt our Snowy for sure.'

Amy clutched Eileen's arm and Eileen smiled at Jimmy. Even if the fish tails didn't cure Snowy, at least Amy was relieved.

'I wish you'd told me about the cheap fish before,' she said to Jimmy. 'See if he's got any white fish for our tea while you're there.'

'The man's only been there the last week or so or I'd have said before. He's a big man, looks like he ought to be off fighting rather than bellowing like a fishwife. Come to think of it, Amy, he's got an accent just like yours.'

Neither Eileen nor Jimmy noticed Amy's eyes widen at this piece of news.

It was Monday morning and George was up and ready to go to work, early as usual. These days, Morag got up extra early herself so that she could make up his lunch pieces.

'Do you have to go now?' she said as she handed them the slices of bread with fish paste, carefully wrapped in a cloth.

He stared at her as if he didn't know her before tucking the package into his bag. 'Of course I do. Rob Gunn is now my direct supervisor. He used to work alongside, now he's in charge even though I was working the yards before he arrived. I have to show I'm working hard.'

'Only, we never have time together any more.'

There, she'd said it. And for once, it seemed like George was listening. Morag suddenly realised just how much she missed their easy, loving relationship. How George would come and sit in the kitchen while she washed up the dishes from their evening meal, how they'd waltz around the room and kiss. The way he charmed the lodgers and talked politics with Mr McLeod. Come to think of it, she hadn't heard him laugh in a long while. Not since they had argued so terribly. His horrible words often came unbidden to her and they hadn't been intimate in ever so long.

'I've got to go. Someone's got to bring in the money.' He put on his coat and hat.

Morag waited until he turned back to pick up his bag and reached up on tiptoe to kiss him. His lips didn't return the pressure. He set her from him without a smile and she noticed the lines around his mouth and along his forehead as if the muscles were taut. Then she was alone in their quiet hallway.

She was upset. Didn't he realise she was hurting too? He kept shutting her out. All the anger and upset over their baby had become intwined with his imagined slights at work. If only he would talk to her. Suddenly her upset turned to anger. How dare he destroy their marriage, their intimacy, with his behaviour. She was trying so hard to be a good wife, but for naught.

All through her morning shift, Morag felt her resentment rising. She sewed fast and furiously, gaining praise from her supervisor and envious looks from the other women as her pile of finished uniform jackets rose. She didn't stop to chat with anyone as she walked home at midday. Her mind was on cleaning the house and making a pie for dinner, anything that stopped her thinking about George.

The house was quiet, and she remembered that Mr McLeod had mentioned that morning he was going to play chess with a friend and wouldn't be back for dinner. She put on her housecoat and took a polishing rag. The ornaments could do with a dusting in the dining room. It was nice to be alone in her house for once. She began to relax.

'Whatever it is, it can't be that bad.'

Morag jumped, and the glass vase, George's mother's favourite, slipped from her hands.

Ricky's hands shot out to catch it and missed. They collided as Morag heard the vase thump onto the rug and bounce and then skitter onto the wooden floor. Ricky's face was next to hers, and she saw the tiny bristles on his chin and smelled a woody aftershave. Afterwards, she couldn't have said who made the first move. Only that they clung together, the kisses deep and urgent, all her tension changing into a surging desire to be held, to be loved. To obliterate the misery of the last months.

Without a single word, they shed their clothes as they hurried upstairs to Ricky's room. In a fever, she felt his body hard and heavy on hers. He thrust into her with little tenderness, and when it was done, he lay beside her. Morag's sweat cooled on her body unpleasantly. She got up, grabbed at the blanket and wrapped it around her. Ricky didn't move. He smiled lazily. *Like the cat that got the cream*, she thought hazily. She stumbled on the edge of the blanket. She made it into her own bedroom and sat on the edge of the bed. Her mind was blank. She wouldn't reflect on what she'd done.

Not yet.

Chapter Fourteen

The shouting woke Eileen up. She struggled to sit, eyes trying to adjust to the darkness.

'Jimmy?' She felt for him beside her, but there was only air.

'Look out, they're coming. Duck!' Jimmy screamed from under the bed.

Eileen scurried to the floor, kneeling to find him. 'It's all right, my darling. It's all right. You're at home in Kiltie Street with me. Come on out. You're shivering with the cold.'

She managed to coax him out and somehow get him up onto the bed again. He was hardly helping and although he wasn't a big man, he was a dead weight against her slender body.

'It's happened again,' she said gently as he groaned and rubbed his eyes. 'But it was worse this time.'

His pyjama jacket was damp under her touch and his shoulder muscles twitched as if small animals ran under his skin.

'Is it really you, Sheena?' Jimmy said urgently, gripping her arm. 'It was so real. As if I was back there. Where I copped that shell and lost my sight and injured my shoulder and leg.'

'It was only a nightmare,' she comforted him. 'But I think they're getting worse. That's the third one this week.'

'I'm sorry. I've broken your sleep too.' His breath was ragged.

The bedroom door creaked open and Amy peered in. 'You've woken up the neighbourhood. I've got to get up in the morning.'

Eileen went to her and pushed her gently back into the hall, closing the door behind them both.

'You're not the only one who has to get up in the morning. But Jimmy's health is more important than that. I'm worried about him.'

Amy rolled her eyes and yawned. 'He's going a bit nuts, is what's going on. All that yelling about not being able to see and telling folk to dive in the mud. What's that all about? It's getting to be a habit. Maybe you ought to take 'im back to the 'ospital. Get them doctors to fix 'im up.'

Amy's suggestion touched on Eileen's deepest fear. What if she did take Jimmy back to the hospital and explain his night-time terrors and they kept him in. What if he never got out and they locked him up. There had been a man in their street, when she was growing up, who had wandered around shouting at folk. Her parents had said he was harmless enough. He'd fought in the Great War and was a hero with a medal to prove it. Eventually, he had lunged at the local priest, and they'd carted the old soldier off to the insane asylum and no one had seen him ever again.

'Go back to bed please, Amy,' Eileen whispered wearily.

The peace between the three of them had lasted only as long as Snowy's illness, which was less than a couple of weeks ago. They had taken it in turns to sit with the cat, to tempt him with small morsels of food and to stroke his dull fur. After a few days, Snowy had perked up and was soon his old self again, demanding to go outside and bringing in dead mice for Eileen to find on the floor of a morning.

It had been a very pleasant atmosphere in the flat while it lasted, she thought. She hadn't realised just how tense she felt when she was with both Jimmy and Amy. As if she had to defend one to the other and that somehow she was to blame for everything.

'I will go back to bed. I need my beauty sleep. I 'ope that's an end to tonight's shenanigans,' Amy said tartly.

Eileen resisted the urge to stick her tongue out at her cousin's retreating back. Instead, she went back into her own bedroom. Jimmy was lying on his side of the bed, covers up to his head. She slid into bed beside him and hugged his shape through the blanket.

'It's going to be all right. I promise,' she said. She didn't believe it herself, but what else was there to say?

Jimmy's snores were his answer. It took a lot longer for Eileen to fall back to sleep. She lay staring at the ceiling, worried about the future. It was harder being a married woman than she had imagined. In some ways, it was marvellous. She and Jimmy got along so well; they had the same sense of humour, and they were in love. Their love-making was tender and satisfying and she anticipated it eagerly on those nights when wordlessly they went to bed early.

But then there was Amy and all the tiptoeing around her that had to be done. It was awkward going to bed to make love, knowing there was someone else in the flat who had sharp hearing and thin walls separating them.

'Every married couple has this problem,' Jimmy had said that night as they snuggled into each other and Eileen had voiced this. 'If it wasn't for the fact you have this flat, we'd have moved in with either my parents or yours until the end of the war. Then you've got parents and brothers and sisters and nephews and nieces all crammed into a wee flat with walls you could spit through. Much as I wish your Amy would move out, we don't have it so bad that way.'

'After the war, if we work hard, we'll get our own wee house, I hope,' Eileen had said.

'Aye. Just for the two of us until the weans come along.'

'I'd like to have children,' she'd murmured, sleep almost upon her.

'Me too. And your cousin will be gone back to London where she belongs. There'll be no one to interfere in our life together.'

The image Jimmy described hushed Eileen to sleep, finally imagining the future she would have with her husband.

The next day, Jimmy was grumpy with lack of sleep. His hand shook as he lit a Player's, puffing on it like a lifeline. Eileen hurried to wash with a jug of cold water and then got dressed for work. She glanced around the flat with something like despair. Amy's coat was slung on the back of a kitchen chair. She tripped over Amy's boots, which had been left carelessly on the floor. Jimmy's cap was on the table. She bit back a sigh as she lifted it and took it through to hang on the coat stand in the hall.

'Can you remember to put it somewhere useful?' she said, as Jimmy went past into the kitchen.

'I'd know where it was if you didn't keep moving it,' he grumbled. 'Is there porridge?'

'Sorry, I didn't have time to make breakfast. I'll be late for my shift if I don't leave now.'

She heard him muttering as she went out. She felt guilty for not making breakfast as a good wife ought to but also relieved to be out of the flat where no doubt Jimmy and Amy would be arguing over the porridge or lack of it. It was hard to guess these days whether Amy would cook a meal or not. Sometimes she left it to Eileen, and at others, she produced something delicious. Eileen was always caught on the hop. She needed to discuss it with Amy. They should have a rota now that Amy wasn't cooking every day. When she had a momen she'd organise one. Eileen raced to the bus stop and caught the bus just as the driver was about to pull away.

—

'It's harder than I thought, being a married woman,' Eileen admitted, later that evening.

She'd gone straight to the Boyles' home after work. Agnes was cooking tripe and onions, and there was a rice pudding with raisins in a bowl, cooling on the work surface. With a surge of guilty pleasure, Eileen anticipated eating such a lovely meal without having to queue for ingredients, struggle with a recipe and serve up while exhausted after a hectic day bent over the sewing machine on the noisy factory floor.

'A marriage is more than a wedding party and foolish romantic notions,' Agnes remarked, passing the plates and cutlery to Eileen to set the table.

'I know that, Mum.'

'How well did you know Jimmy before you tied the knot?' Agnes sniffed. 'You fell in love at first sight, that's what you told me, but then you were apart for years. You don't really know him at all.'

'I thought you and Dad were happy for me,' Eileen gasped.

Agnes sat down at the table, her hands on her lap, folding the tea towel neatly.

'All we want is your happiness. I don't mean to be suspicious of Jimmy, but your father and I, we hardly know him. I hope you haven't married too quickly and live to regret it.'

'I love Jimmy, and I always will,' Eileen said simply.

'Then there's no problem, is there. You have to work at marriage, which is what I said before. It's not all wine and roses. It's mostly hard work. Keeping the house nice, making sure dinner's on the table at six o'clock when your husband's hungry. And keeping yourself pretty too. No one wants a slovenly wife.'

'It sounds tiring.'

'Really, Eileen. You young women want it all these days,' Agnes said reprovingly. 'There's a girl down the road who works on the buses, all scarlet lips and nails, and out every evening dancing too. I can't see any man wanting to marry her.'

'I like to paint my lips too,' Eileen said. 'Besides, you just said to keep yourself pretty.'

'There's pretty and then there's overdoing it. Never mind, help me serve up the tripe and onions before it burns. And call your father in for his tea.'

Eileen hadn't found her mother's advice particularly useful. Agnes and Robert had been married for so long that their relationship sailed along peacefully with little excitement or spontaneity. She decided that she couldn't expect her mother to remember how it was to be a new bride. A few more nights of disturbed sleep and Jimmy's nightmares found her knocking at the Dougals' door.

'Come away in. Is Jimmy with you?' Mary smiled. 'He was only here an hour or so ago.'

'No, it's just me, Mary. Looking for some advice, if you don't mind.'

Eileen was surprised to hear that Jimmy had been at number four that afternoon. He had said he was going out to look for work.

'Did he drop in for a wee while?' she asked, as she hung up her coat and followed Mary into the neatly kept parlour.

'He always comes after his dinner and stays until teatime, when he rushes back. He says your meals are worth going home for.'

Eileen smiled proudly. 'I'm glad he likes them. To be honest, Amy does most of the cooking, but I've learned a few recipes that are Jimmy's favourites.'

She was distracted by feeling proud that Jimmy liked her cooking. Then she frowned. 'I didn't know he was spending his afternoons here. He told me he was looking for work.'

Mary raised her eyebrows. 'Is that so?'

Eileen blew out a long sigh and sat on the comfortable sofa without waiting to be asked.

'Actually, I need to talk to you. That's why I'm here.'

'Wait. Let me get us a wee pot of tea and then we can have a blether.'

Soon, Mary bustled in with the tea tray and poured two cups, pushing one towards Eileen along with a piece of parkin.

'Is there trouble between the two of you so soon?' Mary asked with concern.

'It's not trouble... I don't think so anyway.' Eileen described Jimmy's nightmares and her helplessness in dealing with them. 'They're not getting better. Amy says I ought to get him back to see a doctor or get him into a hospital.'

'My poor son. He never mentioned nightmares. Says he gets headaches.'

'I'm sorry. I don't want to worry you. I just need some advice. I want to help him, but I don't know how.'

'By loving him,' Mary said, taking Eileen's hands between her warm ones. 'That's the best cure there is.'

'I love him more than anything. I'm not certain it's enough,' Eileen said, glad of the comfort of Mary's touch.

'Sure it is. Don't you give up on him. Promise me that,' Mary said, holding Eileen's gaze.

'Of course I won't. But Mary... why does he come here so often when he's got his own wee home to sit in?'

Mary shrugged. 'Says he likes it here. I don't mind. It's company for me when Harry's down the allotment.'

Eileen felt hurt. Jimmy liked his mother's house better than his own. Her thoughts ran on. Perhaps it was lonely for him when she was out working. Amy was often out too. She hadn't thought of that. Still, if he got a job then he wouldn't be lonely. Although, who was going to employ a man with dodgy eyesight and a weak arm?

'How's that cousin of yours?' Mary asked. 'Marlene says she's a wonder with the weans in the crèche.'

'I wasn't sure she was still helping out there, to be honest. That's nice; I must tell Amy she's appreciated.'

'Aye, Marlene also says she can be a wee bit clingy with them. I don't like to pass along the gossip, but one mother complained. She went to pick up her boy at the end of the day, and Amy... well... she wouldn't let him go. They had to pluck him out of her arms. Or so the story goes. Marlene always was a one for exaggeration.'

—

Amy admired the shining brass nameplate beside the doorbell at the top floor flat, number one Kiltie Street. She didn't admire the person who answered the ring of the bell. It was the sallow-faced sister. She couldn't remember her name.

'Yes?' That single word managed to combine disdain and rebuff in one.

'Is Leo at home?' Amy smiled.

'My brother is not at home.' *To the likes of you*, was implied.

'Where is he, then?' Amy said. She tried to see behind the thin figure. Perhaps Leo was at home and his annoying sister was just trying to put her off.

'His wife is poorly, and he has gone to her bedside. I don't expect him back within the week.'

That explained it then. After all the chat and offer of a posh meal, she hadn't heard a thing from him. She craved a bit of excitement and pampering. If only she'd met a rich man before she'd married Ricky. He had been all charm and good looks and she'd been a young fool swept away by her lust for him. She'd lived to regret it. After their wedding, it had been mostly a grind, trying to get by on what Ricky gave her for housekeeping and dodging his blows. Wartime had given her an opportunity to reinvent herself and find a better life. She could wait a week for Leo.

'Thanks ever so. Tell him Amy called round,' she said breezily with a little wave of her hand.

She chuckled at the sight of Ada's outraged expression, but her spirits dropped as she went down the steps and back to number four. She couldn't put it off any longer. She had another visit to make, but this one was quite different.

The flat was empty. Amy loved it when she had it to herself. She loved the cluttered kitchen with the blackened range taking up most of one wall and dominating the room. She loved the smell of the coal in the bunker and its burned ashes in the range. She liked the way Eileen had displayed the crockery on the shelves, and the enamelled bin with *BREAD* written on it. It was all so homely. She'd made some lovely meals here for her and Eileen. And Jimmy now, of course, too, which was less enjoyable.

Snowy wound round her legs and she picked him up, burrowing her face into his soft fur.

'I've got to know if it's really 'im, Snowy,' she murmured. 'Course, there's more than Ricky what has a London accent, obviously. London's a huge city. Doesn't mean it's 'im what's selling fish at the docks, does it. But I 'ave to be sure.'

She shivered as she set the cat down gently and brushed white hairs from her woollen top. She had an idea. She took off her good clothes, which she'd put on especially to visit Leo, and threw them into the bed recess. Instead, she put on her oldest dress, which was somewhat baggy, and relaced her boots. In Eileen's bedroom she found a shawl. It was part of the hoard of clothes left in a suitcase, which Eileen was gradually reworking into other garments. The shawl was a charcoal grey.

'Perfect. No one will notice me in this,' Amy told Snowy as they both stared into the mirror in the bedroom.

The docks was a busy place. The Clyde was full of warships and tugs and other craft. The activity at the shipyards never stopped. The ships were all painted battleship grey, and the skyline seemed full of masts and rigging and flying seagulls crying in the breeze. Men were busy moving cargo, there were navy personnel swarming up a gangplank onto the largest ship while an officer shouted orders, and a pile of lobster creels, still glistening wet, sat waiting to be hauled aboard the fishing vessels.

Someone pointed out the direction of the fish sellers, but Amy smelled the area before she reached it. The aroma of fresh fish, salty water and cockles was enticing, and her stomach grumbled. She drew the shawl over her head. She'd taken Eileen's wicker basket too and she fitted right in with the other housewives crowding the stalls, looking for bargains. A fisherman stood at the dock edge, straight off his boat, chopping the heads off mackerel and cod and bellowing to the throng. The fish blood stained the cobbles, dribbling through the cracks between the stones.

A louder voice rang out. 'Come and get them, ladies. Fresh fish for sale. Cheap as chips, that's my promise. I've got coley and whiting, dab and gurnard. So fresh they'll bite yer 'and off.'

Amy froze. There was no mistaking his voice. Her husband, Ricky, was right here. He had followed her to Glasgow. And if she knew Ricky, he'd be determined to find her and get back what he believed was his. She risked going closer to see him properly. The wicker basket scraped her inner elbow and banged against the other women, who exclaimed in annoyance. Amy didn't care. She had to see him. It was unbelievable. He was here, in the flesh. She felt part horror and part fascination, seeing her husband for the first time in months.

His broad shoulders and height made him stand out above the sailors and fishermen. He was handsome, was her Ricky, there was no denying it. Still, as Pearl had often said, handsome is as handsome does. He might woo the ladies with his looks, but they hadn't felt the pain of a fist lashing out. Not to mention how tight with money he was, unless it was spent on him.

Whatever happened, she wasn't going to go back to him. He could whistle in the wind for that. And he wasn't getting his cash back neither. She'd spent half of it. The rest was nestled safely in a tin in her bed recess. It was dwindling, though. Hence her need of Leo. If she played her cards right, she might end up as his wife. Awful though it was, when Ada had said he was at Alice's bedside, a tiny hope had popped up that Alice was dying.

If Alice died, Leo was going to need comforting. And Amy had every intention of being in the right place, close by, to do so. She'd make a wonderful wife for him; she knew she would. She'd learn to speak proper, wear the right clothes, whatever was required to fit the role.

But what about Alfie? Amy's fingers tightened on the shawl. She'd always intended to go back for him. She just hadn't figured out when or how. If she married Leo, that was unlikely to happen. There was no way he'd take on her son. She knew that instinctively. Leo Mearns liked to have things his way. A small boy, not his own, hardly fitted. Alfie was needy. He clung to Amy and kept clear of Ricky. She'd need to give Leo her undivided attention, so no, it would never work. Alfie had to stay with Pearl. Even if it broke her heart.

There was a little boy at the crèche who reminded her so much of him. She'd cuddled him something rotten last week, but the mother hadn't liked it. They'd wrenched him from her arms and she'd hidden her sobs. Perhaps if it worked out with Leo, she could sneak away and see Alfie in secret from time to time, she thought, missing him all over again.

She kept her head lowered and made a swift left turn, out of the dock front, away from the tang of the polluted river and back into the city.

—

When Amy got back to the flat, Eileen was in.

'Ain't you at the factory today?' Amy asked, peeved to find the flat occupied.

She'd been looking forward to a cuppa on her own to mull over what Ricky's appearance meant. At first, she'd been afraid, seeing him there on the docks. But then, walking home, she'd had time to think it over. Glasgow was a large city. How could he possibly find her? Gradually she calmed down, until by the time she'd caught a bus from the city centre out to Maryhill, she'd convinced herself that she was fine. Life could carry on nicely and Ricky would give up and go home to London to bother someone else. She hadn't thought further than that except vaguely, but as the bus jolted around a bomb crater, Amy decided that if Leo did propose, she'd accept. After all, who was to know she was already married?

'I'm on a half day,' Eileen said. 'Do you want to add to my shopping list? I thought I'd get ahead with the queuing for dinner.'

'I'm not cooking tonight.' She was annoyed.

'Oh, well. I'll manage to rustle up something,' Eileen said.

Honestly, did she have to look so bloomin' miserable? Amy almost relented. She did enjoy cooking but resented making meals for Jimmy. No, she was doing Eileen a favour. She had to learn somehow to cook and bake to a reasonable standard. She ignored Eileen's puzzled frown at the sight of the grey shawl and took it off. It was time to get dressed properly again.

'I was thinking... I might ask my friend Morag if she knows of lodgings,' Eileen said.

'Why? Who needs lodgings?'

'Look, Amy, we need to talk. It's not really working out, is it... you, me and Jimmy sharing. It's just... me and Jimmy being newly-wed and all, we need our own space.'

'Is that you or Jimmy saying that?' Amy muttered.

Eileen flushed. Amy stalked away. Usually that was enough to shut Eileen up, so she was shocked when her cousin persisted.

'I'm away to see Morag this afternoon. I'll ask her then,' Eileen said firmly.

'Suit yourself,' Amy said. She tried to be calm and not to show how this had thrown her.

She didn't want to move out. She loved it here. Besides, Kiltie Street was tucked away near the canal where Ricky was unlikely to find her. She was determined to dig her heels in. Eileen and Jimmy couldn't force her to leave.

—

Over in Bridgeton, Morag found herself in an equally awkward situation. It was ten days since she and Ricky had abandoned all decency and made love. Except it hadn't been love; it had been pure animal lust. She regretted it. It didn't matter that she and George were barely speaking and that she didn't seem to be able to fix things between them. She was married. That was the point. She had betrayed her marriage and George.

She brushed her thick, dark brown hair and pinned it back in a victory roll. She carefully pulled on her lisle stockings. It wouldn't do to ladder them. They were hard to come by. She sighed a little. It was a long while since she'd had any new clothes. Rationing coupons had put paid to that. She did have a new apron, of course, courtesy of Eileen. She was looking forward to seeing her friend in the afternoon. George was barely at home these days so she had invited Eileen to the house instead of meeting out in a café.

But first... she had to go downstairs, where Ricky's smug grin and swaggering gait were waiting. He never said anything directly about what they had done. Yet he managed to remind her in small ways, nonetheless. A brush of his hand, his touch on her back. All so slight that George and Mr McLeod didn't notice. Morag was reluctant every morning to leave her room and face him. And it was all her own fault. She deserved it.

She put on her housecoat and picked up her stump of lipstick. Her fingers paused before it touched her lips. Slowly she twisted the lid back on and put the lipstick down. She didn't want Ricky thinking she was encouraging him. In the end, she went downstairs bare-faced, no powder or cream either.

'Mrs Kincaid, good morning. I wonder if I could have a moment of your time.' He was waiting for her at the bottom of the stairs.

'Of course, Mr Smith. How can I help you?' she said politely as Mr McLeod wandered past them with a good morning grunt and wave.

It was like a game of cat and mouse. Here they were pretending to be landlady and lodger as if they hadn't lain naked together, their moans and cries ringing out in the house. What if he tried to kiss her again? Morag knew she didn't want that. She looked at him now with no desire at all. There had been a madness in her that day. It frightened her. She'd lost control and now she was paying a heavy price.

'Shall we go into the kitchen? Mr McLeod is in residence in the dining room,' Ricky said smoothly.

He steered her into the kitchen, the fingers of one hand pressed to her shoulder blades. To anyone watching, it looked mannerly. For Morag, it seemed to hold a threat. She was being controlled in her own home, led into a room she owned by a man whose latent power was expressed in those strong fingertips pressing just a little too hard into her skin.

'I have a small problem, Mrs Kincaid,' Ricky said. 'I find myself a bit short for rent this week.'

If she had been simply the landlady, Morag would have said that it wasn't her problem and that she really had to have the right amount of rent paid up. As it was, she hesitated.

'You won't mind if I pay a reduced rent this month?' Ricky smiled.

'I can't...' The words tumbled from her mouth.

'Of course, I could ask Mr Kincaid instead.'

'No, that's all right. Pay what you can and please make it up next month.'

Morag tried to find her dignity and her rightful place in control as landlady. She guessed Ricky wasn't going to pay up next month either and there was nothing she could do about it. How was she going to tell George? She'd have to hide the fact there was less money. She kept a little book of incomings and outgoings, and George rarely asked to see it. He trusted her to balance her book. Now it was going to be another thing she was cheating him on.

Ricky grinned. 'That's sorted, then. Good girl.' He brushed past her, whistling.

Morag stood in her kitchen. Numbly, she got out a pot and the bag of oats and began to make breakfast. She moved in a daze, and continued so throughout the day, until Eileen arrived that afternoon.

'I'm glad to see you,' Morag said to her honestly.

'Are you all right? You look tired.' Eileen hugged her.

'I'm fine, really. Come through. Mr McLeod is out playing chess with his pals and my other lodger is out somewhere.'

Morag busied herself making ersatz coffee and offering up scones made with potato and sweetened with carrot.

'Sorry, I'm a wee bit low on ingredients, but these don't taste half bad.'

'Before I forget, you don't know of anyone looking for a lodger, do you? Only my cousin needs a place to stay.'

'Isn't she staying with you?' Morag frowned.

'It's become complicated,' Eileen sighed, setting down her half-eaten scone. 'Jimmy and Amy don't get along, and so I'm hoping if I find a good alternative, that Amy might agree to move out.'

'Oh dear. I see. I'd love to offer a room here, but we only have the two spares and no sign that either Mr McLeod or Mr Smith wants to move. More's the pity.'

Morag's hand went swiftly to her mouth in dismay. She hadn't meant to say that. But Eileen's eyebrows rose in surprise.

'Aren't you happy with them?'

'Can you keep a secret?' Morag asked.

'Of course I can. Is everything all right?'

'I've done something terrible, Eileen, and I don't know how to make it right.'

The whole story poured out, and as it did, Morag felt a weight lifting. Eileen's expression was sweet and concerned, and although she was afraid to see disgust on her friend's face, when she dared to look up again, Eileen only looked worried too.

'So you see, I'm in a right pickle, and it's all my own fault,' she finished quietly.

'Oh, Morag. You're only human. You made a mistake, but it sounds like you've been having an awful time. I wish you'd confided in me earlier about you and George. Still, what goes on inside a marriage is personal, as I know myself.'

'Are you and Jimmy having problems?'

Eileen shook her head. 'Nothing that can't be sorted. Anyway, this isn't about me. We're talking about you. What are you going to do about Mr Smith?'

Morag shrugged helplessly. 'I don't know. I want to ask him to leave but he has this power over me now. He'll tell George I was unfaithful. I've had to let him pay less rent.'

'It's blackmail, pure and simple,' Eileen gasped. 'Maybe you should confess to George. If you love each other, he'll forgive you. Then you can both get rid of Mr Smith.'

For a moment, Morag believed Eileen was right. Only, when she thought of how George was so glum and kept her frozen out of his life, she knew she couldn't. She really didn't know if he loved her any more. They were so far apart these days. How had it happened? She stifled a sob.

'Och, no. Come here,' Eileen cried and pulled her into a warm hug.

Morag wished she could stay there, safe in her friend's comforting embrace. The sound of the front door banging made her stiffen.

'He's back,' she whispered.

When Ricky came in, the two young women were drinking tea. Morag glanced up to say good morning, determined not to let him have the upper hand and saw he was staring at Eileen. Her friend was very pretty, but it wasn't the stare of a man who saw a woman he fancied.

It was more the look of a man who had seen a ghost.

Ricky couldn't believe his eyes. It was as if Amy was sitting in his landlady's kitchen. Only it wasn't her. This young woman was Amy's twin for looks, except she had blonde, curly hair instead of straight, light brown. She was curvier too. In a good way. In a different life, he'd definitely have gone for her. She was a right looker. But he had other things on his mind. He had to find Amy. His money was low, and then there was Alfie. Pearl swore she didn't know where the boy was. He'd searched her house anyway as she stood back, afraid of him, but Alfie wasn't there. So where had Amy hidden him?

After a polite exchange of greetings, he went into the dining room to wait. He was going to follow the blonde when she left. He had no idea if she was a relative of his wife or if it was a coincidence.

But with no other leads after all these months, he had nothing to lose by following her.

Chapter Fifteen

Eileen stayed with Morag for as long as possible, hoping to give her comfort and to shield her from her lodger. It was daft, really; she knew that. She couldn't solve her friend's problem, nor could she protect her. Morag's predicament continued to bother her as she walked back from Bridgeton through Glasgow Green.

It was a breezy late afternoon, and the iron poles on the Green were still full of people's washing, drying in the open air. Citizens of Glasgow had had the right to bring their washing from the tenements or the washhouses and let them dry in the open air at Glasgow Green since the fifteenth century. The poles were so busy today that some women had laid their clean, washed clothes flat on the ground to dry.

There were groups of women talking and laughing. Their hair was caught up in turbans and snoods, they wore wraparound housecoats or dresses and quite a number of them were smoking. What they had in common, Eileen realised, was their good humour as they waited for their washing to dry. They smiled at her as she passed. Glasgow had a reputation for friendly citizens, and it was well earned. People were generally good, she thought happily. But there were always a few bad apples. Morag's lodger being one example.

If only she could help. But how? Morag had slept with a man who was not her husband. Eileen ought to be shocked. Instead, she felt only compassion. How sad that Morag and George were drifting apart. When she'd met them at the parade in George Square, she had thought them a handsome couple. They had seemed to be in love with each other. Yet within the space of a few months, something terrible had happened and perhaps it couldn't be mended.

She couldn't imagine a rift between her and Jimmy. She loved him so much and she knew he loved her too. But Morag had talked so lovingly about George when Eileen first met her. Oh dear, life was complicated. Even without a war to make it more so. In some ways, the war had accelerated problems because it made life very intense. People wanted to be happy, to have experiences because life was short and could be taken away at any moment. It wasn't so long since the Glasgow and Clydebank blitz, which had destroyed so many lives and properties. One only had to pass by the bomb craters to be sombrely reminded of those two awful nights in March 1941 that had obliterated communities and sent folk fleeing to the hills outside the city.

Eileen caught a bus in the city centre out to Maryhill. She was quite unaware of the man following in her footsteps. He had waited while she wound her way through the throng of other women on the Green before following her. He boarded the same bus but made sure to sit at the back while she sat, unaware, at the front, next to a young woman with a wailing baby. He watched as she distracted the baby by offering a notebook to grab and chew.

I'll get some fish before I go home, Eileen decided. She had no idea whether Amy would cook or not. *I can make a fish pie and peas if there are any to be had. Maybe I should take over the cooking in any case. It's not fair on Amy to expect her to cook the tea every evening.*

She stopped at the fishmonger's, next to Heaney's butcher shop. The light was fading as she chose three coley fillets, always cheap, and waited for the cheerful fishmonger to wrap it in paper and ring up the bill. He winked at her as he passed it over.

'Anything for you, hen,' he said. 'Are you free for a wee dram the night?'

Eileen laughed and flashed her wedding ring. 'I'm a married woman now, Mr Benzie, so I am.'

'You'll hear me greetin' the night, so you will,' came the reply, using the Glasgow expression for crying.

'Och, you'll survive. There's plenty of pretty lassies to choose from.' Eileen grinned.

She put the fish fillets carefully into her bag and left the shop. It had started to rain, and she shivered. Darkness had fallen while she was in there and now she could hardly see her way. The so-called 'dim-out' wasn't so much better than the full blackout and formed shadows of the buildings and trees as she hurried towards home.

Suddenly the rain pelted down, hard and cold. Eileen shrieked. She ran towards the nearest bomb shelter. It was a low brick building with an entrance and exit. Normally she avoided it because it smelled of urine and damp. But tonight, with the rain ever increasing, she stumbled inside, her heart beating fast from running. Rain trickled from her scalp down onto her nose and dripped off her chin. She wiped the moistness away with her sleeve. The rain drummed down on the shelter roof.

In the darkness, Eileen felt a prickle of unease. Was there someone else in the shelter with her?

'Hello? Is there someone there?' she called out. 'Show yourself.'

Her heart pounded. The shelter was thick black, like treacle unstirred. Yet something primitive in her responded to danger. Eileen felt, rather than saw, another presence. Tiny hairs on her neck stood up.

'Show yourself,' she repeated. She clutched her bag at her chest to ward off attack.

When all was silent, Eileen dashed out of the shelter with a scream. She ran up the road and turned left into Kiltie Street with relief. But she didn't feel safe until she had clattered up the stone steps and hammered on the door of number four.

Amy let her in with a look that said she was mad. Eileen gasped for air, her chest heaving. The bag, with its precious parcel of fish, slid from her grasp to land on the floor.

'Whatever's the matter with you?' Amy said.

'Nothing,' Eileen managed, before her legs gave way and she kneeled on the cold linoleum. 'Nothing at all.'

—

'I still think there's summat the matter wi' you,' Amy said suspiciously as the three of them sat at the dinner table.

'It's fine. I was simply running to get out of the rain,' Eileen lied.

She felt foolish now that she was in her home. Her imagination had run riot, that was all. She'd been alone in the shelter, but the darkness had scared her. Jimmy touched her hand.

'You're sure you're all right, doll?'

'Honestly, I said I'm fine. Stop going on about it,' Eileen snapped.

There was a moment of frosty silence broken only by the clink of Jimmy's knife as he set it down on his plate.

'I'm sorry,' Eileen said. 'I didn't mean to be angry. I'm glad I've got the both of you caring about me, but nothing happened, and I'd like to forget about it and concentrate on eating.'

'Aye, it's a grand bit of fish. Well cooked.' Jimmy winked as he stroked her hand.

'A sauce might have been nice,' Amy remarked, turning her own fillet suspiciously with her fork.

Eileen rolled her eyes. It was on the tip of her tongue to say that if Amy wanted fish sauce, perhaps she ought to cook the meal, but she held back. The rest of the evening went by peacefully enough. The rain outside hammered down, making the flat feel cosy. Jimmy smoked steadily as he sat beside the wireless listening to the news. Amy read a magazine at the kitchen table, elbows on the table, hands propping up her chin. Eileen got out her sewing box, but her mind kept returning to the dark shelter. Had she been alone there?

The next few days passed without incident and spring rolled cautiously in with the beginning of March. Eileen felt as if she should be more cheerful. The newspapers gave hope that the war should soon be over. She read that Allied planes had continued the intensive bombing of German transport and industrial centres in Berlin. And that Soviet armies had 'gone over to a grand attack' all along the southern front in East Prussia. At the bottom of the page was a recipe for mock cutlets made out of haricot beans, which was a far more cheerful topic. She had the curry powder, dried eggs, flour and dripping, so decided she'd make it for their evening meal.

'Where are my bloody fags? I bet she's hidden them again.' Jimmy's bellow came from the bedroom.

'Amy's gone out,' Eileen called. Her hands were covered in breadcrumbs as she moulded the mock cutlets into what she hoped looked like pork chops.

She prayed that Amy was out looking for lodgings. She'd offered to put an advert in the newspaper, but her cousin had ignored that. The atmosphere in the flat veered from a fragile peace to outright war most days.

'I can't find them.' Jimmy came in. His hands were shaking. 'I need a smoke.'

'Let me look. You have a seat,' Eileen soothed. She rinsed her hands at the sink.

She went round the flat, looking under their bed and between the pillows, moving magazines and bowls on the kitchen table. She hesitated, then pulled back the curtains on Amy's recess bed in the wall. Amy's bedclothes were rumpled and messy. On her pillow was a pack of Player's. Jimmy's cigarettes. Amy didn't smoke as far as Eileen knew. She paused. If she gave them to Jimmy, he'd have a smoke and calm down. But if he saw where she'd found them, he'd be furious.

She whipped the packet into her apron pocket and went back into her own bedroom, pretending still to look for them. A few minutes later, she went back and put them on the table in front of him.

'There you go. They were on our bed. You must've missed them.'

'I could've sworn they weren't there,' Jimmy murmured, flicking a cigarette out and lighting up.

Thinking that was the last of that, Eileen went on happily making the tea and setting the cutlets aside in a covered dish for later. She kissed Jimmy before going out to her shift.

'What will you do today?' she asked, forcing brightness into her voice.

'Usual. I'll go and see Mammy. Maybe I'll hang out with the lads, see if there's work going anywhere.'

'We could use some money coming in,' Eileen said cautiously. 'Your army pension doesn't go far.'

'We've got enough to get by, haven't we?' Jimmy said, putting on his thick coat and cap.

'Only because your mammy and mine help us out with a wee bit of food here and there. And we've got Amy's rations too.'

He didn't answer that. They walked out of the flat together and he pressed a kiss to her lips as they parted. She watched his stiff-legged gait as he went towards number four and let out a sigh. She was sick of the war, as everyone was. People's faces were drawn and grey and tired. Glasgow itself was shabby and worn, covered in scars from the bombings and almost six long years of making do. But Eileen wondered what would happen to her and Jimmy after the war. Would it be any better? Their dreams of a wee house with its own garden and maybe children wouldn't come true without some money coming in.

—

'I reckon I could make a living by being a seamstress after the war,' Eileen confided in Morag at the break.

They leaned against the wall with groups of the other women spaced out. Faces turned up to the watery sunlight in the hope of a bit of warmth.

'But what can Jimmy do? Who's going to take on a man with weak, damaged limbs and poor eyesight?'

'Something will turn up,' Morag said. 'He won't be the only man returning from war with injuries. Employers will have to make adjustments.'

'I hadn't thought of that,' Eileen cried. 'That's worse. He'll be up against so many others.'

'Och, I didn't mean to make it worse for you,' Morag said. 'There'll be jobs. You wait and see, they'll kick us women out of our jobs and give them back to the men.'

'That's no solution either.'

'Life's not fair.'

The two friends let that sink in while they shared a flask of tea that Morag had brought. Around them, the other women also ate their pieces in the short lunch hour they had.

'Anyway, enough of my moans. How are things with you?' Eileen asked meaningfully.

'It's all very quiet. Mr Smith is hardly in the house. When he is, he barely speaks to me or George or Mr McLeod. He goes up to his room or, after the evening meal, he goes out again. It's most mysterious, but I'm just glad he's not bothering me.'

'And George? Will you tell him?' Eileen whispered, although no one else was listening to their conversation and the raucous laughter from the next group would have drowned out their words in any case.

The bell sounded and the women began to drift back into the factory.

'Let sleeping dogs lie,' Morag told Eileen as they entered the building. 'That's my new philosophy. I've done George a terrible wrong, but confessing isn't going to help. Now, I just wish I could mend my marriage but don't know how to begin.'

Eileen heard the shouting before she got inside her flat. The neighbour across the way came out and indicated with a nod of her head.

'They've been at that for a wee while, Eileen, hen. My man's no' too happy. Wants quiet to listen to the wireless after a hard day's work. Will you sort it out?'

'I'm so sorry. I'll tell them to keep the noise down,' Eileen said, scrabbling for her keys in her bag.

She winced as she entered the hallway and shut the door firmly so that her neighbours didn't get the full blast of the angry voices. Two flushed faces turned to her as she struggled to get her coat off while they both sought her backing for their argument.

'She's a bloody liar!' Jimmy roared. 'She knows she took my fags and now she's gone and stolen my book what my pal lent me about railways.'

'I never took your bloody book. What would I want with a boring old book about trains?' Amy screamed. 'You're blaming me cos you bloomin' hate me. That's what.'

'Aye, I do hate ye. Put that in yer hat and eat it.'

'Will you calm down, please, both of you,' Eileen pleaded.

Neither of them heard her as they glared at one another. Eileen ran into the bedroom. Jimmy's book wasn't in sight. She went back out onto the landing and stood there for a moment. It was draughty and she shivered. She pushed open the door to the shared toilet and let out a sigh of relief. Jimmy's book was on the narrow shelf next to the newspaper squares. Luckily, no one had decided to tear out a page for personal use. She grinned at that.

'There's your book.' She gave it to Jimmy, who looked momentarily shame-faced.

He mumbled his thanks, body-swerved Amy, and they heard the sound of the wireless being tuned in the kitchen.

'He needn't think he's got that room to himself,' Amy said indignantly. 'I've got dinner to prepare. Not even a bloody apology from his nibs. As if I'd take his smelly old book.'

Eileen hoped for a truce. It seemed as if her prayers were answered when they eventually sat down for their tea. Amy had fried up the mock cutlets, telling Eileen she could manage by herself. She was bristling, so Eileen left her to it. She'd have to tell Jimmy to apologise to Amy before bedtime or there'd be a terrible atmosphere the next day too. The problem was, she could see by Jimmy's clenched jaw that he wasn't ready to do so.

She took a mouthful of her mock cutlet and gagged. It was disgusting. She'd forgotten to add any salt or curry powder and the whole thing tasted of sawdust. Ruefully, she had another bite. They couldn't throw food out, so it had to be eaten.

'This is absolutely vile.' Amy spat hers out and shoved her plate away with a grimace. 'What did you do to it, Eileen? Surely even you can cook summat that simple.'

'Don't you speak to her like that, missy.' Jimmy jumped up with rage. 'Say sorry right now. You're living in *our* house, at *our* table, so mind your manners.'

'I will not say sorry for the truth.' Amy jumped up too and glared at him. 'You can apologise to me first for saying I stole your belongings.'

'You know you did. Took my fags, didn't you, to wind me up.'

'You smoke too much anyway. Makes the flat stink.'

'Right, that's it. Out you go and don't come back,' Jimmy snarled, pointing to the hallway. 'I've had enough of your cheek.'

Jimmy sprang out of his chair, and Amy's face was red with anger. Eileen followed them, worried. By this time, all three were in the hallway, almost at the front door.

'Och, no, Jimmy. Please… don't make her go. Don't do this. It's not worth it. We can all live together. She's my cousin after all. Jimmy!'

She hammered on his back as he flung open the front door. Amy shook her head and refused to budge from the hall. Jimmy looked suddenly older to Eileen's concerned gaze.

'If she won't go, then I will. I cannae take it any longer. Until you decide who ye want living with ye, I'm away tae Mammy's.'

'Jimmy, please. Amy's got nowhere to go. I can't just throw her out. Shall we go back in and sit and talk about it? Please…'

Jimmy stared at her and shook his head. He looked so utterly sad that Eileen almost pushed Amy out onto the landing herself. Anything so that Jimmy didn't look at her that way. But how was she to choose? It wasn't fair. Morag was right. Life wasn't fair. She wanted both her husband and her cousin to have a place to live with her. Why was that so impossible?

Before she could make another move, Jimmy rammed his cap onto his head and ran down the stairs. The clatter of his boots echoed in her head until they too disappeared. Eileen stifled a sob and turned blindly back into her flat. She shut the door slowly, hardly believing what had just happened.

'He'll come round. Course 'e will. You'll see. Give it a day and he'll be back wanting yer cuddles,' Amy said.

But Eileen knew in her guts that Jimmy wouldn't be back. He was a proud man. Unless she got rid of Amy, he wasn't going to change his mind. She wiped the tears from her eyes. Once again, Eileen was alone with Amy. And completely lost.

Amy hummed a little tune as she got dressed the next day. She put on Eileen's brown skirt and a cream blouse that Eileen had altered from the suitcase trove. It was meant for herself, but Amy knew her cousin didn't mind sharing. Lovely it was too, with a big bow at the neck and pearly buttons down the front. She had a pair of stockings that she'd nicked from the WVS pile when no one was watching so she slid those on, feeling the cool, smooth, delicious texture next to her skin.

Leo had invited her to lunch. She hoped it was somewhere posh since she'd made such an effort to look pretty. It was nice in the flat without Jimmy. She could leave her stuff about without him commenting. She'd made a real effort to cheer Eileen up. Eileen was moping, which did no one any good. Besides, Jimmy was only down the road. She could visit him there. In a few weeks' time, maybe Amy would move her bed back into the main bedroom wall recess. She set her hat on her carefully curled and bleached hair and stepped back to admire the results. Leo wouldn't be embarrassed to be seen out with her, she reckoned, blowing herself a kiss in the mirror.

He took her to lunch at Kelly's in the city centre. Amy's gaze widened at the crisp white linen tablecloths and silver napkin rings and the ivory-handled cutlery, but she smiled confidently as if she dined thus every day of her life. She let Leo guide her in and pull out a chair for her. She smoothed her skirt and placed a giant linen napkin over her knees. She watched the other diners and Leo for clues as to how to act. She didn't want to admit this was the poshest place she'd ever been.

The first course was consommé. She hadn't a clue what that was but nodded when Leo asked if he should order it. When it arrived, it wasn't more than watery stock. And tasted like it. Amy wasn't impressed. Still, the chicken and veg that followed was tasty and she liked the fawning of the waiter and Leo's brusque manner of dealing with him. Dessert turned out to be custard but quite fancy, with a bit of whipped cream decorating it. She hadn't tasted cream since before the war. She sighed contentedly.

'Happy, my dear?' Leo said, patting her knee as if they were a married couple.

They sort of were a married couple, Amy thought dreamily, on her full stomach. After all, he wasn't taking that Alice out to lunch, was he? She knew better than to ask after Leo's wife but wondered how ill Alice was. If only she'd have the decency to fade away, leaving Leo a widower. Amy was right there, ready to step into Alice's shoes.

'Shall we go back to my house after coffee? Or shall we take a little walk first?' Leo said, crooking a finger to bring the waiter back.

Amy had seen the waiters bringing silver coffeepots to tables and was pleased to think they'd get their own very soon, along with the dainty cups and saucers she could see nearby painted with tiny pink flowers. Lovely. All of it was simply lovely.

'Eh? What's that?' she said, not having heard a word that Leo said. 'I meant, pardon?'

He repeated his question with an edge of impatience. Amy drank her coffee. She didn't want to go back to his house. There was the bitter sister for a start. There was also possibly Leo's wandering hands. She wanted to keep him keen and that meant keeping him interested with no more than tiny tasters of what he might enjoy once they got engaged.

'A walk might be pleasant,' she said in her best accent.

They walked down towards the river, Amy's arm in the crook of Leo's. Trams went by, along with the occasional horse and cart. It was busy in the city centre, but the crowds thinned towards the Broomielaw and the edge of the River Clyde. They admired the boats and the bridges crossing the water to join the south side of the city.

'I could get used to this,' Amy sighed, patting her stomach and thinking of Kelly's.

'And perhaps you will,' Leo said, glancing at her with his flat, black eyes that gave nothing away. 'We'll see.'

What did that mean? She guessed he wanted to keep her unsettled. He liked to be in control. Men did. Ricky was just the same. Except he used physical strength to keep Amy in order, as he put it. Leo's method was more about mind games. Amy smiled up at him. Two could play at that. He needn't think he was getting it all his own way.

'Yes, we'll see, won't we. I'm not sure when I can get away again. I've got me cousin always at me to 'elp in the house, and I'm working at the crèche. Still, you've got your own hours to put in at the railways, I suppose.'

Leo's lips pursed thoughtfully. 'Next time, I'll invite you to the house. My sister Sarah is a good housekeeper and will make us a meal.'

So she'd have to dance around that and make it work. Keep him interested but out of the bedroom. Ah well. They were walking back now up the Saltmarket. She shivered. What if Ricky came out of the fish market right now and saw her? A thrill of fear verging on excitement ran up Amy's spine. It made life sharper, more focused. Surely, she was safe. How could Ricky possibly find her in a city of a million souls?

Chapter Sixteen

'Oh, the poor thing,' Eileen exclaimed. 'It's broken its neck.'

She and Amy stared at the blackbird. Its eye was dulled, and its head lay at an odd angle to the body and wings. A few stray feathers lay on the doormat too.

'Why's it 'ere? It can't 'ave flown up all them stairs,' Amy said. She stepped forward, glancing around the landing as if expecting a whole flock of birds to suddenly appear.

'Probably Snowy has dragged it up as a gift. You know what he's like for sharing mice with us.'

'I never thought of that.' Amy laughed. 'That's what it is. Old Snowy up to his tricks. I thought for a moment...'

'What *did* you think?' Eileen asked. 'You looked worried. Look, Amy, I know you've got secrets. I read Pearl's letter that time.' The words were out of her mouth before she'd realised, and her heart hammered then, waiting for her cousin's reaction.

'You never did!' Amy said indignantly. 'You had no bloody right. How dare you!' she steamed on.

'I shouldn't have, and it was wrong, but you've kept everything close to your chest since you arrived here.' Eileen desperately tried to explain. 'You never answered any of my questions about your family or your life in London. I suppose I hoped it would give me some answers. Instead, it gave me more questions. Who is Ricky? Pearl said he'd gone, and it sounded like he was looking for you. Tell me, *please*.'

'I don't know what you're talking about. Let's go back inside and get the coal shovel. We can't leave this thing 'ere.'

Eileen could tell from Amy's shut expression that she wasn't going to share. What was it Amy had thought for a moment? She'd looked really scared. Eileen sighed. Her cousin was as stubborn as they come.

'Did you go and see Mrs Margolis about her room to let?' she said, changing the subject.

If she knew Amy at all, whatever she would share would come when she was ready and not before.

Amy shook her head. 'I haven't had time, have I. What with the crèche and the WVS stuff you wanted me to do.'

'Och, Amy. You have to find somewhere else. I'm really sorry, but we've talked about this. Jimmy's my husband, and it's only right and proper that him and me are together. It's a shame you two don't get on, but I'll help you find somewhere nice if you don't want to go back to London. Although I don't understand why you can't stay with Pearl or Norman?'

'I don't mind if 'e comes back. It's him wot's causing the problem, not me.' Amy shrugged.

'I don't want to argue again,' Eileen said softly. 'Please, have a look about. Morag gave me a wee list of possible lodgings today at work, so I'll pass that to you. There's bound to be something suitable.'

Amy rolled her eyes, showing her frustration. 'All right, all right. Keep your hair on. I'll go and see some. Anyway, got to rush. Leo's invited me over to hear his new gramophone record.'

'Is that wise? You know the neighbours like to gossip. It's not seemly, you and him like that when he's got a wife.' Eileen sounded prim to herself.

'As if I care about a few old trouts letting out hot air. There's nothing wrong with me visiting a friend. Besides, Leo's sisters are there acting as chaperones.' She stepped gingerly over the dead bird and towards the stairs.

Eileen watched her go, somewhat mollified. It was true; if the two older sisters were there, it was hardly likely that anything unsuitable was going on. Still, she wondered why Amy was fixed on Leo. He was older, not very attractive in Eileen's opinion, and gave her the creeps to be quite frank. What did Amy see in him?

After dealing with the corpse, she grabbed her own coat and headed over to number four.

'Is he in?' she asked Mary, who answered the door with a sympathetic smile.

'Aye, he is. Just had his tea, so he has, and he's in the parlour discussing the war with Harry. In you go, love.'

Eileen hesitated. 'Mary… is there any chance he's coming home with me?'

'I've spoken to him, and I've told him his place is at home with his wife,' Mary said. 'But he won't budge until that cousin of yours is gone. That's his words, not mine, love. If you want my advice, you get rid of Amy. Send her back to her own home and her own folks. Then Jimmy'll be back. I'll make sure of it.'

'Can't you send him home now?' Eileen asked desperately.

Mary's kind face wrinkled as she looked at her daughter-in-law. 'Honest to God, I'd like to, but then I think of all those months in hospital and how frail he was, and I wonder if I push him too hard… if we push him between us both... what will happen? Will he get sick again? I don't want to have that on my conscience. He's my son as much as he's your husband.'

Eileen was envious when she went into Mary's neat parlour and saw Jimmy sprawled on the sofa, his arms animated as he argued with Harry. The British and American troops had crossed the Rhine the day before and the two men were betting on when the last day of the war was going to be. Neither noticed Eileen at the door.

'Not a chance.' Jimmy laughed. 'I'll bet you a shilling it's over before the month is out. Stands to reason. They'll be in Berlin, shoot Herr Hitler, and once he's down, the other Nazis will be begging to surrender.'

'Ever the optimist.' Harry grinned. 'No, my lad, I'm telling you. We've a tough few months ahead yet. Remember, every year for the past five years, we said it'll be over by Christmas. Well, this year maybe that'll be true, but I guess we might see another autumn of warfare before there's peace. Don't forget the Japanese and the Americans are fighting in other far-flung places too.'

Harry glanced up and saw Eileen. He struggled to his feet from the softly cushioned armchair. 'I'll leave you two alone now.' He pressed Eileen's shoulder gently as he passed.

'How are you?' she said, once they were alone. She sat in Harry's vacated seat.

'Give me a kiss, darling.' Jimmy went over to her and kissed her thoroughly. 'I love you, doll. You know that.'

'Aye, Jimmy. I do know that. So why are you staying away from me?' Eileen burst out.

He flushed and looked away before turning his gaze back. 'Is she gone?'

'Not yet. She's promised to look at lodgings soon.'

He made a noise of disgust in the back of his throat. 'Aye, soon. Whatever that means.'

'Look, does it matter? Come back with me tonight. Please. I miss you.'

She craved his touch, his warmth in bed, their lovemaking and his tenderness. Didn't he miss all that too? That awful loneliness that had inhabited her all her life, the loneliness that had evaporated when she fell in love with Jimmy and got married, was edging back in. It created a hollow in her very centre, and she was afraid of it.

'See, the thing is,' Jimmy said carefully, taking her hands, 'I don't trust myself around Amy.'

'What do you mean?' Eileen asked. She felt the familiar rough calluses on his fingers, the warmth soaking into her fingertips from his and the awareness and desire that his closeness caused.

'I was that angry. I was spitting nails,' he said slowly. 'I was mad at her, and I frightened myself. So, you see, I can't come home until she's gone.'

'So, you're leaving me,' Eileen said, standing up.

'No, doll. Never that.' Jimmy jumped up too. 'Once she's away in her new lodgings, I'll move back. At the moment, Mammy's feeding me fine so don't go worrying about me. And you call me if you need me. For lifting or whatever...' He trailed away.

They both knew she wasn't going to call for that. His weak arm meant he couldn't lift much, and he felt dizzy if he exerted himself. Eileen was scared his sight would go again if he tried too hard. Instead, she and Amy had done the lifting of the coal bucket and the baskets of wet washing.

'I'll be seeing you,' she said, kissing his lips and having to tear herself away.

'Aye, soon as can be,' came the reply.

Eileen hurried out into the evening air, avoiding Mary and Harry's sympathetic gazes, tears too close to the surface. She held them in until she got home.

—

A week after the dead bird, Amy came home to find a trail of dried rose petals leading up to the front door. Her heart pounded and she felt sick. It had to be Ricky. He was playing with her, taunting her. Only Ricky knew that roses were her favourite flower. She picked up the scattered petals and held them to her nose. There was a faint scent, but they crumbled in her fingers. They were old, brown-tinged and rotting.

She should move out. Only if she did and he was watching her, she'd be quite alone when he came to confront her. Of course he'd come at some point. Much better to be here with Eileen. Even better if Jimmy was here. Oh, the irony. She'd spent so much time wishing he'd vanish so she could have Eileen and the flat to herself. Now, here she was wishing him back. Safety in numbers. Ricky was a big powerfully built man, though, while Jimmy was slender and not much taller than her or Eileen. It wasn't likely to be an even match.

Snowy shot out as she opened the flat door.

'Don't you be long out there,' she called after him. 'It ain't safe.'

That was true. The darkness held terrors, if only for her. Her gaze darted about but saw nothing. She slammed the door shut and leaned against it on the inside, her breath making her chest heave.

'That you, Amy? Did you get a cabbage?' Eileen called.

'Yeah, course I did.'

Amy's fears subsided at the homely gesture of removing the cabbage from her string bag and handing it over. It was Eileen's turn to cook. Tonight's dish was bubble and squeak. There was a tiny, chopped onion on a plate and a bowl of mash. A bit of salt and dripping to fry it in and there was a delicious meal. Amy instructed Eileen in the simple meal, crowding out her thoughts, which were none too happy.

There was a scratching at the door. Amy clutched Eileen's arm convulsively.

'What are you doing? It's Snowy. Go and let him in, will you. My hands are covered in grease,' Eileen said.

Cautiously, Amy approached the door. She listened, her ear pressed to the wood. Out of the corner of her eye, she saw Eileen, hands on hips, at the entrance to the kitchen, staring at her and shaking her head. A faint mew came from the landing. She opened the door and Snowy scampered in. Amy shut it quickly.

'You're like a cat on a hot roof. Snowy's got nothing on you,' Eileen remarked. 'Whatever's the matter?'

'Nothing. Is dinner ready?'

—

After the blackbird and the rose petals, there were no more portents. Until a week later when Amy came home from the crèche. Amy's imagination had calmed, and she had begun to believe that the bird was one of Snowy's catches and that the petals had fallen from a bouquet bought by the neighbour opposite. Never mind how she'd managed to buy them in this time of shortages. There was always the black market.

There was an envelope pushed under the door. Amy crouched to retrieve it. Another of Pearl's letters, she thought, sliding her finger under the flap, although Agnes had clearly left this one in person as there was no address written on it. Pearl wasn't a good correspondent or a regular writer, but she sent occasional short notes about Alfie, and the Boyles redirected them without complaint to Eileen's home. It was the closest Amy could get to her son.

Only it wasn't Pearl's handwriting. In fact, the postcard inside the envelope didn't have any writing on it at all. Amy's brows knitted together as she turned it over to see the picture. It was of Buckingham Palace. It couldn't have been any clearer than if Ricky had materialised beside her and admitted it was him. Amy scooted inside in case he did appear. She was edgy because she had no idea what he was going to do next.

—

Ricky grinned to himself as he pushed the postcard into the envelope. He wanted to scare Amy a little more before he made his move. It had been a lucky day for him when Morag's pal had come to visit her. She was a pretty girl, and he'd enjoyed following her through the darkening streets. Her hips swayed in that natural way women's do, and her golden hair bounced attractively with each step she took. In another place and time, he'd have been interested. But he wanted to find his wife.

As the raindrops began to fall, he'd nipped inside the bomb shelter. He had overtaken her by going round the side into the second entrance so that he stood in the darkest spot and heard her enter. It was so dark he couldn't see a thing and knew that neither could she. She had sensed him, though. Calling out if someone was there before rushing out into the rain. It had been amusing. Although it was Amy he wanted to scare. If she screamed and ran, it would serve her right.

He'd continued to follow at a distance. Her figure became less clear as night fell but he saw her stop at a tenement and run up the steps. After that it was easy. He simply went home and returned the next morning. There were convenient trees and shrubs opposite the tenements beyond a muddy patch of grass with a single bench. He hid in the trees and watched. Sooner or later, he'd see Amy. He was sure of it. And then there she was. Trotting down the stone steps as if she hadn't a care in the world. She had a new hat and clothes, and she'd changed her hair. Strangely, it was now blonde and curly, just like the other girl's. He didn't bother to ponder that. It was enough that he'd found his erstwhile wife. And where there was Amy, there was his cash. And his son.

He posted the envelope when he knew no one was home. Amy worked at another tenement where women and children came and went. Was Alfie there? He didn't know. His priority was punishing Amy and getting the money. He'd worry about Alfie after that. But he was certain he was taking his son back with him. Unless that bitch, Pearl, did have Alfie after all. She had denied it, and he hadn't found him in her house, but it was possible she had hidden him. Wouldn't Alfie cry out for his old dad? Ricky's mouth twisted. Maybe not. Amy had poisoned their son against him. Of course he'd never hit the boy. Alfie was his. To be moulded in his own way. To grow up just like him.

He wished he could see Amy's face when she saw the postcard. That would put the wind up her, as he intended. He wanted her to know he was coming. He whistled, hands in pockets, as he walked back through the city. He couldn't afford the tram or bus, but he didn't care. Soon, he'd have enough once he got his savings back. Amy bleated about how it was their savings, but she'd done nothing to earn it. She and Alfie spent it all right on food and coal, but it was his by rights. He'd stashed it away against a rainy day and given Amy enough to keep their household going.

It took him two hours to walk from Maryhill to Bridgeton,. He was full of restless energy, fuelled by thoughts of Amy and what he'd do and say to her. He went into his lodgings to plan it out. The doddery old fool who rented the other room was out, or at least not in the parlour where he was usually rooted. There was no sign of the lovely Mrs Kincaid either. Ahh, he'd enjoyed their little affair. She had avoided him afterwards, and he couldn't be bothered pursuing her, but it had been a pleasant interlude. Handy too, when he ran out money for the rent. The flickering in her dark eyes had amused him. They both knew what he could tell the husband if she didn't agree. It was quite useful. There would be other reasons, no doubt, when he needed to get his own way, and dear little Morag would have to oblige.

'Is that you, Mr Smith?' A belligerent voice came behind him.

It was the husband. Ricky hadn't expected him to be home. He rarely was, and didn't say much when he was in residence.

'Mr Kincaid. How can I help you?' Ricky put on his most charming tone.

'You can help me by stepping out into the back court. I've got something to say to you.' The man was shaking and his face infused with red colour.

'All right. Let's step outside.'

Ricky wasn't worried. He was a half foot taller and a lot broader than George Kincaid. Whatever was coming, he was going to win.

Chapter Seventeen

The back garden had a high brick wall surrounding it, with a green wooden gate for entry and exit to a cobbled lane that ran behind the houses in the row. It wasn't overlooked except for a side window from next door, but that was shuttered. It was a private place for a dispute, so no wonder George Kincaid had led them out there.

Ricky felt a laugh bubbling up. The man in front of him was literally dancing with rage. His heels lifted and slapped against the stone slabs and George's hands were balled in a pugilistic stance.

'I've seen the way you look at her. Did you touch her? Did you?' George's voice was shrill.

'Who?' Ricky said lazily.

'My wife, that's who. You know fine well I'm talking about Morag.'

Ricky thought about denying it. After all, it was finished, and he had other things on his mind, namely his own errant wife. But the man was irritating. It would do him good to hear a few home truths.

'It wasn't as if *you* were touching her. Poor girl practically fell into my arms, asking for it.' His arrogance oozed from him.

'Why, you...' George growled. He lunged towards Ricky, flailing his arms, trying to land a blow.

Ricky deflected him easily. He'd been an amateur boxer in his younger days. He'd made a few bob in the clubs in London. He moved easily out of reach of George's swings. George was shouting, but Ricky didn't listen. The other man might be shorter and with less muscle, but his fists could still sting. He concentrated on his moves, feeling it all coming back with muscle memory. You didn't forget the wins. The adrenaline high as the referee lifted your arm and the crowd roared. You didn't forget losing either when the stiffness of bruising and injury mingled with your shame and that need for revenge fuelled the next glorious round. The money hadn't been half bad either.

'Can't get your own woman, is that it?' George yelled. 'Left you, did she, you piece of shite.'

That cut deep. Ricky felt his own anger rise, mixed with an image of Amy raiding his box, which he'd hidden under the floorboards, believing it safe. Thinking of Amy taking Alfie and sneaking away in the night like the thief she was.

He gave a great bellow and landed a single punch to George's jaw. George dropped to the ground and lay still. Ricky saw a trickle of blood run from behind the man's ear to stain the damp slab. He fled.

—

The noise of the sewing machines hurt Morag's ears. The motion of guiding the material through and the constant bobbing of the needle up and down was making her feel queasy. The whole room was full of movement. The women's heads were bent over their machines, pale necks exposed under snoods and turbans and pinned rolls of hair all tidied away to prevent accidents. Beside her, Eileen was concentrating on her sewing, her foot pumping rhythmically and fast. She must have sensed Morag's glance because she returned it with a brief flash of a smile before returning to her task.

Even the smell of the fabric was off-putting. Why was it so sharp and unpleasant? Why hadn't she ever noticed the odour before? She stifled an acid burp with the back of her hand but felt the nausea roll up through her stomach and into her chest. Morag stumbled away from her position and ran out of the room. The supervisor called, and she vaguely heard Eileen saying that Morag wasn't well. She made it outside and threw up in the grass. She retched until her guts were hollow and empty. With a groan, she walked away round the side of the factory so she was out of sight of the vomit.

Morag cradled her belly. She stared out at the Green. It was so flat, all the way from the factory to the River Clyde. Mostly it was lawns with flowerbeds. The flowerbeds were black soil so early in the season and the flower displays had been replaced a couple of years before with vegetables. The river was fringed with trees, but through their leafless branches, the great brown flow of the river was visible.

She began to walk down the path that led to the riverside. She didn't care who saw her. The supervisor was a kind woman, and in any case, she wasn't going to want a sick worker throwing up all over the army fabric. Production had to continue at a fast pace. There were always efficiency drives. As if they could work any faster than they already did.

Her monthly visitor hadn't arrived in the weeks after she and Ricky… Morag shied away from saying it, even in her head. No, she had to be honest now. This baby that was growing inside her was the result of her infidelity. 'I'm pregnant,' she whispered to herself.

There, she'd said it. So how did she feel? Morag gave a strangled cry to the wind that was half joy and half regret. She was at the very edge of the river now, standing on the path with the big tree trunks to each side. The water churned and roiled with the current, the colour of tea splashed with milk.

It smelled of brine, being tidal up to the weir. It stank of chemicals from the factories on the other bank and the flotsam floating past included crates and sticks, bottles and dead fish. Weird then that she didn't feel sick any more. She even enjoyed the breeze that ruffled her hair, coming across the water.

She didn't know how she felt about the baby. She had wanted one so dearly. But she had wanted a baby that was hers and George's, made from love. A child that they wanted to bring up and care for together. Her miscarriage and George's awful reaction had spoiled that dream. Now, here she was, expecting another man's baby. What was she going to do?

Morag wandered the Green without noticing how long she was there. No matter how she thought it through, she could see no solution to her dilemma. She ought to be thrilled she was having a baby, but it was all so complicated. If George reacted so badly to their own pregnancy, how was he going to react to her news now?

Eventually, the drizzle started up and Morag shivered. She felt quite tired now and a little bit hungry. There was nothing in her stomach and her nausea had passed. She had to go home. Where else was she to go? She had to face her husband at some point. Her watch told her it was six p.m. George would be home expecting his tea. In the last couple of weeks, he had been home more. Instead of disappearing out to the men's working club, he'd stayed in reading the papers and listening to the wireless with Mr McLeod the way he used to. She hadn't asked him why. It was difficult to have a conversation at all with him. They were stilted with each other.

She couldn't put it off any longer. Drawing her collar up against the rain, Morag walked steadily from the Green along the London Road. Spray from the buses dampened her skirt. A coal merchant passed by, his old Clydesdale horse, with its coat steaming with the heat of its body and the cold rain, pulling at the cart full of hessian sacks. Her breasts tingled painfully where they brushed against her bra, and her mouth tasted metallic. She knew from friends that these were early good signs that a pregnancy was secure, but she no longer knew if she was happy or sad about it.

She let herself into the house and stood for a moment in the hall, listening. The house creaked a little, as old houses do, but apart from that, there were no sounds to indicate that anyone was home. Mr McLeod was away visiting an old friend for a few days, so she didn't expect him to be there, but she was greatly relieved that Ricky Smith was absent. What would he do if he knew Morag was having a baby? His baby. He might vanish, which would be a great relief. But what if he demanded to play a part in her baby's life? Morag clutched her tummy in horror. She'd never get rid of him then.

There was no sign of George. When he was home, he was very punctual about meal times. He liked his tea on the table at six p.m. promptly. Morag was already too late to manage that. The stew was in a covered dish in the pantry. All she had to do was heat it up. He wasn't in the dining room, at the table, impatiently holding his cutlery. How odd. She put the stew in a pan on the range and rustled up three plates, assuming that their horrible lodger was going to want to eat too.

When no one turned up in the dining room, Morag left the neatly laid table and took the stew off the heat. She put a pan lid on and shrugged helplessly. She went upstairs, intending to go into the bedroom and brush her hair. Instead, she found herself turning the other way and opening the carved wooden chest that held the baby clothes. The familiar waft of mothballs was oddly comforting. She lifted the blanket and took out the linen bag. From it, she spread the tiny outfits onto the landing carpet. If her baby was a boy, he'd wear the wee sailor suit. If it was a girl, the pink dress. Whatever it was, boy or girl, it was surely going to wear the white christening robe and get use out of the pale yellow shirt. She gathered the clothes and buried her nose in them, breathing in their scent. One day soon, they'd smell of her baby. A sweet, soft baby that cooed and tugged at her hair and cuddled into her. A real baby. A wave of excitement and a sort of terror flooded through her. What a responsibility it was to be a mother.

George was still absent when she'd folded the clothes and returned them to the chest. She realised how much she missed him when he wasn't there. Not so much the George of recent months, so sullen and absent even when he was physically in their home, but the George she had fallen in love with and married. The man she had danced and laughed with and kissed in the kitchen. It was an age since he'd winked at her behind the lodgers' backs and made jokes and been happy.

She put the stew back on the range and decided to fry a leek with it. George liked the taste of leek; it was one of his favourite vegetables. She put on her coat. The rain had stopped, but it was a cold day. She had a small vegetable patch in the back garden with some overwintered leeks, Brussels sprouts and kale, which helped supplement their meagre rations.

She had hardly turned the corner when she saw him lying there.

'George!' she screamed, rushing to him and kneeling on the cold stone.

He gave a moan and Morag thanked God fervently that he was alive. He tried to sit up and she helped him. There was blood behind his ear and more on his collar. A livid bruise blossomed on his jaw, a purple-black mess.

'You're alive. I thought… for a minute I really thought you were dead,' Morag said.

He touched his jaw gingerly and let out a hiss of air. The blood on his neck was sticky and coagulated when she mopped at it with her handkerchief.

'I think I blacked out for a bit,' George mumbled. 'I have a real thumper of a headache.'

'Can you walk?' Morag asked. If he couldn't, she wondered how she'd get him up and into the house.

'I think so. Here, can I rest on your shoulder?'

'Of course. Let's take it slowly and gently.' It seemed like the first real conversation they had had in weeks, where they actually spoke and listened and responded to each other. How awful that it was only because of a terrible accident.

George's arm was heavy, draped around Morag's neck as they both staggered very slowly out of the garden and round and into the house. She helped him into the dining room, and he sat in one of the chairs. She ran into the kitchen and came back with a damp cloth to sponge off the blood. He sat like a child and let her clean him up. She tried to avoid his bruised jaw.

'I'll get the doctor,' Morag said, putting the cloth down, heedless of her lovely set table.

'No, no, don't do that,' George said. 'I'll be fine.'

'Did you slip in the garden?' She couldn't imagine how he had done that but was horrified with his answer.

'It was Ricky. He punched me. Look, I need a drink. We've got brandy in the corner cabinet; will you get me a glass?'

Morag's head buzzed as she poured a medicinal brandy into one of George's father's brandy snifters. They never drank brandy. The older Mr Kincaid had liked a snifter or two after dinner along with a thick Cuban cigar. The brandy bottle dated from George's parents' days in the house, but it didn't go off, brandy, did it. Her mind gabbled away, avoiding the truth until she had to face it. Ricky Smith had tried to kill George.

They didn't speak again until George had emptied the snifter and Morag insisted on making a pot of tea for him too. They drank a cup each. They couldn't avoid the subject any longer.

'Ricky attacked you. Why?' Morag asked, dreading the answer.

George's lovely brown eyes met hers for the first direct gaze since Christmas. In them she saw a mix of emotions that she didn't care to tease out and name.

'I accused him of having an affair with you. He admitted it, and when I tried to punch him, he did the same to me. Only he was a better shot.'

Morag sat heavily in the chair opposite George's.

'Have you nothing to say to me?' George said quietly.

'It was only the once. You were so distant to me… But I'm to blame. I'm so, so sorry. It was a terrible thing to do. Can you ever forgive me?' She was crying now, hot tears that streamed down her cheeks and dripped off her chin.

'I guessed it. That man, I won't say his name he's so vile, the way he looked at you and spoke to you. I just knew it. It almost killed me. But… I do forgive you.'

'You do?' Morag whispered incredulously.

'Yes, because I'm to blame too,' George cried, reaching out and grabbing her hands. 'I was awful to you about the baby. I blamed you and then I was ashamed of myself for the way I behaved to my own sweet wife. It wasn't your fault you got pregnant. Then I was too proud to apologise, too afraid you'd hate me, so I pushed you away. It was easier to stay late at work and to go to the club, to avoid you. I felt guilty seeing the sadness in your eyes. And I mourned our baby too once I let myself imagine how it could have been. I was a damned fool, and I pushed you straight into that man's arms.'

'Oh, George. We've both been fools,' Morag wept. 'I didn't see that you were hurting too. I missed you so much. You never spoke to me; you never touched me any more. Our marriage seemed like it was over.'

'Can we start over?' he asked, still holding her hands tightly. 'Go back to how we were? We were so happy, weren't we? Tell me it's true.'

'We were so very happy,' Morag agreed, wiping away her tears with one hand and holding on to George's hand with the other.

'And we can be again. I know it. I'll stop working so hard at the yard. It's not as if I'm getting up the career ladder as it is.' George's face darkened. 'I wanted to make something of myself, for us and our future.'

'I don't care if you make manager or not,' Morag said. 'We'll be all right the way we are. We've got the house and we've enough to eat or will do once rationing stops. What more do we need?'

'At least we're both working.' George smiled.

Morag removed her hands from his slowly. All this baring of souls and she'd forgotten her unfortunate truth. She wasn't going to be able to stay on working in a few months.

'I've got something to tell you,' she said. 'You might hate me when you hear it.'

'I can't possibly hate you when I love you so much,' he exclaimed. 'Nothing you say can change that.'

'I'm not so sure.'

'Try me. What can be so bad compared to what's already happened? I don't blame you for that. Not any more. I'll never mention it again. But that man is not coming into this house ever. We'll put his belongings outside for him to take away and keep the door locked. He can find other lodgings.'

'I don't want to see him ever.' Morag nodded.

She gazed at George, taking in his handsome features and imprinting his loving expression in her mind because once she told him, she might never see that expression again.

'Tell me, then,' he prompted. 'I'm getting nervous.'

'The thing is… I'm… well, I'm having a baby.'

The words felt like poison as they left her mouth. Now Morag cast her eyes down to her lap, concentrating on the tartan pattern of yellow and brown and the bobbled material where age had rubbed the yarn. She loved the skirt and there were a few more years of use in it. Not that she'd be able to wear it once her pregnancy began to show. The silence lengthened and she was afraid. Slowly, she raised her gaze upwards to George's face. He stared at her and rubbed his sore head, leaving his curly hair springy instead of smoothed with hair cream. A strange certainty overcame her.

'And I'm not giving it up. No matter what,' she heard herself say. 'I want my baby. I love you with all my heart, but if you want to walk away from this, then you do that. But I'm not giving it up.'

She felt suddenly strong and determined. Her path was clear. She did love George. She was *in* love with him and always would be. But there was a new life growing inside her and it was part of her. She'd been desperate for a baby for over a year and now she had one. He or she was a gift from God.

She waited for George's answer. How hard it was for him. She was asking him to take on another man's child. A man that they both now hated. The minutes ticked by.

'I want us to be together,' George said finally. 'And if that means the baby too, then so be it. I'll accept and bring him up as my own.'

'You said we couldn't afford to have a baby yet,' Morag reminded him. 'I need you to be absolutely certain about this. It's all or nothing, George.'

'We'll manage. Somehow, we'll make it work.'

'Even if you don't get a promotion and I have to give up work to be a mum?'

He winced. 'Even if I don't get my promotion that I've worked so hard for. I promise I'll be a good dad to the wee one.'

Morag came round to his side of the dining room table and leaned down to kiss him. 'That's good enough for me.'

Their kisses deepened and George pulled her down to sit on his lap. She cradled his head so gently, conscious of his bruises and possible concussion.

'Is Mr McLeod still away?' George asked when they came up for air.

'Mmm, he is. Why?'

'For once, it's just us in our home with no interruptions. Shall we go upstairs, Mrs Kincaid?'

'Yes, please, Mr Kincaid. That would be just perfect.'

Their love-making was tender and gentle and made Morag want to cry. She did shed a few tears, which George wiped away. He tipped up her chin and kissed her lips.

'Are you sad, dearest?' he murmured, kissing the tip of her nose, her cheekbones and nibbling on her earlobe.

'No, I'm crying with happiness,' she whispered, snuggling her body closer into his so that there wasn't a gap between them.

'I love you, Morag. We'll make our wee family together.' He stroked her flat stomach as if in wonder. 'The next one will be mine and maybe there'll be a third or fourth.'

Morag laughed. 'I love you too. I don't mind how many weans we have. Tell you what. My ma will be pleased. She's always hinting about babies.'

'Aye, that's so. Does that mean she and your dad will be round the house even more?' George gave a mock groan.

'Don't be so mean.' Morag poked him in the ribs playfully.

'Ow. Is it not enough I've a sore jaw and crown? You've to give me a sore rib to match? Come here.'

Morag's heart was singing. The old George, the one she loved so much, was back. Somehow, they'd work things out and make the best of what they had.

Chapter Eighteen

'What is that awful smell?' Amy said, sniffing and screwing up her face.

'It was our dinner,' Eileen replied. 'I was frying fadge, and I left them too long in the pan.'

'What is fadge?'

'Don't sound so suspicious.' Eileen couldn't help laughing at Amy's expression. 'It's Irish potato scones. My mum's recipe. They're delicious.'

'Delicious, is it.' Amy picked up the blackened skillet and inspected it. 'Don't look too tasty to me.'

'Well, not now they're not,' Eileen groaned. 'I've wasted all the potato and flour on them and there isn't much else in the house for dinner besides.'

'I can nip out for sausages.'

'Mr Heaney will have shut up shop for the night already. As have all the other shops on the main street. I saw the awnings being pulled down as I walked up from the bus stop.'

'This is why you should let me do the cooking,' Amy grumbled. 'I'm starving and there's no grub. 'Ere, move out of the way and let me have a root about. I'll cobble summat together.'

'I made that lovely cauliflower cheese for Jimmy. Second time I made it was a success, and I made other nice food for him,' Eileen said wistfully. 'That's part of

257

being a wife. If Jimmy and I have children, I want to be able to make more than jeely pieces for them.'

Amy wasn't listening. She was kneeling down at the cupboard, taking out the few tins and frowning. Eileen went through to the bedroom and sat on the bed. She longed for Jimmy. He'd laugh and put his arms around her and tell her not to be daft. He loved her whether she could cook or not. If only he'd come home. Mary was right, though. He wasn't fully healed, whatever he believed. If they pushed him too hard, his health might fail. It was better to wait. Soon she'd ask Amy again about moving out. Only there was a fragility about Amy too these days. She was nervous and jumped at sudden noises. She snapped at Eileen and then said sorry too quickly.

They ate bread and dripping for dinner followed by a can of peaches. Eileen had been keeping the peaches for Jimmy's birthday but wisely she didn't say anything. It was good that Amy had saved them from a miserable evening of empty stomachs. Afterwards, she did the washing-up while Amy sat and flicked through *Woman's Own*. She picked up the skillet and scrubbed at it in the soapy water. No matter how she scrubbed, the black, encrusted grime wouldn't shift. They'd run out of baking soda and warm water.

Amy came and peered over her shoulder. 'Eggshells and lemon.'

'Sorry?'

'To scour the dirty skillet.'

'If only we had eggs to eat and provide shells. Powdered eggs aren't quite the same. As for lemons... pigs might fly.'

Amy thought for a moment. 'You need a handful of sand for that, then. It'll take the gunge off something lovely.'

'Sand? Where can I get sand from? Unless I steal a sandbag from the front of the shops. I don't suppose we'll get any more bomb blasts.'

'Have you ever stole a thing in your life?' Amy said, amused. 'Bet you ain't.'

'Certainly not. That's wrong. Have you?' Eileen was afraid to hear her cousin's answer.

Amy laughed and shrugged her shoulders. 'Come on, it's our turn for the laundry room today. I'll bring the washing and you can take the skillet. There's grit in the back court, which is a good enough substitute for sand.'

'Did you heat the boiler?'

'You might be surprised to hear that I did. I can be organised, you know. You like to think I'm scatter-brained or lazy, but I'm not.'

Eileen felt the heat rise in her face. She did think that. Although she admitted that Amy did her fair share of the cooking and cleaning in the flat. It was only when it came to going out to work that she shirked her duties sometimes. She made excuses not to go to the crèche or was too tired to go to the WVS centre. Instead, she put her feet up and read magazines.

The wash house was a tiny brick building at the back of the tenement that was shared by all the tenants. As a fair system, each flat was allocated a particular day to do their washing. The clean clothes were then pegged outside in the back court to dry when the weather permitted. On dreich damp days, it was a matter of hauling the wet, clean clothes back up into the flat and hanging them on the pulley above the range to steam and hopefully dry.

Dusk was settling in as they went slowly downstairs. Amy carried the wicker basket with their dirty clothing in both arms and had to watch her step, moving like an older woman. Eileen went ahead with the skillet and a candle. The skillet was heavy iron and made her arm ache. She didn't want it to touch her dress because it was so grimy and greasy.

It was a cool, drizzly evening and she shivered as she put the skillet down and unlocked the wash house door. Inside, it smelled of damp wool and carbolic soap. She put the candle on the window ledge and fumbled to light it. There was the cast iron boiler, making odd yet comfortingly familiar noises as it strained to heat the water from the coal fire set beneath it. There were two large sinks and a mangle. Someone had left an empty basket, which Eileen put to one side carefully. There was also a wrinkled wet sock, which she laid on the edge of the basket to be retrieved.

They could, of course, have gone to the steamie, as many Glasgow women did to wash their clothes. She and Amy had gone before, and Eileen had enjoyed the friendly atmosphere and camaraderie of the working wives and grannies who did their laundry there. There were children there too, who were washed along with the clothes, and many screams and yowls were to be heard as dirt was washed from behind the ears after a day running free. The children's reward was hot rolls that were sent out for, and the tears quickly dried. Eileen smiled remembering it. Still, it was good to have their own wee wash house, and they didn't have to walk far to get to it. She kneeled to stoke the coal fire, which was almost out. A few tiny tongues of flame flickered into life among the grey ashes.

Now, where was Amy? She'd only been behind Eileen by a few feet, going along cautiously, her vision obscured by the large wicker basket. Eileen turned away from the boiler and heard a muffled scuffling outside the wash house.

'Amy?' she called.

A scream, cut short, chilled her blood. Eileen dashed outside and a shocking scene met her eyes. A large figure struggled with a smaller one. Amy! Eileen froze for a second.

'Where's my cash, you bloody cow?' the figure snarled, shaking Amy like a ragdoll.

'I ain't got it, Ricky. That's the truth,' Amy cried out.

'You wouldn't know the truth if it hit you in the face, *wife*. Which is what I'm going to do. Now you tell me quick, first about my cash and then where's Alfie?'

As if in slow motion, Eileen's brain turned. This was Ricky. *Wife*, he said. He looked horribly familiar, his face just visible in the dull glow coming from the wash house, and Eileen realised she'd seen him before. He was Morag's lodger, and he was Amy's husband. No wonder Amy had been so nervy. She knew he was coming after her. The pieces all fitted into place, and Pearl's letter now made sense. Eileen watched in horror as one of Ricky's giant hands wrapped round Amy's neck and his other arm pulled back, that hand clenching into a fist. He was actually going to do it. He was going to hit Amy in the face. She couldn't let that happen.

The rowing couple were oblivious to Eileen's presence. There was no way she could fight off Ricky by herself. Even with Amy helping, Ricky was too large and strong for them. But Eileen had the element of surprise. She glanced about frantically. She could run for help. But to do that, she had to get past them. She imagined Ricky grabbing her as she ran. No, that wasn't going to work. She might scream and hope that the other residents had their windows open to the back court and would hear her and come to help. It was impossible to see if any of the windows were open. The night sky was too dark. She couldn't take that risk. One scream and Ricky would spin round and see her.

Her frightened gaze landed on the skillet where she'd left it beside the wash house door. There was only one thing to do. She lifted it up and swung it as high as she could. It hit Ricky a solid blow to the back of his head. He gave a low cry and crumpled to the ground.

'Amy,' Eileen screamed. 'Are you hurt?'

Amy let out a sob, stuffing her hand into her mouth to stifle it. But when Eileen reached out to comfort her, she pushed her away, dry-eyed. Amy pointed to the still body at their feet.

'You've killed him,' she gasped.

They stared at the body. Eileen kneeled down and forced herself to touch Ricky's wrist, searching for a pulse. With relief, she felt the constant flicker in his vein.

'He's unconscious. Oh God, what will we do?' Eileen said, feeling sick to her stomach.

'We'll drag him out of sight behind the ash pits and then think hard. Don't just stand there, help me,' Amy whispered savagely.

No wonder they called it a 'dead weight', Eileen thought, her heart thudding against her ribs as they pulled at Ricky's coat and then tried to grab him under the armpits and drag him across the cobbles. It seemed to take forever, but they managed to move him out of sight behind the wash house where the ash pits were heaped. It was very unlikely that anyone was going to come down there that night.

Amy ran upstairs with Eileen following. They shut the flat door and leaned against it, panting. Eileen glanced across at Amy and felt she saw herself mirrored there. Amy's face was a chalky white, her eyes like blackcurrants, and there was a drip of sweat trickling from her hairline onto her temple.

Amy belched and ran into the kitchen. Eileen heard vomiting. She stepped slowly into the kitchen as if in a nightmare and saw Amy bent over the sink. When she stood straight again, Eileen saw the livid mark of red fingerprints on her neck.

'He's your husband?' Eileen said. 'I don't understand…'

'Look, I'll tell you everything. I promise. But first we need to move Ricky before he wakes up.' Amy wiped her mouth on the tea towel and threw it into the sink. She was trembling.

'I'll go down the street. Leo Mearns has a telephone,' Eileen said.

'What are you talking about?' Amy hissed.

'He's hurt. I gave him a wallop with that skillet; I was so afraid he was going to kill you. He might need an ambulance.'

'Ricky's got a thick skull. He'll be all right, but he's going to be angry as a bull when he gets up, so we need to get rid of him. He can't be 'ere.'

Amy sounded suddenly calm, and Eileen was horrified. 'This is your husband. Aren't you upset? Don't you love him at all?'

'Oh, never mind all that. Me and Ricky 'ave a history, and it ain't all chocolates and roses. We 'ave to focus. What can we do with him?'

Eileen was shocked at how callous Amy appeared. Only the fact that her cousin's whole body was trembling gave her hope that inside she felt some remorse, some shred of feeling for her husband.

'We have to go and check,' she found herself saying. 'We have to go back down to the ash pits and see if he's woken up. How awful, we ran away, and we didn't even try to help him.'

'He was about to bash my brains out. It was lucky for me that you got in there first,' Amy commented.

There was some truth in that. If Eileen hadn't hit Ricky with the skillet, he would have throttled Amy and hit her in the face with his fist. He might have killed her. She had saved her cousin. That was some measure of comfort. But she had a tight knot in her tummy at the idea of going downstairs and outside in the dark to see him. She recoiled from it, but it had to be done.

'Get the torch,' she told Amy firmly. 'Come on. Let's get this over and done with. If Ricky needs medical help, you can run for Doctor Graham, and I'll phone from the Mearnses' house for an ambulance.'

Her hand was slippery with sweat on the torch handle as they went down the stairs quietly. Luckily, none of their neighbours came out. Eileen feared her face would give her away that something awful had happened. Amy had a lot of explaining to do. But first they had to get this done.

As she peered out from the ground-floor door, the outline of the wash house was just about visible in the weak moonlight.

'Let's do this,' Eileen whispered to Amy. She took her hand and felt how cold it was.

Hand in hand, they crossed the short distance to the wash house and paused. Eileen turned on the torch, making sure that its light was cast downwards in case anyone inside the tenement happened to look out the window right at this moment. She gulped and moved towards the back of the wash house where the ash pits were piled. Amy moved with her. In disbelief, Eileen stared at the spot where they had left Ricky. He wasn't there.

—

Four tenements further along Kiltie Street, Jimmy was restless. He lit another Player's, grimacing to see that the packet only had one fag left. He sucked on the ciggie, enjoying the taste and sensation of the smoke drawing deep into his lungs and relaxing him. He sat in the armchair, his head resting on the antimacassar for a moment before he sat up and leaned forward. He missed his Sheena. If it wasn't for that cousin of hers, he'd be sitting in his own kitchen, smoking and talking through his day with his beautiful wife. But he had frightened himself with his anger towards Amy. That day he'd tried to force her from the flat he hadn't been himself. But, he wondered, if it wasn't him in his right mind that had shouted at her, who was it? And could that man appear again? What if he and Eileen had an argument? Would that anger spill up and make him act that way with her? That was what kept him here at Mammy's home.

He went through to the kitchen. Mary had just come in from the WVS centre and taken off her green hat with the purple ribbon. She was proud of that hat, and rightly so. She worked hard as a volunteer, doing her bit, as she called it.

'Och, Jimmy, there you are son. Are you after a wee cuppa? Put the kettle on the range, won't you, and I'll make us a pot. Harry'll be back from his allotment soon with the veg for tea. He promised me the last of the Brussels sprouts.'

Jimmy grinned and good-naturedly filled the kettle and put it on the hot range. He'd make the pot of tea and all for his mother.

'You have a wee seat there,' he suggested, pointing at the kitchen chairs. 'I'll get the cups and saucers.'

'You're a good son, so you are.' Mary paused and smiled at him. 'Are you doing all right?'

'Aye, I'm getting there.' He wasn't sure if that was so but he felt that's what Mammy needed to hear. His arm ached and his headaches bothered him, but his sight was sharp enough, and his greatest fear, that he'd go blind again, hadn't happened. The doctors had said he wasn't to worry, it was unlikely, but still…

'I'm worried about you,' Mary said, sitting down a little stiffly and rubbing her legs as if they pained her. 'I'm concerned about you and Eileen. It isn't right, Jimmy. A man and his wife… they should be together.'

'Aye, Mammy, but I've explained it to you. That Amy… well, while she's there, I can't be.'

'It's not just that you have to share the wee house with her, though, is it?' Mary said shrewdly. 'There's more to it. I think you're afraid of what you did. You didn't hit her, son. You never touched her.'

'But I shouted at her, and I wanted to move her bodily out of the flat.' Jimmy tried to describe it honestly even though it made him wince. 'It wasn't how a man should treat a woman. Even if he dislikes her.'

'You're scared there's violence in you. After what you've seen and done in the war.'

It wasn't a question, so Jimmy hung his head. His cigarette burned down on the ashtray beside him, and he didn't notice.

'You were always a kind boy and good to your sisters. Good to me and your dad too. When your dad passed, you were the head of the family, and you took on your responsibilities despite being only young. You went into the army at eighteen well before the war started and you've played your part ever since. Maybe you are angry at your injuries and being discharged but I don't believe you're a violent man, Jimmy Dougal. I believe you're kind and loving and gentle and I know you love Eileen with all your heart.'

'I do love her, Mammy. I've never felt for another woman what I feel for my Sheena. She's the only girl for me.'

'It's time to go home, love. Even if Amy still lives there. Eileen's stuck between the both of you. She loves you and wants to be with you, but she feels a duty towards her cousin too. She wants to look after Amy, and she can't throw her out because that's not right.'

'Eileen tells you more than she tells me,' Jimmy joked.

'Maybe I'm the better listener,' Mary said gently.

Jimmy blushed. Mammy was right. He hadn't really listened to Eileen's point of view. He'd been angry and jealous of Amy. Yes, jealous. He finally admitted it. He wanted all of Eileen's attention and instead had to share it with Amy.

'What if I lash out again?' he said.

'You've got control over your actions. Go and punch a pillow or go for a walk if you're annoyed. Better still, get a job and a focus for your life. There's plenty of life left in you, unlike for some poor lads who didn't come home.'

'I don't know what job I can find. I've not found anything yet.'

'That's for you and Eileen to figure out.'

They heard the front door open, and Harry came in with an old sheet of newspaper wrapped round whole stems of Brussels sprouts.

'These do, my love?' He kissed the top of Mary's head and whistled as he washed his soil-stained hands at the sink.

Mary winked at Jimmy. Not much got Harry down. He was a cheerful presence in their home and the best stepfather the Dougal offspring could wish for.

'You still here, then?' Harry teased Jimmy as he did every day.

'No, I'm not.' Jimmy stood up, decided. 'I'm going home. Where's my coat?'

The look of surprise on Harry's face was comical. 'I was only joking, lad.'

'Mammy's right. I belong at number eight on the top floor with my best pal, my wife. I cannae linger here any longer. Enjoy the Brussels sprouts, the both of you. And thanks for giving me a breathing space here.'

'This is your home and always will be,' Mary said, hugging him. 'We'll miss you staying here, won't we, Harry.'

'Of course we will, but don't you worry, my lad. Your mammy's still got me. I'm not going anywhere.'

Jimmy put on his coat and cap and grinned. 'Wish me luck. I hope Sheena doesn't kick me out for being a daft eejit and staying away.'

The night was sharp-aired and the watery moon cast the shadows of the tenement blocks onto the pavement as he walked along Kiltie Street. There was a spring in his step as he anticipated Eileen's happiness that he was coming home. Tonight, he'd make love to his wife in their own marital bed. He'd never let her go again.

Amy still had to leave, but he promised himself he'd be more tolerant towards her. He could manage a polite distance, surely. And if he caught himself feeling annoyed or any hint of a surge of that terrible anger that had consumed him, well, he'd be out the door like a shot. He'd walk it off by the canal. Aye, it was going to be all right.

He'd get a job too. It didn't matter what it was. The problem was he'd been in the regular army all his adult life. He didn't know anything else. What was he good at? What could he do with one weak arm and possible damage to his eyesight? He sighed. He'd figure it out. He had to. His shoulders went back. With Eileen at his side, it was all possible. They had their dream of the wee house and the children and the garden. They'd do it together.

His attention was caught by a figure emerging from the gloom further up the street. It staggered like a drunk. Jimmy grinned. It probably was a drunk who had managed to get lost going up the main street and had swerved into Kiltie Street by mistake. It was too dark to make out the man's face, but the figure was too bulky and tall to be a woman. Around here, there were a few women who imbibed to excess too. And who could blame them, with their menfolk away at war and the worries that melted away with a swig of gin.

Jimmy heard the sound of a motor car behind him. Leo Mearns owned the only car in the street, so he knew it was him. A fine machine it was too with a polished exterior and leather and walnut interior. Mearns kept it immaculate. Jimmy knew him as a snob and a show-off.

He glanced round as the car drove slowly past. The headlights were uncovered now that the dim-out had replaced the blackout, and the beams shone as cones of yellow.

Leo Mearns turned and waved to Jimmy. What was it with the man? It wasn't a friendly wave to a neighbour. It was a 'look at me' kind of wave. His superior smile, just about visible in the dark, irked Jimmy. Then, as if in slow motion, Jimmy watched in horror as the drunk wobbled out onto the road and Leo, still watching Jimmy, almost ploughed right into him. There was a squeal of tyres as the car braked suddenly.

Leo got out of his car, the smug smile wiped from his face.

'You idiot, I could have run you down. I didn't see you. What were you doing in the middle of the road?' he shouted.

The man's answer was to roar with rage and take a swing at the older man. Jimmy stepped forward quickly to block the blow with his good arm. He had learned a few fighting tricks in the army and wasn't afraid of the fellow now breathing loudly and leaning on his knees.

'Let's have none of that,' Jimmy warned. 'We don't want any trouble here in Kiltie Street, so take yourself off or it'll be worse for you.'

The big man looked as if he might be up for a fight, but Leo Mearns stood forward too and Jimmy saw he had a walking stick with a sharp ivory handle in his grip. Eileen and Amy ran out into the road and stopped at the sight in front of them. Jimmy saw the man stare at Amy and take a step towards her. Jimmy stepped out too, protectively in front of Amy, and instead of out-of-control anger, he felt sharp and strong and incisive.

'Amy, you come along with me now. You're my wife,' Ricky said plaintively.

Listening in astonishment, Jimmy saw Amy shake her head and Eileen curl her arm around her cousin's shoulders protectively.

'It's over, Ricky,' Amy said, sounding tired. 'I ain't coming back to you and I want you to leave.'

The commotion of the car brakes and their shocked voices had brought people out onto the dark street. Mary rushed over to them, Harry at her heels, to make sure they weren't harmed. Leo was staring in surprise at Amy while Eileen looked to Jimmy and gave a hesitant smile. Ricky looked at them all standing with Amy and he rubbed the back of his head, winced, and lumbered off, his shoulders down and an air of defeat about him. They watched until he disappeared out of Kiltie Street.

'Let's go inside,' Eileen urged, taking Jimmy's arm. 'There are things you need to hear. There are also things Amy needs to explain. Come on, the both of you.'

Chapter Nineteen

In the end, they didn't get to talk to each other properly until later that night as more people came out onto the dark street to stare at the car and hear the events that had taken place. Eventually, reassured that no one had been hurt, the crowd of neighbours thinned as they went back into their homes.

'Will you be all right?' Mary said quickly, as Harry pulled her arm and indicated with a jerk of his head that they ought to go too. 'Because if not, I'll stay with you. You've had an awful shock.'

It was Eileen who soothed her mother-in-law. 'You're very kind, Mary, but we're fine, so we are. I'll come by tomorrow and tell you about it. You and Harry go on up. It's cold enough out.'

She hugged Mary, who smiled reluctantly and followed her husband back into the close at number four with many a concerned glance back at her son and her daughter-in-law.

Eileen pulled Amy's arm and led her cousin back up to the flat. Amy didn't resist and Eileen wondered if she was more affected by Ricky's actions than she was letting on. She put the kettle on to boil, more for something to do than because of a desire for tea.

Jimmy arrived soon after and he went immediately to Eileen and pulled her into a hug.

'That man... Ricky... he attacked Amy, and I hit him on the head with the skillet. He dropped like a lead weight, and I thought I'd killed him. But when we went to check, he'd gone. He was dazed and wobbling about and... that's when the car nearly hit him. It's my fault.' Eileen slumped against him, her chest tight and her hands suddenly cold and clammy.

Jimmy's arms were around her and he hugged her tightly, kisses pressed to her hair, her cheek and her mouth as he comforted her.

'It's not your fault, doll. If it's anyone's fault it's Leo Mearns's for not looking where he was going, driving that big bloody car.'

He glared at Amy above Eileen's head. 'Why did he attack you, then? Did he have a reason?'

Much as Eileen enjoyed Jimmy's closeness, she had to hear what Amy said. Gently she wriggled free of Jimmy's embrace so she could see her cousin's face. Jimmy pulled up his chair close to hers and they both waited to see what Amy would say. She took her time, sipping from her cup before putting it down deliberately.

'All right, I'll tell you. It had to come out eventually, I suppose.' She straightened her back, ready for confession. 'You remember the day I arrived 'ere, I had an almighty bruise on my cheek?'

Eileen nodded.

'That was courtesy of Ricky. He was always free with his fists when he got in a mood or had too much to drink. I'd 'ad enough of it so I took off. But I wasn't going to go empty-handed, was I. Ricky had stashed what he called his savings but what I called *our* savings. He gave me a pittance for housekeeping, kept the rest for 'imself for drinking, and what he didn't use, he piled for 'is rainy day. His, mind. What about me? We was married but it was all about 'im.' Amy grimaced. She jumped up from her chair and walked over to the kitchen window to stare out before walking back towards them and continuing her story.

'Anyway, I grabbed the cash and took off while he was out at work. He'd paid a local doctor to say he wasn't fit for active service, so he didn't go to the front. At first I didn't know where to go. I knew he'd find me if I stayed in London and then I remembered Norman's brother. Your dad. I got the address from Norman and used some of the cash for a train ticket.' She looked at her cousin.

'And you know the rest, Eileen. I hung about at your parents' house, but I didn't ring the bell. I knew they'd ask awkward questions that I wasn't ready to answer. When I found out your address I turned up and waited on the doorstep until you came 'ome. You're a good 'un cos you let me stay.'

'I couldn't turn you away.' Although if she had, Eileen thought fleetingly, all this might not have happened. Despite Jimmy's words, she felt guilty for her part in Ricky's downfall.

Amy shrugged. 'And that's the simple truth of what 'appened.' She glanced over at Jimmy, and for once, she had a smile on her face as she looked at him. 'Thank you for standing up to him. He wasn't a kind husband. Although I wasn't the best of wives, I suppose.'

Jimmy nodded and returned her smile. 'I wasn't going to let him bully you, husband or not. I'd have given as good as I got if he'd tried anything on.'

'I know I've got a lot of faults,' Amy said, glancing at them both with a smile that was now hesitant. 'I'm lazy and selfish but I've 'ad to fight for what's mine. It's not an excuse, I know. But I've been happy 'ere with Eileen and you've both been good to me. I want you to know that I appreciate it.'

Eileen was so very pleased to see them get along finally. Jimmy was a good man, through and through. And Amy was more vulnerable than she'd known; all her tough exterior was bluster really, and inside, Eileen had suspected, was a kind heart at her core.

Eileen got up and refilled the kettle, putting on the range to heat. They could do with another cup of tea. Her throat was parched. She went to get the cups off the table and paused. Amy's simple truth hadn't included everything. She straightened up, the tea things forgotten.

'Just before Ricky was going to hit you, he said something. He wanted to know where his money was and…'

Amy stiffened.

Eileen looked at her. 'Who's Alfie?'

She never found out what Amy would have told her because right then there was a hammering at the front door. Jimmy got up to answer it. Eileen and Amy waited, Eileen's accusatory question floating in the air.

A short woman with grey curls under a yellow headscarf and holding a child by the hand came in, with Jimmy close behind.

'Alfie!' Amy cried, rushing around the kitchen table and grabbing the little boy in a hug so wide that all Eileen could see were two blonde heads together.

The older woman sank into a chair with a beseeching glance at Eileen. 'Thanks, love, I could do with a cuppa. Me feet are killing me.'

'What are you doing 'ere, Pearl?' Amy snapped, her arms still around Alfie.

Jimmy looked at Eileen, baffled. Eileen wasn't sure she knew what was going on either. She made a fresh pot of tea with the last of the week's ration and put it on the table along with the last drop of milk. She had managed to let it steep and then pour it before anyone made any sense. Alfie pulled away from Amy and went to lean against Pearl, his thumb stuck in his mouth and a hole in his shorts just above the knee.

'Pearl?' Amy said.

'I ain't doing it no more, Amy. Alfie's *your* son. I've hidden 'im from Ricky for long enough. I'm on tenterhooks all day long waiting for 'im to catch me out and find Alfie. So it's time for you to step up and be a proper mum again.'

Eileen gasped. 'You've got a child. You never told me.'

'I couldn't, could I. Ricky was after me and he wanted Alfie back. I'd hidden him with Pearl so that Ricky couldn't ever treat my son badly.'

'To be fair to Ricky, he never hit Alfie. At least, that's what you told me,' Pearl said.

Amy shook her head. 'He never, but that doesn't mean he never would as Alfie got bigger. I couldn't take that risk.'

Alfie's eyes were wide and round as he sucked his thumb. It couldn't be good for him to hear all that about his own father, Eileen decided. She kneeled down to his height.

'Do you like cats?' she asked.

Alfie nodded. She took his hand and led him through to her bedroom where Snowy was curled up in a fluffy white ball, his tail covering his whiskery face. Alfie scrambled up onto the bed and she left him stroking the purring cat.

'Ricky's gone for good,' Amy told Pearl.

'He's never! 'Ow did that 'appen?' Pearl squawked.

Eileen barely heard Amy explain again the events of the night. She was thinking of how, for all his faults, Ricky must have loved Alfie. He'd followed Amy all the way to Glasgow to find his son. How sad that he had gone without seeing him. Amy might argue that Ricky was a danger to Alfie. Eileen had no way of knowing if that was true. Pearl claimed he had never lifted a finger against the little boy. Ricky was violent, it was true. Look at the way he'd treated Amy. But wasn't there some good in him when it came to his son?

Och, it was all so complicated. It explained why Amy was so good with children, though. And why she'd chosen to work at the crèche. She must have missed Alfie dreadfully. It was quite a transition for Eileen to realise that Amy wasn't young and single after all. She was a wife and mother.

When she checked in on Alfie, he was asleep beside Snowy. She tiptoed back out of the bedroom and into the kitchen, where Pearl was yawning and Amy and Jimmy both looked tired.

'Alfie can stay here tonight,' Eileen said. 'If you can have him in with you, Amy? He's too sleepy to walk anywhere else. Pearl, we'd love to put you up too, but we don't have much space. I'll go and borrow a truckle bed from Jimmy's parents if you can wait a wee while. It'll fit in this room under the inset bed. There's not much privacy in a tenement flat, I'm afraid.'

Pearl waved her hand. 'Don't worry about me, love. I've got a room in a boarding house nearby. I'll be off soon after I've 'ad a little chat with my daughter and I'll come back tomorrow to see Amy before I go 'ome.'

Eileen and Jimmy tactfully went into the bedroom to give the two women a chance to talk alone.

For a moment, Amy and Pearl didn't speak.

'Spit it out, then,' Amy finally said. 'Tell me what a terrible mother I am.'

Pearl sighed. 'I haven't been that great a mother myself. You and me, we aren't close, I know that. It's my fault; I didn't want a kid when you came along. I wanted to dance and sing and enjoy myself without being tied to the stove and all the washing and whatnot. I should never 'ave married yer dad.'

'That's all under the bridge.' Amy sniffed. 'Don't bring it up now. Just tell me how come you've arrived 'ere all of a sudden with my Alfie.'

'It ain't all of a sudden,' Pearl said sharply. 'Honest to God, Amy, you never think about anyone except yourself. It's been ages and poor little Alfie misses you summat awful. He loves his granny, but he wants his mum.'

Amy flushed. 'He's safer with you. Look at my neck. Ricky done that with his great big hands. He'd 'ave rearranged my features too if it weren't for Eileen clocking 'im one.'

'I know you ain't had it easy,' Pearl said, her voice softening. 'He's a bad 'un, your Ricky.'

'He's not my Ricky. Not any more. Jimmy sent him packing and I'm sure it's for good. I won't let him hurt me or Alfie. Not ever,' Amy said fiercely.

Pearl nodded. 'I don't believe you will, neither. I'm proud of you, girl. It took guts to stand up to him. But it's time to think about Alfie now and the future. I'm getting old and I can't be mum to him forever, much as I love the boy. Now, I'm going to go to my lodging house what 'as a lumpy mattress but I'm that tired I won't notice. I'll see you in the morning and we can catch a train south together.'

Pearl patted Amy's hand awkwardly. Amy put her hand over her mother's fleetingly, feeling the knotted veins and swollen knuckles. A rare moment of tenderness for Pearl almost overwhelmed her but she covered it with a cough.

'I'll say to Eileen that you're on your way so they can say goodbye,' she muttered.

They saw Pearl out the door and then Amy picked Alfie up and took him through to the inset bed. Pearl had left a small bag of his clothes and Eileen took the bag through to give to Amy. Alfie had woken up just long enough for Amy to help him out of his school jumper and shorts, and she rummaged in the bag to find his brushed cotton pyjamas. Eileen left them sorting out his possessions.

'Jimmy, are you staying?' Eileen asked, holding her breath for his answer.

'Aye, darling. That I am. If you'll have me?' he added sheepishly.

'You're my husband. You belong here,' Eileen said simply.

They said good night to Amy, who was drawing the covers over Alfie's sleeping body with a tenderness Eileen had never seen in her before. She barely acknowledged them, her focus on her small son.

Lying in bed in their own bedroom, Eileen took Jimmy's hand.

'I can't believe you're back for good. I'm so glad.'

'I'm ashamed of myself,' Jimmy said, raising himself up on his elbow to look at her. 'I should never have left you alone here. If I'd known that man was prowling, looking for trouble, I wouldn't have. I couldn't bear it if something happened to you, my darling.'

'He wasn't after me. He wanted revenge on Amy.' Eileen shivered. 'I'm sure it was him that left the dead bird and the rotting petals. Maybe he hurt Snowy too. We'll never know.'

She sat bolt upright in the bed. 'I bet it was him in that bomb shelter.' She saw Jimmy's puzzled expression in the dim light. 'I was in there because of the rain, and I felt a presence. I just knew I wasn't alone. Maybe he thought I was Amy because we look so alike and wanted to scare me.'

'Aye, you two could pass as twins.'

'I think she dyed her hair and borrowed my clothes to hide from Ricky.'

'It's over now; come here,' Jimmy murmured.

'Is it over? I blame myself for Ricky's accident. I gave him a nasty blow with the skillet and then Leo nearly ran him over, but if Ricky hadn't been stunned from the blow I gave him, then maybe—'

'Maybe, if and but,' Jimmy interrupted. 'No one knows what might have been. You could equally blame Amy for running away from her husband. That's what brought

Ricky here to Kiltie Street. Or blame Ricky for being the kind of husband who hits his wife. If he hadn't done that, Amy might not have left him.'

'You're right,' Eileen said. 'It's all so sad.'

'Now promise me you won't blame yourself any more.'

'I promise.' It was easy to say but harder to do, but Eileen knew she'd have to work at it. Jimmy was right.

'Come here,' he repeated, and this time Eileen snuggled into him.

He kissed her softly and then more urgently until their bodies entwined and desire took over from comfort. Jimmy made love to her with a pent-up passion, and she clung to him until the sensations took them both to a crescendo and they shuddered with the exquisite tenderness of their bodies and an overpowering love for each other.

'I'll never leave you again,' Jimmy promised, his voice gravelly with feeling.

Eileen's reply was to kiss him once more and cover him with her body, wanting that closeness, both physical and emotional, never to end.

In the morning, Amy lay in bed and listened to Alfie's soft breathing. The kitchen was dully lit where the blackout curtain had wrinkled at its edge. Now that the dim-out was in place rather than full blackout, no one had complained or issued a fine. The daylight seeping in made the glass jug on the table glint. It was lovely being in the inset bed with Alfie. She'd missed him dreadfully all these months, although she knew he was safe with Pearl. Besides, Ricky didn't deserve to have his son. He was a rotten father as well as an appalling husband. Now he was gone and Amy felt nothing but relief.

She slipped out of bed, careful not to wake Alfie. It was early and she hoped Eileen and Jimmy were still asleep too. She needed to be gone before they woke. As quietly as possible, Amy got her cardboard suitcase from the shelf under her bed. Her clothes were stored in it, so she got dressed and put her other belongings into the suitcase and strapped it shut. She decided against making breakfast. It would cause too much noise, she reckoned. She slid her feet into her shoes and stood for a moment, thinking.

Pearl was all bluster. She might say she'd had enough of looking after Alfie, but for all her faults as a mother, Amy had to admit, Pearl was a doting grandmother. When Amy left, Pearl would take Alfie and give him a home. She'd miss him something awful, but she could visit, couldn't she, every once in a while. She'd make sure to stay in touch too with letters and little gifts. Alfie would be all right. She loved him with all her heart, but she had to be practical. Ricky's money would run out soon and she wanted a comfortable life for her and Alfie.

Amy had decided that Leo was her best bet. He knew now that she was married, but he also knew that there was no love lost between her and Ricky and that her husband had gone for good. He'd made it clear he found her attractive. His two ugly sisters were off-putting, but she could handle them. She'd be a much better lover for him than his sickly Alice. There was one thing Leo was unlikely to accept, and that was a child. If she turned up with Alfie in tow… well, she couldn't afford to take that gamble.

Yes, she'd be in clover. Leo was well off, he had that big flat with its rich furnishings and ornaments and a posh car and a good job on the railways. Amy needn't work. She'd be a lady of leisure, lunching and shopping with the friends she'd surely make as a rich man's companion. She'd send plenty of money down to Pearl for Alfie.

She bent to pick up her suitcase.

'Mum?' a little voice said behind her.

Amy set the suitcase down carefully and turned round. Alfie's face, creased from sleep, peered out from the curtains of the inset bed. His hair was rumpled and his cheeks rosy. His blue-and-white-striped pyjamas were buttoned wrongly.

'Where are you going?' Alfie asked. He jumped down from the bed recess. 'Don't leave me behind.'

Amy kneeled and hugged him before putting him from her. 'Now, listen 'ere, Alfie. You're better off with Pearl. I'm no good as a mum. I'm too selfish. I've got to leave you. See.'

'No. I want you, Mum,' Alfie wailed. 'Take me with you.'

'Shush,' Amy whispered, pressing her finger to his mouth. 'You'll wake the others.'

'I'll work hard. I'll make money for us both,' Alfie whispered now too. His hands clutched at Amy's coat.

She had to do it. She had to leave now before it got harder to do so. Wasn't it best for both of them? She'd convinced herself of that. If she went to Leo, she had a life of luxury ahead where she never needed to worry about being poor and where the next meal was coming from or how to afford the clothes and make-up she liked. And Alfie would be better off too. He was too young to realise that.

If she stayed… she'd have to get a job and probably live with Pearl. Possibly for years. It'd be an unremitting grind in the poorer part of the East End of London. Exactly what she'd escaped from by leaving Ricky.

From the bedroom, she heard the creak of the floorboard. Either Eileen or Jimmy was awake and in a moment they'd be through. She had to decide *now*.

She looked at Alfie and felt the painful tug of her heart as she thought of all the days she'd spent away from him and all the days ahead, missing out on him growing up. She couldn't do it. Her dream of being a well-off lady melted away as Alfie hopped from one foot to the other. She sighed. 'Come 'ere, then. I ain't going anywhere except 'ome with you.'

Chapter Twenty

In early April, Eileen was glued to the wireless, listening to all the astonishing events playing out in the world. They were taking place in distant countries, but their effects would ripple across to affect them all, even in Kiltie Street. On 13 April, Russian forces captured Vienna. On 24 April, the blackout was lifted, and Eileen and many other people began to cautiously hope and dream about the end of the war and the prospect of peace. At the end of the month, news came that Hitler had killed himself and Eileen knew then that peace had to be declared very soon.

Amy, Alfie and Pearl had gone home as planned and Amy had sent a letter to say they'd got there safely and to thank Eileen for letting her visit.

'I find myself missing her,' Eileen said as she served up their tea of mock cutlets and cabbage.

'Aye, she was a grand cook,' Jimmy agreed, lifting a cutlet suspiciously with his fork.

Eileen hit him on the shoulder. 'Not because of that. Although it was nice when she cooked. It's not my strong point.'

'Och, your cooking's fine. What is this on my plate anyway?'

Eileen went to give a sharp reply then saw her husband's cheeky grin. She kissed him instead and sat with her own dinner in front of her.

'She was a funny mixture, wasn't she. I know she could be secretive and devious to get her own way, but she was also my friend. She kept me company when you were away and then when you were in the hospital. And she was kind to Snowy.'

Jimmy grunted noncommittally. Eileen didn't really expect an enthusiastic response from him. She knew how he felt about Amy. He hadn't hidden his relief and glee after she and Alfie and Pearl had packed their suitcases and bags and gone home. He was glad to be in his own wee home, as he put it, with his beautiful wife all to himself.

'I'm glad she was reunited with Alfie,' Eileen went on, her dinner as yet untouched. 'I did wonder if she'd step up to being a mother again. Half of me thought she might do a runner and leave Alfie with his gran.'

'I'm just glad that she's home with her own folks,' Jimmy said.

He shovelled a mock cutlet into his mouth with every sign of enjoyment.

Eileen's cooking had greatly improved. She thanked Amy silently for that. Her cousin had given her plenty of tips and demonstrations to get her started in married life. Agnes had told her that the key to a good marriage was satisfying her husband's stomach. Eileen smiled. Aye, well, there were more satisfying activities to keep a husband happy. She blushed a little to think of those activities last night. Now they had the flat to themselves, they didn't need to worry about making any noise.

'You look like the cat that got the cream,' Jimmy remarked. 'Care to share?'

'Och, I was just wondering when this war will be over. It can't be long now, can it?'

In fact, they had to wait another week for the announcement. In the meantime, the workers at the sewing factory were all called into the main hall one lunchtime and told they were being let go. There was no need for more army blankets and forces uniforms. Eileen and Morag were among those who lingered after being told that. It was their dinner break, but no one felt like going back to work in the afternoon.

'Do we have to carry on the now?' a large woman, wearing a red turban, bellowed to the supervisor.

There wasn't a clear answer and some of the women left to go home. Eileen and Morag stayed. It was raining heavily and neither felt like hurrying through the weather.

'I'll work this afternoon and until we get our wage packets,' Eileen said.

'Aye, me too. I don't want to give them an opportunity to save on paying us. George and I will need every penny now we've got another mouth to feed on the way.' Morag patted her tummy and smiled happily.

'No sign that food rationing is stopping. I keep waiting for them to announce that but they're awful quiet on that front,' Eileen said. 'How are you keeping, by the way?'

'I'm well past the morning sickness, thank goodness. I feel quite energetic. In fact, I was cleaning the house from top to bottom the other evening and thinking of painting our spare room as the baby's nursery. George keeps trying to stop me. He treats me like delicate porcelain these days. Says he'll do the painting and get a crib and all the trimmings.'

'He sounds like he'll be a doting dad.' Eileen smiled. Morag had told her all about Ricky punching George and

George's reaction to her news of her pregnancy. In return, Eileen had told Morag about Ricky's dramatic appearance at the wash house and how it had all turned out for Amy.

'He will at that. He's sworn this baby will be his. We won't ever tell our son or daughter otherwise.'

'I'm so glad it's all worked out so well for you,' Eileen said. 'What will you do now that we've got no job?'

'I'd like to keep renting out a room. Poor old Mr McLeod doesn't have anywhere else to go. He's got no family left and in a way he's like a member of our family. He's thrilled that we're having a baby so I can see him being like a granddad. With George's parents long gone, that'll be lovely. Miss Linton's room will be our nursery. I won't say it was Ricky Smith's room; I want to wipe that part of my memory out completely. So I can't rent that out, but George has plans to add a bit on at the back extending into the garden, so if we did that, we could rent that room out. Not that there's much chance of getting any building materials just now. The best news of all is that George finally got his promotion.'

'Oh, that is good news.'

'Aye, it turns out that Robb Gunn wasn't terribly good at his job. He only got it because his uncle works at the yard. So they've shifted him sideways to shuffle paper where it won't hurt and given George his job. I can't tell you, Eileen, what a difference it's made to George's confidence and mood. I'm in love with the man all over again.'

They had wandered across to the benches now and sat to unwrap their sandwiches.

'What about you?' Morag asked. 'What will you do now?'

'I don't know. I was a parlourmaid before the war in a big house in the countryside. I liked it well enough, but I don't think I could go back to that way of life now that I've had a bit more freedom. Then it was living in and a half day a week and one Sunday off a month to go home. Besides, the pay was poor compared to wartime pay in the factory.'

'You've got a knack for the sewing. I've seen the gorgeous clothes you've made yourself. I remember once you said you might set up as a seamstress.'

'I'd forgotten that. It's been a hobby of mine, but perhaps I could make money doing it.'

'You could try. After almost six years of war, women will want some new clothes, fresh and pretty to brighten their day. And surely the clothes rationing will end once the war does. It can't be long until Churchill tells us it's all over.'

'We'll stay in touch, won't we?' Eileen said, suddenly worried that their friendship would fade away.

'Don't be daft, of course we will. It's not that far a distance from Kiltie Street to Bridgeton and they do have things called trams and buses. Besides, Jenny or Jamie will need a godmother to tell them right from wrong and set a good example.'

'Jenny or Jamie, what lovely names... oh... you're asking me to be godmother? Are you sure? Haven't you a sister or someone else who ought to be asked?' Eileen gasped.

Morag laughed and shook her head. 'Neither me nor George have brothers or sisters. Besides, who else has kept me company day after day on the blasted machines, kept my spirits up and been privy to my darkest secrets? You're my best friend, Eileen Dougal, and we'll always be friends.'

There was a warm glow in Eileen's stomach at Morag's words. Was it possible to have two best friends at once? Because she was that fond of Morag and also Jeannie. She was the luckiest girl ever. Not only did she have two women who liked her, but she had Jimmy too, who was a friend as well as her lover and husband. She felt so different to the girl she'd been at the beginning of the war. That girl, her younger self, had been lonely deep down in her core and no amount of dancing or making herself pretty with clothes and make-up could change it. So much had happened in the intervening years. There had been struggles and sadness but also friendships and love.

Jeannie came home a few days afterwards, bringing her daughter, Flora, and her younger sister Isa and brother Bob with her from the farm where they had been evacuated. Eileen and Jimmy went round to see them. After all the hugs and kisses, Mary steered them into the neat front parlour.

'It's a squeeze today with all the children.' She laughed. 'Sit yourselves down and I'll bring tea. Dennis, mind who you're barrelling into. Bob, take Dennis away outside to play. There's no room in here for youse two and my china ornaments.'

'Wait for me,' Evie shouted, 'I'm coming too. Is it hopscotch or What's the Time, Mr Wolf?'

Bob, who had first been evacuated as a wee boy of five, was now a strapping lad of eleven, looking more like his big brother Jimmy with every day. He was kind-hearted and easy-going and assured Evie they'd be happy to play whatever she wanted. The three of them rushed outside, forgetting to shut the door. With a sigh, Mary closed it and went into the kitchen to prepare the tea and fish paste sandwiches.

Isa, now sixteen, preferred to sit with the adults. She was slim and taller than Mary and Jeannie. Mary said she took after her Irish grandmother, who'd been the tallest woman in her village. She had turned into a quiet, confident young woman and Mary and Harry were sure she'd do well as a teacher, which was what she was hoping for now the war was almost over.

Flora staggered past Eileen to grab her mother's knee. Jeannie scooped her up to rub noses, which made Flora giggle.

'I can't believe she's a year old and walking.' Eileen smiled. 'You've been away so long at your aunt and uncle's farm.'

'Well, that's us back now and not going anywhere. Leastways, I'm not until me and Bill go to Canada.'

'Is that still your plan?' Eileen's heart sank a little. Canada was an ocean away.

'We can write to each other.' Jeannie nudged her, knowing what she was thinking. 'Maybe you and Jimmy will come and visit us too.'

Eileen cheered at that. Yes, perhaps once she and Jimmy were settled and had built up a nest egg they could travel. Something to aim at for the future, along with a house and, hopefully, a family.

'The war's nearly over. It made me think of Janet.'

Janet was their friend who had been killed in the terrible bombing back in 1941 during the Clydebank blitz.

'I think about her often too,' Jeannie said softly. 'We'll never forget her because she's in our hearts, and our memories keep her alive.'

'It's going to be an odd celebration when the war ends because while it'll be wonderful and happy, it'll also be very sad thinking of those who died and aren't here to celebrate. All those lost men and women and children. It's unbearable.'

'But we have to bear it and go on. Otherwise, what was the point of them losing their lives? We have to live our best lives for them.' Jeannie held Flora so tightly that the toddler squealed and wriggled to be set free.

'What about Annie?' Eileen said more brightly, as the mood was getting too sombre. 'I haven't heard from her in a while.'

Eileen, Jeannie, Janet and Annie had all worked at Fearnmore munitions factory together earlier in the war.

'I had a letter that Annie asked me to pass on to you. Sorry, I forgot to, I was so busy with helping Aunt Martha on the farm. Annie's had a little girl called Jane, a sister for Davey. So I'm guessing she thinks about Janet a lot too.'

'So much has happened over the last six years. We've all grown up, haven't we,' Eileen said. 'It's time to look to the future and what we'll all do now.'

'It wasn't all bad,' Jeannie agreed. 'At least not for us. We've made good friends, and we've had a few laughs along the way. Mammy says she can't be happy until Bill and my sister Kathy are home. I can't wait for that either.'

—

Jimmy too was thinking of the future.

'Who wants a man with poor eyesight and an arm that can't lift heavy weights? How am I going to support my family? I've only ever known the army. I've got no other trade or training.'

They were travelling across the city by bus to visit Eileen's parents. It was the afternoon of 7 May and although there had been no official announcement that the war had ended, Eileen noticed all the shops had rosettes in red, white and blue and there were flags too, the Union Jack and the Scottish Lion being prominent but also French flags and a few she didn't recognise but she supposed were of some of the Allied European countries.

The bus continued on in a bumpy sort of way, past the bomb craters and gaping holes where tenements were missing from the Glasgow and Clydebank blitz. The devastation of the bombing that was still clearly visible in the housing and streets of Glasgow gave her an idea.

'They'll need builders after the war,' she said. 'They'll need lots of new housing to replace what's been damaged and destroyed.'

Jimmy looked interested. 'That's true. What about my arm, though? How could I lift things?'

Eileen thought for a moment. 'It's only the one arm. Maybe you should go back to the doctor and see if the muscles can be strengthened. Anyway, even if it's weak, I'm sure there'll be plenty of construction work you could handle, and they'll be crying out for men, for sure.'

Agnes opened the door to them at the neat little house in the west of the city.

'You'll never believe it. The latest on the wireless is that the Germans have announced that it's all over. When is Mr Churchill going to say anything? It's deflating, really. Come in and we'll sit at the wireless with your father and listen in case they say more.'

The four of them sat for a good long while but there was no more news. They shared a pot of tea and some of Agnes's home-made butterless scones and finally Eileen and Jimmy returned to the Kiltie Street flat in time for their tea. On the way home, there were men everywhere up ladders, putting up bunting and pennants.

'I hope they're right and don't have to take that lot all down again,' Eileen said to Jimmy. 'When will they tell us?'

They put their wireless on for the nine o'clock news that evening, and there it was. In a quiet, emotionless voice, the announcement came that the next day was to be VE Day and Churchill would speak at three p.m.

'That's it, then. After all this time… it's over.'

Instead of joy, she felt tired and worn out as if she could sleep for a year. Outside, voices were raised. Jimmy went to the window and grinned.

'Let's go out, half the street's out there.'

Eileen felt her energy perk up when they went outside into the warm evening air. Jimmy was right. All the neighbours were on the street, talking eagerly to each other, laughter ringing out and people embracing each other.

Mary, Harry and Jeannie rushed over to them and they all hugged.

'I can't believe it,' Mary said, tears in her eyes. She wiped them away with a laugh. 'It's finally over. We did it. Tomorrow's a holiday and rightly so. We have to have a street party.'

Jeannie nodded her agreement.

'I'll help with that.' Eileen smiled. 'I'm sure everyone will.'

'We can all chip in with our sweets rations, make it special for the children,' Mary said. 'And I've no doubt everyone in Kiltie Street will bring some food to share.'

The sounds of shouting and raucous laughter wafted in the breeze from beyond Kiltie Street, where celebrations had already begun in earnest with whatever beer and wine could be found.

'Let's go to George Square,' Jimmy suggested, excitement in his voice.

'What about your mum and dad?' Eileen said.

'Och, don't mind us,' Mary told her. 'We need our beauty sleep tonight and we'll have the party tomorrow. You young folk should go on and party.'

'Not me.' Jeannie yawned. 'Flora's a terrible sleeper so I need a few hours' rest myself while I can. Besides, I wouldn't feel right without Bill.'

Jimmy was already tugging at her sleeve, so Eileen went with him.

'Will there be a bus at this hour?' she said as they went out onto the main street.

As she spoke, two buses came down the slope of the road and they hopped onto the first one. It was full, with everyone talking to each other.

'I'm driving youse lot tae George Square and then you can gie it laldy,' the driver shouted.

'Aye, you and all,' someone yelled back, and everyone roared with laughter.

Eileen leaned into Jimmy for the journey, buffered by other bodies all standing and swaying as the bus turned the corners. The bus driver let them out near George Square, the centre of the city, and they followed a snake of people towards the famous square with its statues and wartime bomb shelters and the grand City Chambers on one side.

Men and women in army and naval uniforms clung to the statues, waving to the crowds and singing at the top of their lungs. The revellers swigged from beer bottles and the crowd swayed. The atmosphere was lively and friendly but with an electricity to it as the pent-up emotions of almost six long years of war were released right in the heart of the city.

Someone shoved a bottle of beer into Jimmy's hand, and he offered it to Eileen, who shook her head. She didn't need alcohol to feel enlivened. She watched Jimmy swig it but wasn't worried. His days of heavy drinking were over, thank goodness. He had so much to live for now.

George Square was strangely beautiful with all the flags draped from windows and the coloured lights strung up by the Glasgow Corporation in honour of the occasion.

'Eileen!' someone yelled, and Eileen struggled to turn among the bodies to see who it was.

Morag had a huge grin on her face as she reached her. George was close behind.

'I thought it was you,' Morag shouted over the noise.

Jimmy and George were introduced and the four of them wound their way around the square with no particular destination, just the enjoyment of being part of something amazing.

'It's a moment in history,' Morag yelled. 'Something to tell our children about, that we were here.'

Jimmy and George diverted into a nearby pub to find more beer. The pubs had been allowed extended opening hours for the momentous occasion and the citizens of Glasgow were making full use of them. Someone had lit a bonfire right in the square and there were shouts of glee as more wood was found from somewhere and lobbed into the flames.

At midnight, they heard the sound of the ships' horns from the nearby River Clyde, a cacophony of noise that rippled along the river while searchlights lit the sky with white cones of light.

'Is that fireworks?' Eileen cried as the sky erupted in puffs of colour.

'It's Verey lights from the ships,' Jimmy shouted back as they craned their necks to enjoy the spectacle.

Somewhere, an impromptu eightsome reel had begun, and before long, they were caught up in the dancing, joining a conga line that pushed its way through the throng, attracting more people as it went.

—

The next day, there was the promised street party in Kiltie Street. The local church had lent tables and chairs, and the women brought out their best tablecloths to drape the tables with. Mary and Linda O'Leary brought down plates of sandwiches and a red, wobbling jelly. Leila Connelly had baked a sponge cake, and other neighbours shared what they could from saved rations. The adults had pooled their sweets rations so that the children could all have a lucky twist of sweeties. A few shillings collected by Bob from all the flats had bought what fresh fruit the local greengrocer had and tins of fruit and condensed milk.

Isa, Bob, Evie, Dennis and Flora played on the street along with the other Kiltie Street children, all excited for the party. Jimmy helped Martin O'Leary put up the colourful bunting that Mary and others had sewn over the last few weeks and soon Kiltie Street looked bright and cheerful and welcoming.

'We'll get the makings of a bonfire set up.' Jimmy winked to the children, who whooped and ran off in all directions, determined to bring back any wood they could find.

'Och, Jimmy, is that a good idea?' Jeannie said. 'We've got them all spruced up in their Sunday-go-to-meeting clothes and they'll all be as black as chimney sweeps if you get a fire going.'

'We can't have a party for the end of the war without a roaring fire. It wouldn't be right,' her brother protested.

Eileen laughed and shook her head as Jimmy went off, hands in pockets, whistling while searching for wood. The children ran to him, pulling at him to see their finds.

'He'll make a great dad.' Jeannie nudged Eileen. 'And I'll be a fond auntie. I am already to Dennis, Kathy's wee boy, but I'd like to be auntie to yours too.'

'I hope so. We'd like that too but there's no sign yet. Plenty of time, though. Now the war is over I don't have to fear losing Jimmy for years to fighting away.'

'Isn't it wonderful, this feeling of peace. I can't quite believe it.'

'It is wonderful, but there's a wee part of me, a bad part, that quite misses the wartime fun we had. I know there were terrible things, but we had fun together and there was a spirit of everyone pulling together that I'm afraid is going to get lost,' Eileen said.

'It's up to us to make sure it continues,' Jeannie said firmly, linking her arm with Eileen's. 'Let's help Mammy set the tables.'

'Who lent the radiogram and records?' one of the women asked as big band music began to blare out across the street and couples started to dance amid much laughter.

'Sarah and Ada Mearns,' Mary said, nodding up to the top-floor flat at number one. 'They said they won't come to the party, but they wanted to contribute something and send good wishes to us all. Leo is with his wife, so he won't be coming either.'

'Come along, darling. Give me the first dance,' Jimmy called to Eileen.

'Aye, away you go and have fun.' Mary waved her away with a smile. 'The hard work's done and Linda and me can put our feet up now. Here comes Harry with some beer. I've not seen Martin so sprightly on his feet for a long time, getting to the bottles.'

Eileen went into Jimmy's welcoming arms and enjoyed dancing on the road in among the other couples. It was an overcast but warm day, and maybe, just maybe, the sun was going to peek out soon from between the clouds. Bob and some other boys his age dashed in between the dancers with branches. Behind them came the other children dragging what looked very much like a wooden door.

'Jimmy, where's the fire going?' Bob shouted. His branch dropped as he danced around them, cheeks flushed with exertion.

'You'll have to go and help them.' Eileen laughed.

'Don't go anywhere,' Jimmy warned. 'I'll be back for another waltz in a wee moment.'

She watched him helping Bob to drag the branch out onto the scruffy grass area on the other side of the street from the tenements near where the bench was and hoped the bench wouldn't go up in flames too. She wondered how Amy was doing and whether she and Alfie and Pearl were celebrating in London, where there were bound to be huge parties and a chance to see the king and other royals at Buckingham Palace. Although that sounded marvellous, Eileen knew there was nowhere else she'd rather be than right here in Kiltie Street.

Jeannie's cry made her look up. Jeannie was grabbing Mary and pointing to the end of the street. Harry was behind Mary, his hands on her shoulders and a wide grin on his face. Eileen looked and saw two figures just at the corner where Kiltie Street turned into the main street. They came together and slowly walked towards the tenements, and as Mary and Jeannie began to run and Jimmy, Isa and Bob looked up too, she saw that it was Kathy and Bill – looking tired, but happy – before they were surrounded by their family.

Her vision was then filling with the Dougals hugging each other. She smiled, hurrying along the street to join them.

Acknowledgements

Thank you to Dan, Becca, Lynne and the rest of the Hera team for their excellent editing and support which has made the book so much better and for being a delight to work with. Many thanks, as always, to the RNA Scottish Chapter for the friendships, lunches and zoom calls which keep me motivated on the writing journey. Finally, love and thanks to my nearest and dearest for bringing the coffee and making meals on the days when my word count had yet to be reached.

A Letter from Carol

Dear Reader

I hope you are well. Thank you for choosing *Sheena's Promise* which is the fourth in the Kiltie Street Girls series.

In researching for this book, I visited the Bridgeton area of Glasgow and Overtoun House above Dumbarton and was fascinated by the rich history of both of these locations. Part of the fun of writing historical books is delving into the past and finding new facts and incorporating this history into the background of the story where the characters interact and the plot develops.

For those of you who know Glasgow, the Greenbank carpet factory where Eileen finds a job is fictional. I found out that the Templeton carpet factory on Glasgow Green did make army blankets during World War 1 but despite searching, I couldn't find any confirmation that the factory did the same in World War 2. So I created Greenbank and placed it just next door to Templeton's for Eileen and Morag and the other female workers to sew in!

If you enjoyed *Sheena's Promise* please consider leaving a review. Reader reviews are very much appreciated and make the book more 'visible' for other readers too.

Thank you for your support and I hope you have enjoyed the Kiltie Street Girls series.

You can keep up with my writing news at my website and get in touch with me on my social media pages on Facebook and X (twitter). Best wishes and happy reading,
Carol x

Website: www.carolmacleanauthor.com
Facebook link www.facebook.com/carolcmaclean
X (twitter) link www.twitter.com/carolcmaclean